COLDWATER
DIANA GOULD

COLDWATER
DIANA GOULD

GIBRALTAR
ROAD

A VIREO BOOK
LOS ANGELES | NEW YORK

Gibraltar Road
A Vireo Book
an imprint of Rare Bird Books
453 S. Spring St., Suite 531
Los Angeles, CA 90013
www.gibraltar-road.com
www.rarebirdbooks.com

9780988931244 (trade paperback original)
9780988931265 (ebook)

Library of Congress Control Number: 2012951098
    Gould, Diana, 1944-
        Coldwater : a novel / by Diana Gould.
        p. cm.
        ISBN 978 0 988931244
        ISBN 978-0-988931265
        1. Motion picture studios--Fiction. 2. Television
broadcasting--Fiction. 3. Alcoholism--Fiction.
4. Hollywood (Los Angeles, Calif.)--Fiction. 5. Detective
and mystery stories, American.   I. Title.
    PS3607.O8844C65 2012   813'.6
                QBI12-600207

The author gratefully acknowledges permission to include a selection from *In a Dark Time* by Theodore Roethke, from *The Collected Poems of Theodore Roethke*. Permission granted by Random House, Inc.

Printed in the United States of America

For those who still suffer
in and out of the rooms

In a dark time, the eye begins to see...
—Theodore Roethke

CHAPTER 1

I've spent so much of my life afraid of the wrong thing. Lying awake, fretting what-ifs. My boyfriend will leave me. This headache is cancer. We're in production and on location: What if it rains and we can't make the day? As if fear were a protective shield that could ward off disaster. I'm pregnant. The show I'm working on will be cancelled. Preemptive worrying: what you dread won't happen if only you agonize first. The pilot won't sell. I'm HIV-positive. Why didn't I insist on a condom? Then, when it doesn't rain, you aren't fired, positive, or pregnant, it's a plus, not a neutral; you're not only free, you've accomplished something.

What you fear rarely happens, so worry and be safe.

There's only one thing wrong with that plan.

Sometimes what happens is worse.

That night, what I was afraid of was being late on a script. We'd been prepping off an outline for two days; the messenger was coming at six a.m. to bring the script to the director. I'd run out of coke. I couldn't write without it.

I was a writer-producer, show-runner of a TV show I'd created, two months past my thirty-first birthday. Five years before, I'd been a reporter on the metro desk of a newspaper in San Diego when I'd met Jonathan Weissman at one of those "How to Break into Television" panels. I'd had an idea for a series; he liked the idea, and he liked me. He helped me develop it, and in the process, we fell in love. I moved in with him and his young daughter, Julia. Eventually, miraculously, we sold our show, *Murder Will Out*, about a crime reporter turned private eye named Jinx Magruder.

Now two thirds into our second season, I was having trouble with a script that was already late. I'd called my dealer, Zeke, and asked him to come over, but his car was in the shop, and he said I'd have to go to him.

Jonathan was in New York for the upfronts—the week in May when the networks chose their fall season. It was the nanny's night off. I was alone in the house with Julia.

I stood in the doorway to Julia's room. Julia was not yet thirteen. Sleeping, she still looked like a child; although the fragile beauty of her movie-star mother was emerging as she grew to womanhood. Her hair was splayed over her pillow, an old and tattered Piglet doll nearby, not held, but there, a talisman of the childhood she was leaving behind, sidekick for the journey to adolescence ahead.

What to do? Wake her and take her with me? Leave her in the car while I run in, score, and leave? Or leave her alone and asleep.

What would I say? "I need to get drugs. I can't write without them. Just wait in the car while I go in and get them."

Julia was old enough to be left alone. Wasn't she? Ridiculous to still need a nanny at her age, but with two working parents on a series that demanded eighteen hour days, it helped to have someone who could drive and fix meals. But Julia could be left alone, couldn't she? Besides, she was asleep. What could happen? It wouldn't take me more than—what—twenty minutes. This time of night? No traffic? There and back in...forty-five minutes, tops. Better than waking her and taking her with me, having to explain where we were going and why.

I knew Jonathan wouldn't approve. But he was in New York. And he didn't have to write the script.

You'd have to be a writer to understand.

What if I left her and a fire broke out? Or a burglar broke in? A rapist, the Manson family, the men who killed the Clutters?

In Brentwood?

Why not? Sharon Tate was two canyons away.

The option of finishing the script without coke was not available. Not in those days.

The clock was ticking. It was almost one in the morning. The messenger was coming at six for the script.

I scribbled a note, left it by her bed next to her cell phone, closed the door softly, and left the house.

* * *

Fifty minutes later, I'm flying home. Almost two in the morning on a cold starless night on Coldwater Canyon in Beverly Hills. No sidewalks, only narrow shoulders, expensive homes hidden from view behind protective hedges. No street lamps, barely a moon. My headlights the only illumination on the twisting canyon road.

The taste Zeke had given me was amazing. In a flash of insight, I'd seen the whole last act. Everything Jinx Magruder would need to solve the case. It was perfect! How could I have missed it? It was all so clear. Beautifully and intricately connected, layers of meaning reverberating in on themselves. No wonder I used drugs!

I was watching the scenes play out when, out of the corner of my eye, I saw—what was it?—too late—to keep from hitting it.

The jolt of the impact threw me forward, slamming my chest into the wheel, as it spun the car into a skid. I straightened the wheel into the direction of the skid, and the car righted itself and continued careening down the canyon before my mind had registered what had happened.

I'd hit something. What had it been?

Who. Had it been.

I knew I should stop and find out.

But I had two grams of coke in the car. What if I had to wait for the police to file a report?

I rounded one curve and hurtled towards the next. A glance in the rear view mirror revealed only the familiar sight of a terrified woman struggling to appear okay. The road behind was empty.

I'd left Julia at home. If I stopped, Jonathan would find out.

I rounded the curves without downshifting, the downhill momentum increasing my speed. No lights. No sounds. Just the purr of the Porsche and the thud of whatever my fender hit, which now echoed in the blood pounding in my ears.

What had I hit? Stop, and find out.

What if I was arrested? Production would shut down, and we were already over budget. If I went to jail, it could cost us the season. People with families to feed would lose their jobs. It was irresponsible, selfish even to consider it. It must have been a dog.

I love dogs. I should stop and tell the owners.

It didn't have tags. If it had, I would have seen them.

My sweaty hands gripped the wheel. My foot pressed the accelerator as if I could outpace what I had done. As if, if I just drove fast enough, I could get back to the time before I'd left the house.

Because in some part of my frenzied being, I knew it was no dog. Dogs don't kneel by the side of the road to change their tires in the middle of the night.

I turned on the radio. And I remember now that as I fled down that dark, twisting canyon, eyes like pinwheels, brain on fire, the Beach Boys sang in celestial harmonies, "She'll have fun, fun, fun, 'til her daddy takes her T-Bird away."

Chapter 2

I finished the script in time for the messenger to get it for the six o'clock call.

Jonathan, Julia, and I lived in an old Spanish-style house in Brentwood that had previously been owned by Ida Lupino. Jonathan had turned one of the downstairs bedrooms into a home office for me. My room was on the dark side of the house. Its small windows had a decorative iron grating and let in little sun. I usually kept the drapes drawn anyway. I lay down on the sofa, hoping to catch an hour or so of sleep before I'd have to leave for the studio. As I closed my eyes, the accident replayed in my mind. I rounded the curve and saw in my peripheral vision, too late, a woman changing a tire by the side of the road. My fender had glanced off—what—her shoulder? Knocking her over. But I had already sped round the bend, leaving her behind.

My eyes shut against the scene playing inside them; my heart pounded as it had last night. What could have happened to her?

How badly had she been hurt? Why hadn't I stopped? To offer assistance, to call for help?

Because of the drugs.

Is this who I had become? Someone who'd needed drugs so badly she'd left a child alone in the middle of the night? Someone who would leave the scene of a hit and run?

A knife of pain stabbed me behind my eye. I swung my legs off the sofa onto the Navajo rug on the Mexican tile floor, cupping my eyes with my hands.

If this is how bad a problem I had, I'd better do something about it. And I would. As soon as we finished the season.

Right now, I had a headache only a Fiorinal could cure. I staggered over to the desk and opened the bottom drawer, rummaging through the prescription bottles. I found the Fiorinal and took six, downing them with a swig from my emergency vodka.

I should call the police. Tell them what happened. Tell them it was me.

Then Jonathan would know I'd left Julia alone.

Jonathan hated drugs, couldn't understand why I needed them. He had an occasional drink, socially. He could never understand why I got drunk. Neither could I.

What if they traced the car? I'd been a crime reporter; my show was a detective series. I knew they had methods for finding people. If they were going to find me anyway, wouldn't it be better if I turned myself in?

But we were in production. I'd just finished this script; another was due in six days.

What about that poor woman? What if she had medical bills? I had insurance.

I also had responsibility for a show that employed several hundred people and cost the network over two million dollars an episode.

I saw the remnants of last night's coke. I rubbed my finger in it, put it to my nose, sniffed. I needed it to help me think.

I heard a knock on the door.

"Come in."

Julia entered wearing her Eastman school uniform of pleated beige skirt and white polo shirt. I knew she was at odds with her rapidly changing body, which was sprouting pimples instead of breasts, growing taller but not softer. It pained me to see her dissatisfaction with her appearance; to me, she always looked wonderful. Now she seemed like an image from a time of innocence, before last night, that was already receding into an irretrievable past.

"Did you finish the script?"

I nodded, and she smiled, happy for me.

Julia's real mother had died of cancer when Julia was three. Julia was about eight when we'd met, and when Jonathan first introduced us, she had looked at me the way a shipwrecked passenger would gaze at a boat on the horizon. The longing in her eyes terrified me, given the work I'd done to keep anything like it out of my own. My relationship with my own mother didn't make me eager to recreate the mother-daughter bond. And yet, she'd won me over with her lack of guile. As I fell in love with Jonathan, I also fell in love with her. We'd done our best to be a family ever since.

"I made French toast."

"Oh, honey…" I reached for her, and she came over to me. I put my arms around her and buried my head against her. "You shouldn't have to do that. I should be the one making breakfast for you."

"You were on deadline." Julia had grown accustomed to taking up the slack for preoccupied grownups.

I gave her a kiss and told her I'd be there in a minute and to get herself ready for school. Fortified by the vodka, Fiorinal, and cocaine, I went upstairs to shower and dress. Julia was waiting for me in the kitchen when I came down, and I saw the reason she'd prepared a special breakfast. She had written a story she wanted me to look over before she turned it in today.

My head throbbed; my throat was ash. I poured myself a cup of coffee, though the cocaine had already begun the heavy lifting of getting me up to speed. My stomach turned over at the thought of food, but I pretended enthusiasm for the breakfast Julia had prepared. I took a sip of coffee and tried to focus.

The story was written in longhand on four pages of lined paper. It was about a princess who rescued a pirate from the evil king who was holding him in a dungeon for daring to woo her. It was filled with adventure, larger-than-life characters performing bold deeds of heroism and villainy. My own show, *Murder Will Out* also featured a bold female heroine, Jinx Magruder, whom I had conceived as the anti-damsel. But I suffered so over writing. I agonized over every word. Success had raised the stakes to the point where I needed drugs to catapult me over the fear. Julia wrote for the joy of making things up and writing them down, without worrying about how derivative it was. I envied her freedom; it reminded me of how much I had lost.

"Honey, this is wonderful! I mean it. It's just great!" I added, "I may just have to steal it for next week's show."

Julia laughed with pleasure, not deflecting the compliment. Julia never pretended to feelings she wasn't having. When she was happy, she laughed; sad, she cried; shy, she hid. Everyone else I knew took a drink.

But she would soon be thirteen. That dangerous age, when fearless girls begin to worry about what boys think of them. It was already beginning, I realized, as she asked self-consciously, "Maybe it's too…babyish. I mean, who really cares about pirates and stuff?"

"Tell that to Johnny Depp," I said and gave her an extra hug.

When the phone rang, I jumped.

For a few seconds reading her story, I'd almost forgotten. Now I knew it must be the police, having traced my car. Who else would call at seven a.m.?

The ringing phone pierced the quiet in the kitchen. Julia looked at me, her face reflecting the fear I felt. I knew I must look pale because all the blood had drained from my face. My heart beat so hard I thought she might hear it.

I answered tentatively, a lump in my throat.

"Brett Tanager, please."

"Speaking." My throat so dry, my voice cracked.

"Hold for Danny De Lucci."

Danny was the production manager. He got on the phone and told me they'd gotten the script and were boarding it now. We were too heavy on the outdoor day; were there any scenes that could be rewritten to take place indoors? I went to get my copy of the script, and we talked about it back and forth until we'd come up with two scenes that could be adjusted to fit the shooting schedule. I said to go ahead and board them, and I'd rewrite them as soon as I got in. I bent down to check the damage on my car in the driveway. The rubber protector on the bumper had been pulled off slightly, and the fender was bent. I looked for blood, chipped paint. But, at least to my naked eye, I couldn't see either. It didn't look too bad. Maybe I hadn't really hurt that woman after all. Maybe I'd just knocked her over, and she'd be fine. If she'd been really hurt, my car would look worse.

Julia came out to see what I was looking at.

"I think I hit a dog," I said as explanation.

She whimpered in sympathy.

"Or maybe it was a coyote."

"When?" she asked, concern for the animal all over her face.

"Come on, you'll be late for school."

I had to get into the office to rewrite those two scenes before starting the next script, and I had meetings all day. I didn't take my car in to be fixed. Somehow I thought it was better not to try to hide the evidence. As if not getting the car fixed were the moral equivalent of turning myself in. I searched the newspaper for word of what happened but found nothing. It might be too soon. But when I checked the next day, and there was still no word, I thought with enormous relief that, one more time, I had eluded the consequences of my own bad behavior. I resolved again that, when the season was over, I'd take a good hard look at my drug and alcohol problem. In the meanwhile, there was a script to write.

On the third day, a small item appeared in the back of the metro section. Rosa Aguilar, a housekeeper who worked for a family in Beverly Hills had been on her way home shortly after one in the morning when, changing her tire by the side of the road, she was hit by a car whose driver did not stop. She had been taken to Cedars-Sinai hospital where she remained in serious condition. Police had few leads; there had been no witnesses.

I closed the newspaper, a numbing sensation spreading through my body as all the muscles in my neck arms and chest contracted and blocked off the flow of blood. I don't know how long I sat there, struggling for breath, when my secretary buzzed to tell me Brad Castleman was on the line.

Brad worked for the network. A call from him was never good news. He would have read the script and would be calling with "notes." Getting notes from Brad was like being pecked to death by parakeets. I knew I shouldn't take the call in the state I was in, but I picked up the phone anyway.

"Brad!" I said, trying to sound like someone eager to hear what he had to say, like someone who hadn't caused a woman to be taken to the hospital, someone who wasn't a criminal.

Brad had some "concerns." I looked at my watch. I knew it would be a lengthy conversation. He began giving me his notes.

Not having been high on cocaine when he read it, as I'd been when I wrote it, he had found some story elements that didn't track. He plodded his way through, zeroing in on the moments I liked best, suggesting alternatives I found ponderous and heavy-handed. I tried to concentrate, tried to be polite, but I found myself becoming increasingly sarcastic, ridiculing what Brad was saying, which made him more intractable, until we were shouting. But all the time I was arguing with Brad, I knew he was a stand-in for the real cause of my anguish, the headline in front of me that said "POLICE SEEK HIT AND RUN DRIVER."

Finally, I said there was an emergency on the set and got off the phone. I re-read the article I don't know how many times. I reached for the phone to call Cedars-Sinai, but as I did, I heard a quiet voice warn me that the police would probably put a trace on the phone. I hung up.

I told my secretary they needed me on the set, left my office, walked to the parking structure, got in my car, and drove off the lot to find a pay phone. Do you know how hard it is to find a pay phone now that everyone has cell phones? I knew there was one at the Fonda Del Sol, the Mexican restaurant and bar I often went to across the street from the studio.

I ordered a quick scotch to fortify myself and went in the back to place the call.

"This is Edith Strunk," I said, "from the *Valley Sentinel*. Could you give me an update on the condition of Rosa Aguilar?"

I learned no more than that her condition was listed as serious. Still, it was a relief. She was alive. I had another quick drink to celebrate, got back in my car, and drove back onto the lot.

A few hours later, I was in the midst of a production meeting, when I was once again seized with terror and remorse. I excused myself, drove off the lot, found another pay phone at a gas station, and called again, identifying myself as a different reporter. Again, I was soothed and relieved to find that Rosa Aguilar was still alive, her condition serious but stable.

After that, whenever I became agitated, I found a pay phone and called to enquire about Rosa's condition, addicted to the flood of relief that flowed through me at word that she was alive. I began to imagine that when she recovered, I'd come forward, and we might even laugh about this someday.

On the fourth day after what I was beginning to think of as "the accident," I was driving to meet Brad, who, upset at the turn our conversation had taken, had asked if we could meet for lunch. Brad had no real power. That resided with Marty Nussbaum, who owned and ran the studio that had recently bought the network as well. But it seemed politic to meet with him. Ordinarily Brad would come to the lot, but we had arranged to meet at a restaurant near the studio. I noticed a pay phone in front of a convenience store in a corner mini-mall and pulled into the parking lot in front.

"This is Edith Strunk from the *Valley Sentinel* calling for an update on the condition of Rosa Aguilar."

I was put on hold. I waited in a state of heightened awareness of the dryness in my throat, my speeding pulse, and racing heart, while listening to "Rocky Mountain High, Colorado" on the phone. When the Muzak stopped, I heard the shuffling of papers and muffled voices before a woman spoke.

"Rosa Aguilar died at approximately 6:40 this morning."

My vision dimmed then ended, like a fade out. I felt myself falling, but I clutched onto the pay phone. I must have staggered towards the alley because the next thing I knew I was leaning against the dumpster, retching and heaving. The smell of my own vomit mingled with the smell of rotting garbage brought me back to life— or what would pass for my life from then on. I looked up to see a red-faced, bare-chested homeless man watching me. He seemed not much older than me with long hair and wild red eyes. He held a cardboard sign that said "Why lie? I need a drink," but he held it by his side as he watched me puke.

I straightened up, standing on shaky legs, and realized I had thrown up on my Armani suit, and I'd have to reschedule lunch with Brad. The tinny computerized version of "Eine Kleine Nachtmusik" let me know that my cell phone was ringing. It was Jonathan in New York.

"We did it, babe—we got the pick-up!"

There was silence as he waited for my reaction, but I was too disoriented to respond. A wave of nausea swept over me, my legs felt wobbly, and I thought I might throw up again. Jonathan was too elated to notice and went on, his voice high and fast with excitement.

"A full twenty-two! And we keep our time slot! Marty loves us! The advertisers love us! I'm so proud of you!"

I tried to murmur something appropriate. Jonathan was elated enough for two.

"I couldn't do anything about the license fee, so we're still stuck with the seven-day shooting schedule. But you've turned them out fast enough so far, and I told them you'd have no problem with that. Gold ring, babe, just like I told you! I love you."

I got off the phone, called my secretary, and told her to reschedule Brad Castleman. Then I called my doctor and got a refill for Xanax.

CHAPTER 3

Jonathan flew home the next day. His plane got in at five. The plan was that he'd go to the house, shower, and change, and we'd all go out for dinner when I got home. I managed to leave the office just after seven. But I stopped in at La Fonda del Sol for a drink first. I wasn't sure what I was going to say to Jonathan about what had happened or whether or not I'd tell him. In any case, I felt the need to fortify myself, and I always enjoyed the camaraderie among the grips and gaffers who mingled there after work. By the time I got home, it was after nine. Afraid I'd appear drunk, I snorted a line in the car.

Jonathan was hungry and angry. I arranged my face into what I hoped was a smile. His face fell when he saw my inebriated state.

"Julia was hungry; I ordered take-out. Have you eaten?"

I managed to kiss him, apologize, and mumble something about needing to address the network notes, which were predictably stupid but had to be done.

Our large kitchen was the primary family room. At its center was a full size work station with stools around it for kibitzing with the cook; more often than not we ate there rather than at the dining room table. Large copper pots and pans hung from a circular rack above it. Jonathan took out the containers of Thai food he'd already put back in the refrigerator and set them out for me. He took two plates from the cupboard—hand-painted ceramic plates we'd bought on our last family vacation in Italy. As he served me he told me his ideas. The pickup gave us a platform. The studio and network were solidly behind us, willing to spend money on guest stars, promotions, tie-ins. Now that it was an integrated media universe, we could cross-pollinate.

"Sounds sexy."

He laughed, giddy with excitement at the fulfillment of our dreams. I got a beer from the fridge and picked at my food with chopsticks, pretending to eat. Jonathan was too excited to notice. He said that Marty had promised to open the Poseidon purse for us. Kate McKenzie, the actress who played Jinx Magruder, would be featured on every talk show on all the Poseidon networks and channels. There would be stories about her in every Poseidon magazine and fan book compilations in the bookstores. He even talked about a cartoon spin-off for Poseidon's kid network. With Poseidon behind us, there was no limit to the saturation we could achieve.

When Jonathan and I had first begun developing the show, he'd been working for Trident, a small independent studio. By the time we sold the pilot, the studio had been bought by Poseidon, a conglomerate that was quickly becoming an entertainment behemoth. Last year, Poseidon had bought the network as well, so both studio and network were under the same ownership. Marty

Nussbaum, Poseidon's driving force and CEO, held power over a vast entertainment universe, and liked to keep, as the saying about him went, "a finger in every eye."

Poseidon owned publishing companies, radio networks, cable channels, theme parks, hotels, newspapers, magazines, Internet portals, and a satellite and distribution service that allowed it to broadcast its product into every reach of the globe. All entertainment short of daydreams. If they could figure out a way to sell ads during REM sleep, they would. Once they decided to publicize us, there was little chance of any person in the world not being aware of our show.

As I listened to Jonathan, I imagined telling him that while he was away, I had killed someone in a hit and run accident and not (yet) gotten caught. I pictured his expression. Horror, shock, revulsion. Anger, disappointment, helplessness. Would he remember that he loved me? Or only feel the loathing I now felt for myself?

"Marty has ideas about a new direction for the show. Just a few changes, a slightly different slant, which I assured him would be fine with you."

"What kind of changes?"

I knew that once I came forward, our show would forever be branded with my crime. Even with Poseidon money behind us, I would go to jail. I *should* go to jail. It would be the end of everything Jonathan had worked towards. Telling him would break his heart. And if I told him and didn't come forward? I'd burden him with a secret whose weight I was only beginning to fathom.

"Now, don't get defensive. Just some ways to broaden the appeal. Bring up the ratings. I'd rather you hear it from him directly."

How could I live with him and not tell him?

"Let me guess. He wants to find more ways of getting Jinx Magruder into a wet t-shirt."

How could I live with him once he knew?

I could see Jonathan's annoyance with me for not getting on board with his excitement.

"I wish you wouldn't dismiss his ideas before you've even heard them. It's just possible they might be good. You can't deny his track record."

Our conversation was interrupted by Julia bursting into the kitchen.

"You got the pick-up! That's so awesome!" She sat on one of the stools and picked a peanut from a Styrofoam container of Pad Thai. "What are we going to do to celebrate?"

"What do you think we should do?" Jonathan's face flushed with pleasure at our triumph and at the sight of his daughter, who, since his wife had died, had been the love center of his life.

"Whatever you guys decide. You're the ones who sold the show."

Jonathan went to a calendar we kept in the kitchen, which showed, in addition to play dates, doctor's appointments, and family obligations, our production schedule, around which everything else needed to be arranged.

"Let's see…we're finished with post on the twenty-third, and we don't have to start shooting until…" He flipped over two pages. "The fifteenth of July. Of course, it would be good to have two or three scripts ready before we start prepping…" He turned to me. "Could you write in Hawaii?"

A few months after Jonathan and I had begun working together, we'd all gone to Hawaii. Julia was eight. The two weeks we'd spent there as a family were among the happiest any of us had ever known. Julia's delight at the Oz-like underwater wonders she saw while snorkeling was contagious; the world seemed wondrous through her eyes. I loved to tell her bedtime stories, her body snuggled next to mine as she thrilled to the adventures of Susie-Q, a character I made up. We ate meals together, saw sights together, played and ate and laughed together. After Julia fell asleep, Jonathan and I made long languorous love on crisp hotel sheets that were rumpled in the morning by the tumult of our desire. When we got back from that vacation, I'd moved in. In Hawaii, we'd become a family.

"Sure." Julia squealed with delight. She high-fived Jonathan then me, while Jonathan's eyes twinkled.

I knew I was never going to say a word.

* * *

In bed that night, Jonathan pulled me close.

One thing that had gotten Jonathan and me through everything and anything was sex. From the first day we met, it was as if we were pulled together by some cellular magnet, a tug of longing, for connection, possession. Hurt feelings, misunderstandings, all could be subsumed in our body's need for one another. We could always turn to each other in bed and find something that made everything else less important.

Now, I recoiled from his touch. I felt dead inside; worse, detached and removed. I did not want to be reached at my deepest recess; I needed to keep that place hidden from now on. Even having a secret had to be kept a secret.

"What is it, babe?"

I reached for him, clasping him in my arms and legs, and tried to will myself to respond with the passion he'd come to expect. I tried to use the heat from our bodies to quell the images that came whenever I closed my eyes: a woman changing her tire by the side of the road as I struck her and careened past. I tried to respond as if there were only the two of us in bed, but Rosa Aguilar was there between us.

I wanted to go to the funeral but didn't dare. I sent flowers instead and included some cash, in small bills.

Honestly, I didn't think I'd get away with it. Every time the phone rang, every time a door opened, I thought it would be the police. But it never was. I was the only one who knew that there was an uncrossable barrier between me and the rest of the world; that everyone else was on one side, and I on the other.

CHAPTER 4

Cut to, exterior, beach, day. Tufts of white clouds billow in a bright blue winter sky. The sun is high and white, the ocean glassy and smooth. The tide unfurls carpets of foam as sandpipers scamper at its edge. A woman stands at the shoreline looking out to sea trying to work up the nerve to walk in.

I hadn't had a drink yet that day, and it had been almost five hours since I'd awakened, or come to. But the craving was intense, and I knew that any minute now I would smoke a joint, or take a Xanax, and then think, oh, just one to take the edge off—and one more time I'd wake to find myself caked in vomit, or soaked in urine, or next to a man whose name I didn't know, promising myself that today would be different.

I had long since lost house, home, and family. It took so many drugs in ever increasing quantities to blot out the memory of Rosa that I'd lost whatever ability I'd had to write scripts that made any sense. Jonathan had no choice but to replace me—on the show and, not long after, in his life. No longer fettered by the need to function, I hurtled into darkness. I spent days and nights in behavior so noxious that the only solace I could find was in removing myself from anyone or anything good.

And yet somehow, a few weeks ago, I'd run into Gerry Talbot, a director I'd once worked with. He was shooting a film in Toronto and needed someone to stay in his house and water his plants. God knows why he thought he could trust me, but he had, and I'd jumped at the chance. Gerry lived in a spectacular beachfront home in Malibu, and I was unemployable, $180,000 in debt, and sleeping on my dealer's sofa. A show-runner who could no longer run the show. This gave me a place to stay and a car to drive—mine had been repossessed—but most importantly, I thought that living at the beach would be the chance I'd been looking for to finally clean up and get my act together.

And yet—and yet. Every day I'd wake with the same resolve, but before long, I'd take that drink, and often that was the last thing I could remember. I'd come to behind the wheel of Gerry's Range Rover, with no memory of where I'd been, heart jack-hammered at the thought that I might once more have done what only I knew I'd done before.

Since I could not stop drinking, nor prevent its consequences, my only recourse was to stop waking up.

I put one foot tentatively in the water. It was icy cold. *You'll get used to it*, I told myself, *Just walk in*. I was barefooted, in jeans and t-shirt, and even though I had a sweater wrapped around me, I shivered in the bright winter sun. I tried to urge myself onward but couldn't take the next step. Maybe if I were drunk, I could do this. I'll drink, and this time I won't try to stop, I just have to remember to get back here and walk in.

But I knew I couldn't trust myself even to do that. Oh, God, help me. What was the matter with me?

"Brett!"

A young woman came towards me, negotiating the sand awkwardly in her chunky platform boots. She wore a high-cut denim skirt which showed off her long legs, tights with the kind of holes in them that used to be cause for throwing them out but which now made them more expensive, and a blousy spaghetti strap top revealing a thin collarbone leading to narrow shoulders and delicate arms. A tattoo of a serpent coiled round a rose on the top of her arm. It was only those big doe eyes and the juxtaposition of the beauty mark next to the chicken pox scar on her cheek that allowed me to recognize her at all.

"Julia?"

Had it been that long? She'd still been a child when I knew her, but her slender body had softened and curved; she was becoming a young woman. Her hair was cut well, in a subtle, expensive haircut that showed its natural wave to good effect; her skin was clear of any lines or blemishes.

If I'd thought I was dead inside, the sight of Julia proved me wrong. Like the wings of a great bird taking flight, I felt a wild surge of—could it be joy?—opening in my chest. It lasted only a heartbeat, and then it was gone. But for a moment I remembered what it was like to live in a world with good in it. A tide of love and loss overtook me, powerful as the wave I'd hoped to die in a moment before, from the time when I was her mother, and life seemed to work. I longed to hug her, but held back, paralyzed by my own unworthiness.

"Brett. I need to talk to you."

"How did you find me?"

She looked puzzled, as if I'd seen her, and told her where I was staying. It was a look I was used to, on the faces of people who assumed I'd remember moments we'd spent together while I was in an alcoholic blackout. But surely, if I'd seen Julia, I would remember.

Wouldn't I?

I ransacked my memory of the nights before, but there were hours, days, of lost time, when I truly had not known where I'd been or what I'd done.

"Did I tell you?" I asked tentatively.

But I thought I saw relief in her eyes. "My dad told me you were house-sitting for Gerry Talbot."

"How did he know?"

In her face, I could see the dimpled cheek and chin of Jonathan, also the delicate bone structure and pale, haunting beauty of her "real" mother, the shiksa goddess Jonathan thought I might be but wasn't.

"Maybe Gerry told him? I overheard him talking to someone about it on the phone, and I asked him."

"Who was he talking to?"

What must I look like to her? My clothes hung off me; I had lost interest in food. I never combed my hair, never wore makeup, barely showered or changed my clothes. I was glad I was wearing a sweater and jeans, because I had scabs and bruises all over my body. I made a gesture to primp my hair, matted by the ocean air. My appearance didn't seem to bother her.

She cast a quick glance behind her. I followed her gaze, but saw nothing but the multi-million dollar beach "bungalows" that lined the road.

"You're all grown up! I can't believe it! Look at you!"

It wasn't only that she was beautiful; it was the layers of time her appearance carried. A teenager stood before me, but in her, I saw the little girl in a tutu I'd sprinkled with fairy dust before sending out to trick or treat. The eight-year-old in a snorkel mask whose squiggling body I held in the shallow water in Kauai. I remembered the two of us baking a cake for Jonathan's birthday, collapsing in giggles at the sludge we produced but eating it anyway because, after all, it was chocolate. If only I could have been the person Julia thought I was when we snuggled as I made up Susie-Q stories how different my life would have been.

She shifted from foot to foot, scanning the beach from one end to the other, her eyes filled with fear. She still said nothing about why she'd come.

"You want something to eat? A coke or something?"

The beach was a private one, shared only with the neighbors, and at eleven o'clock on a Tuesday morning in February, it was empty of all but a few sandpipers. She agreed, and we began walking back up to Gerry's.

"How did you get here?"

For the first time, she smiled. "I drove. I'm sixteen now. Dad and Lynda gave me a Prius."

"Sixteen!"

When was the last time I'd seen her? I tried to think back. For a while after Jonathan and I split up, I'd had an apartment on Sunset Plaza Drive, and occasionally Jonathan would let me see her, although he wouldn't allow her to stay overnight. I railed at him for taking her away from me, but she was his, not mine, and in some part of me, I knew he was right. It wasn't long before it was more important to have money for drugs than for rent, and I was forced to move to a cheaper place on Hollywood Boulevard, and I was embarrassed for her to see it. I'd kept the same cell phone number, so she could reach me, and for a while she kept me abreast of news of school, or friends, or Jonathan, who quickly began seeing another woman, whom I was gratified to know she didn't like.

On her fifteenth birthday, I'd arranged with Jonathan to drop her off at Musso and Frank's, a restaurant not far from my house. But I'd fallen the night before, and as I was leaving the house to meet her, I caught a glimpse of myself in the mirror. I had a big black and blue mark on my face, and I'd chipped a tooth. I thought she could only have the same feelings for me I had for myself—disgust, contempt, and hate. I got drunk and didn't show up. I thought the best thing I could do was stay out her life. Now I realized how much I'd missed.

"Wait till you see this house. It's incredible." As we walked back up the beach, I couldn't help but ask, "What's with the tattoos?"

"They're stick-ons. Cool, huh?"

"Way cool."

Gerry's house was a designer showcase, pristine and sleek, photo ready. The ocean side of the house was glass; the kitchen and dining room looked out over a large wooden deck. A few grasses sprouted on the dunes by the house then the sand extended, clean and bright, to the shoreline, where it turned darker and wetter in the low tide. The sun was high, the sky bright blue, the ocean calm. I opened the Sub-Zero refrigerator, took out two Diet Cokes, and poured them into two glasses over ice. I was about to add a shot of rum into mine but stopped myself. In that moment, I knew for the first time that, for me, there was no such thing as one drink. I didn't want Julia to have to watch me get drunk. I put the rum back and took the two Cokes out to the deck, where Julia had her back to me. Instead of the ocean, she was looking at her cell phone and texting someone.

"Incredible view, isn't it?" I said. "I've got this place until April when Gerry gets back."

Julia finished texting but still wouldn't meet my gaze. If there was one thing I was familiar with, it was fear, and I recognized it in Julia's eyes.

"Something's happened to Caleigh."

Caleigh (whose name rhymed with 'gaily') Nussbaum had been Julia's best friend since first grade. Marty and Erika Nussbaum's only child was as close to a princess as American democracy allows.

"She's disappeared."

"What do you mean, 'disappeared'?"

"She's not at school, she's not texting back, hasn't posted on her wall; nobody knows where she is."

"Did you ask her parents where she is?"

"You know Marty and Erika. Anything they said would be a lie."

I certainly knew Marty. We used to say about him that the way to tell if he was lying was to see if his lips were moving. I'd met Erika a few times, but she'd made little impression on me, other than being the sort of woman who always defers to her husband.

"When was the last time you saw her?"

I recognized this too: riffling through the mental alternatives before coming up with the most presentable story. How awful to see Julia taking on my worst characteristics.

"At school. Two days ago."

Somehow, I knew it wasn't the truth. A liar can usually recognize another.

"Are you sure she's not just home sick and not answering her phone?"

My suggestion didn't even warrant a reply.

"What do Jonathan…and Lynda say?" I tried not to choke on the name. Jonathan and I had lived together but never married. We'd talked about it, and each of us wanted to at different times but never simultaneously. He married his next girlfriend quickly. There'd been some overlap. It had been a sore point. To say the least.

"They work for Marty. They're not going to want to rock the boat." She turned towards me, and I could see the apprehension in her eyes. "I need you to help me find her."

I was startled. "Me?"

"You used to write that detective show." She paused. "And you're not all caught up in that Hollywood bullshit."

In my show, Jinx Magruder solved a murder a week. The more scared I was, the braver she became; the more my life spun out of control, the more commanding was Jinx.

"Honey, that was television! Make believe. It doesn't have anything to do with real life. You should know that better than anybody." I took a swig of my Coke. "If you're really worried about Caleigh, tell Jonathan and Lynda. Let them talk to the Nussbaums. It sounds like maybe the police should be involved."

The sun was warm, but a breeze rippling from the ocean was salty and cool. My palms were starting to sweat, and yet my skin felt clammy. A wave of nausea turned my stomach, and I thought perhaps I should have poured myself that shot of rum after all. I pulled my sweater close to me, hoping Julia wouldn't see that my hands were trembling.

"There's this big merger in the works. Poseidon is being bought by Alliance. If it goes through, everyone is going to make a ton of money, including Jonathan and Lynda."

"But surely, if something's happened to Caleigh that would be more important than money…"

The words weren't out of my mouth before she shot me a look that reminded me that to Marty Nussbaum there was nothing more important than money.

"…at least to Jonathan?"

Julia looked out at the ocean, as if weighing how much it was important for me to know. I followed her gaze. A few sandpipers scampered at the shoreline, leaving tiny footprints in the wet sand as the tide rolled towards them and away. A lone seagull flew low over the water.

"If I tell you something, will you promise not to tell my dad?"

Deep inside, where my heart used to be, I felt something stir, something furry, that had slumbered but now stretched and yawned, touched that Julia sill thought she could trust me.

"Of course."

"Have you ever heard of 'enjo kosai'?"

"No. What's that?"

"It's Japanese. It means 'paid dating.'"

I waited for what came next.

"It's really big in Japan. It's like when older men want to be with teenage girls. They like pay to take her to dinner and buy her presents and stuff. Caleigh was really into it."

"Wait a minute. What do you mean they want to be with teenage girls?"

She shrugged. "I don't know. They really get off on being with young girls. It's like some sort of father-daughter thing. Except for the sex."

Somebody told me once that you learn a lot more from kids when you don't react to what they tell you but just listen without judgment. So I just said, "Oh?"

"It's like a secret thing. Old guys who are into teenage girls. Caleigh was making tons of money at it. You can make like $1000 a night. Sometimes even more."

I sputtered on my Coke. "But Caleigh's parents have all the money in the world. Literally. What does she possibly need money for?"

I remembered the year that Marty made headlines for receiving a bonus worth more than the Writer's Guild was asking for its entire membership for a three-year contract.

"She won't even let Caleigh have her own credit card. When you think of what she spends and she won't even give Caleigh a credit card?" Julia made it sound like child abuse. "She treats Caleigh like one of her dolls that she can dress up any way she wants."

I remembered now that Marty's mansion was famous for its enormous size with an extra wing to house the booty of Erika's compulsive shopping. And that Erika was famous for having a collection of dolls.

"This way she can buy anything she wants. Like, she got two Prada dresses? And three Balenciaga bags. That's why a lot of girls from my school are doing it. So they can buy whatever they want."

"Girls from your school?"

"Caleigh got a bunch of us into it."

I felt my stomach knot. "You too?"

Julia held my eye for only the briefest moment before looking away and shrugging, like it was no big deal. I was speechless. It wasn't only the idea that rich girls from one of the most expensive private schools in Los Angeles were working as prostitutes. It was more the look I'd seen in Julia's eyes—defensive, false bravado concealing—what?

Shame? Embarrassment? A cry for help? Whatever it was, it was layered and false, which Julia had never before been. I sipped my coke, noticing that it had no power to take the edge off the pain of how I'd let her down.

"Caleigh was into it more than anybody else. And now she's disappeared. And I think something's happened to her. And I want you to help me find her." She turned towards me with urgency. "You made up everything Jinx Magruder did. You'd know how to do it, if you try."

"Honey, those were stories. Pretend people. I wouldn't know the first thing about how to find someone in real life. You need real help."

"I know! That's why I'm here."

"Not from me, from someone who knows what they're doing. Ask Jonathan."

"I can't."

"A teacher then, or a guidance counselor. Someone at school."

"No. There isn't anybody else."

In the distance, white sails dotted the horizon. The air was still with only the sound of the breakers lapping softly in a gentle rhythm. I wanted so much to be able to help her, to make up for all the times I'd let her down, but I knew, even if she didn't, that I was not someone who could do anyone any good.

A runner, bare-chested, loped along the shoreline leaving footprints in the wet sand. Gerry's house was on the exclusive Broad Beach Road, and his neighbors were among the elite of the business. The exquisitely sculpted body of this beautiful runner belonged to Campbell McCauley, one of Gerry's movie star neighbors. I was starting to point this out to Julia, when I noticed the desperation in her eyes.

"Please?" she asked.

"Hold on. I have an idea."

When I was doing the show, I'd been referred to an ex-cop turned private eye whom I could call for research. He'd been so helpful, we'd put him on retainer. I'd liked him. He'd always had an air of competence I admired. I hadn't spoken to him since I left the show, but I thought maybe he could help Julia now.

"I know this guy; he was the tech advisor on the show. He's a private investigator. I'll bet he could help you. Maybe I've still got his number. Hold on."

I went back in the house to look for my phone. I found it in the bedroom, but I'd gotten it too recently to have his number in it. We'd have to Google him. I went back to report to Julia.

She was gone.

"Julia…" A moment before, her presence was so unexpected; suddenly, her absence was desolating.

I looked up and down the beach, as she had done a moment ago. The beach was empty. The runner's footprints by the water's edge were already washed away; he was nowhere in sight.

I walked through the house and opened the front door, hoping to see her car, but saw only the garbage bins lining the block waiting to be collected. Other than that, the street was empty.

CHAPTER 5

After Julia left, I thought about what she had told me and decided to try to find Mike Drummond anyway. I'd always enjoyed talking to Mike. When he was our tech advisor, I had often called him frantic, staring down a deadline that loomed like an oncoming truck. I knew I could count on him, not only for ideas, but also for his comforting presence. He walked through life with confidence that he'd have what he'd need when he needed it. It wasn't arrogance; it was, well, faith. I thought I could probably use a shot of that now, and it would be great if I could help Julia out, a feeble stab at recompense for the times I'd let her down. I found his number, called him, and arranged to come down to see him.

It was only as I was driving Gerry's Range Rover down to the address he'd given me in Playa del Sol that I remembered something else about Mike that he'd made no secret of at the time: He was a drunk and junkie who was sober now. There was nothing anonymous about Mike's alcoholism.

Mike was in his garage as I drove up, working on the engine of a car up on blocks. Mike was a big gruff bear of a man, a fifty-year-old surfer, strong and lean, with powerful arms and shoulders. I remembered that Mike's passion for surfing was equaled only by his enthusiasm for restoring old "woodies"—the cars from the 40s that hauled surfboards in the 60s, and it was one of those he was working on now. A beat-up jalopy that looked like I felt was parked on the street. A 1948 Ford Station Wagon, its paint was faded, its wood panels chipped, springs and stuffing burst from what used to be upholstery. It had been stripped of its V-8 engine, which was up on Mike's worktable, its parts spread out before him. He put down the piston he was oiling when he saw me walk towards him, grinning broadly.

"Hey, kiddo. I was wondering when I'd ever see you again. What's it been, a couple of years?" He apologized for not hugging me, gesturing to his hands, dirty with oil and grease.

I was fine skipping the hug. He wore a t-shirt, cut-offs, and old sneakers. The top of his head was balding, sunburned, and freckled, fringed by hair bleached white by the sun. His face was craggy, with a deep furrow between his bushy brows, but the lines extending from his eyes and the ridges of his cheeks showed how often and easily he laughed.

"I had to go back to real work when the show was cancelled," he said. "It was no fun after you left anyway." The show had gone on for two years without me and had been off the air a year.

"So, what's this about a missing kid?" He fitted the piston into the cylinder bore and began tapping it gently with a rubber mallet, listening to the sound it made with careful attention, then picking up the oil can and giving a gentle squirt before tapping gently again.

I told him about Julia coming to see me and her concern that she couldn't find Caleigh. I'd promised Julia not to tell Jonathan, but it didn't seem to violate that promise to talk to Mike.

"They've been fooling around with some dangerous stuff. They've kind of been playing hooker."

Mike looked up, startled. He put down the oil can; I had his attention.

"Going out with older men and getting paid to do it. Supposed to be a fad in Japan called 'enjo kosai.'"

"Nussbaum's kid?" He'd worked for Poseidon too. He seemed as incredulous as I'd been.

"Anybody go to the cops?"

"No. Caleigh's parents are denying anything's wrong, and Julia hasn't told her parents because they both work for Caleigh's father."

He wiped his hands clean on a rag. His garage smelled of oil and grease, mixed with freshly varnished maple, mingled with the breeze from the ocean just a block away. The music that came out of his speakers was an eclectic mix of surfer music, reggae, blues, and songs that might have played on the radio when the car he was restoring was new.

"The first thing I'd do is talk to her friends. Kids know everything. They'd know where she was if she'd run away, or what kind of trouble she was in. That's where I'd start."

He picked up the piston rod and fit it into the crankshaft. "Hand me that torque wrench, would you?" He gestured to some tools on the table.

As I handed him the wrench, he held my gaze in his open, clear blue eyes.

"How are you, Brett?"

It had been a long time since anyone had looked at me with kindness or caring. Was that the reason? Or something within me I hadn't known was there? How to account for the words I heard myself say to him; the secret I'd I never admitted to anyone before.

"Actually…" My face burned with shame. "I think I may have a problem. I drink…too much. I try to stop, and I can't."

He broke out into a grin so wide, it was as if I'd just told him we'd won a first class trip for two to Fiji.

"Brett, that's wonderful."

I stared back at him, dumbfounded he could find anything marvelous in what I'd just said.

"That you're admitting it. That's the first step."

I felt sick to my stomach; I thought I would faint. If I could take back the words I'd just said, I would have.

"Come on inside. I'll make you a cup of coffee. Let's talk."

* * *

This was a man who took his coffee seriously. He brought me into his kitchen, sat me down at the table, and began a process that began with grinding whole beans, then boiling filtered water to pour over the grinds in a French Press. In moments, the house was filled with the smell of strong, freshly brewed coffee. He poured me a cup. My hands were trembling, and I spilled it on myself. He seemed to have anticipated this; he'd brought a napkin and wiped up what I'd spilled.

"Just alcohol or drugs too?"

"Both."

He wasn't surprised. "Hardly anybody just drinks anymore. They call it 'alcoholism' because that used to be the main drug. Now there are so many. But addiction is addiction—it's all the same disease. You ever have a blackout? Where you wake up and can't remember what you did the night before?"

That had been happening to me since high school. But lately, it would happen while I was up: I'd come to in the middle of a conversation and have no idea who I was talking to, or where I was, or how I'd gotten there. It was terrifying beyond description.

"Congratulations! You're an alcoholic!" He beamed again with that inexplicable delight I would soon learn people in AA found in the most sordid of admissions.

Mike tried to put me at my ease by telling me stories about himself. He talked about using the drugs he was supposed to be confiscating, testifying in court to things he'd been too drunk to see. He told a story about thinking he was going to a law enforcement conference in New Mexico and ending up at a stripper's convention in Texas. He made me laugh, but when it came time for me to tell him stories of my own, I held back.

"Why'd you quit?" I asked instead.

"I blew a murder case. A girl got killed, and the perp got off because I screwed up. I got fired and was about to eat my gun."

He paused to make sure I knew what he meant. I thought about my plan to walk into the ocean right before Julia arrived. I said nothing, but he knew I understood.

"Instead, I called a sober cop I knew, and he helped me get sober."

"How?"

He looked at his watch.

"I'll show you." He told me there was a clubhouse a few blocks from his house that held meetings every night. He suggested he make me a bite to eat, and then we'd walk over there together.

If I told him I had other plans, he'd know I was lying.

The clubhouse was in an old log cabin a few blocks from the beach. It had one large room for meetings with folding chairs facing a podium and AA slogans, steps, and traditions all over the walls. Another room functioned as a lounge, with ragged sofas and several easy chairs, none of which matched, and an old beat-up TV in the corner. There was also a counter, behind which a young man in a sleeveless shirt, little gold earrings, and rock and roll hair, sold coffee, soft drinks, and sandwiches.

"Boots!" Mike called to a large brassy dame, age indeterminate, from another era. She had bouffant hair the color of Raggedy Ann's. An unrepentant cigarette between her lips curled smoke up into her false eyelashes, bold with mascara, ample as awnings.

"I'd like you to meet Brett. She's new."

Boots' eyes lit up as if she'd found a mink stole beneath her Christmas tree.

"Welcome, precious. We're so happy you're here."

Mike knew everyone in the room and introduced me to more people than I could ever remember. Everyone shook my sweaty hand, greeted me warmly, and expressed delight at meeting me. It had been a long time since anybody had been happy to see me, and before I knew what was happening, I found myself smiling too.

The first speaker that night was a grandmother in long skirt and crocheted vest. When introduced, she put down her needlepoint, got up to the podium, and regaled the group with stories of dancing on tabletops, jumping naked into pools, and eloping to Tijuana with one man forgetting she was already married to another. Everyone laughed uproariously, including, I was surprised to find, me.

But when the second speaker got up, I cringed. It was an actor I'd worked with on the show. I was mortified that he should see me here. I whispered as much to Mike.

"Brett, he's here too."

He told a story of broken marriages, shattered lives, opportunities squandered, and then—the happy ending. Sobriety! Music up, pull back, fade out, the end.

As if.

When we left the meeting, Mike exuded satisfaction like a man who'd had a good meal, great cigar, Turkish rubdown. He turned to me with his clear blue eyes.

"So, kiddo, think you can go from now till you go to sleep tonight without taking a drink or a drug? I'm not saying you have to stop forever, just for the rest of today. Think you can do that?"

I studied my shoes. I knew I could not be trusted, but I didn't want him to know that.

Whatever showed on my face, Mike said, "Shit, what was I thinking?"

He looked around for Boots, or some other woman he could commandeer, but the parking lot was empty.

"Look," he said, "please don't take this the wrong way. But I don't think you should be alone. Stay with me tonight. Don't worry, I've got a spare room. I'm not after you. I just don't want you to have to go through this by yourself."

I knew I shouldn't give Mike the wrong idea. He thought I was going to be joining this group, and I knew I couldn't. AA expects you to tell all the horrible things you've done, and I knew that was for people with secrets more benign than mine.

But I also knew that if I went back to Gerry's, I would drink.

I watched as Mike made up the spare bed and loaned me a pair of pajamas. I, who had followed men out of bars to get high, woken up next to strangers whose names I didn't know, felt suddenly embarrassed, ashamed to be the recipient of such kindness. I wondered what he'd want in exchange.

But as I fell asleep that night, I remember realizing with amazement that I'd gone one whole day without a drink or a drug.

CHAPTER 6

The next day, I woke without throwing up. A milestone. But I
had a pulsing headache, my skin was clammy, and I ached all over. I
thought I was getting the flu and should maybe put off this sobriety
business until I felt well enough to handle it. Mike explained that my
body was like a toxic waste dump, that while I was using, my liver
and kidneys had all but stopped even trying to eliminate poisons,
knowing that more was on the way. With sobriety, my body would
finally begin to purge itself of years of ingested chemicals. It might
be a while before I felt better. But it would happen.

"When? How long will it take?"

He wouldn't say. The way to do it was to go to a lot of meetings.
Everyone there would be sympathetic; they had all gone through
it and wouldn't expect anything of me. He appointed himself my
sponsor and suggested I go to the morning meeting at the clubhouse.
He was out in the field today, but we exchanged cell phone numbers,
and he told me to call him later to tell him how I was doing.

"Today, there's only one thing you have to do: don't take the first drink. Or the first drug. That's it. No matter what."

I went to the morning meeting, and when it was over, thought I'd better just hang out until the one at noon. I knew I'd have to go back to Gerry's eventually—I was supposed to be house-sitting, after all—but I was afraid to be alone. I'd gone one whole day without drinking and using, but I had no confidence I could do that again. So I sat in the clubhouse, drinking cup after cup of coffee, allowing myself to be introduced as a newcomer to other sober alcoholics who came and went throughout the day.

After the noon meeting ended, I called Mike, told him I'd been to two meetings that day, and thought I'd better go back to Gerry's.

"Have you eaten?"

"No."

"You'd better get yourself something to eat."

"Yes, Mom."

"I'm serious. You need to keep your blood sugar up. Don't get too hungry, angry, lonely, or tired. Those are set-ups for relapse."

I told him I'd found a meeting in the directory not far from Gerry's house. I'd get something to eat, drive back to Malibu, take in the mail, and go to another meeting. I thought I could do that much.

"Call me any time. Don't take the first drink. Or drug. And call me."

I had to admit I enjoyed being fussed over.

* * *

I drove back to Malibu, stopped at a coffee shop near Gerry's, and ordered a burger and a Diet Coke. A TV in the corner was tuned to an all-news station, with the sound off. I'd been too consumed with my own suffering to pay attention to anything happening in the outside world, but as I glanced up, I saw footage of Marty and Erika Nussbaum, standing in front of their mansion. Marty was in shirtsleeves, Erika a designer suit. She clung to his arm and looked frightened and fragile, allowing him to do the speaking for both of them.

For once, Marty's boyish enthusiasm was absent. He appeared haggard and anxious.

I asked the waitress if she could turn the sound up. She pressed a button on a remote.

"I think any parent can understand the anguish my wife and I are experiencing."

His fist was clenching and unclenching by his side. He looked down at the tiny woman clinging to his arm. Erika looked up at her husband and then vacantly out into space, saying nothing. Her suit, neat and trim, had epaulets on its padded shoulders, as if to lend a military snap to the fragile woman within. I remembered that when I'd met her, she'd reminded me of my mother. Maybe it was the combination of hauteur and sadness.

"If there is anyone who has information that will lead to finding our daughter…we beg them to come forward. There will be a reward. And if anyone thinks they can get away with harming her…" His voice came close to cracking. "…they will find that retribution will be swift and merciless." His fist opened and closed by his side.

At the news desk, the anchor turned from the screen showing the live feed to face the audience, ruminating, "The very human side of one of the giants of the corporate world."

He took a moment before continuing.

"To recap, Caleigh Nussbaum, sixteen-year-old daughter of Marty Nussbaum, CEO of Poseidon Entertainment has been reported missing. She was last seen Monday, leaving her cosmetologist's office in Beverly Hills, wearing her school uniform of tartan plaid pleated skirt and white shirt, with a lime green cashmere sweater over the shoulders. She drives a red Mercedes SL63 with the license plate, MY SL63. Anyone who has seen her, or who has any information about where she is, is advised to call this special hotline."

The screen showed a still photo of Caleigh dressed for her school prom. A teenager now, I could still recognize the little girl I used to know. She had inherited some of her father's pudginess, but encased in her strapless sheath, she did not exceed acceptable bounds of beauty. Her hair and make-up had been done with sophistication and style, yet she still had the youthful awkwardness of a newly hatched chick. The professional lighting, accentuating what bones there were beneath chubby cheeks, cast a haunting shadow over her innocent features. It was a portrait of a very young woman striving to be glamorous beyond her years.

The police were looking for Caleigh. Julia would have no need for me now.

I remembered how frightened she'd been when she came to see me.

I looked at my watch. A little after three. I thought maybe I'd just go find her at school and see what she thought about this development.

The next meeting wasn't until 7:30. What else was I going to do with myself?

The Eastman School was a private school that served both sexes, from kindergarten through twelfth grade. It was harder to get into than Harvard; parents applied after the first ultra-sound. Its students were children of the wealthy; friendships and alliances made here were invaluable assets for later success. Sensibly, the administration required a uniform. The campus consisted of several buildings sprawled over a choice piece of real estate north of Sunset in Brentwood, the former estate of a silent screen star, from the days when there was no income tax, and this was countryside.

As I pulled into the parking lot, parents were shepherding kids towards their SUVs and mini-vans, while the teens with licenses headed for their own cars. Julia had been in middle school the last time I'd dropped her off here. I wondered if I'd recognize any of her friends in the long and leggy teenagers I was watching.

A gaggle of Eastman girls in soccer uniforms came towards me, laughing and razzing each other about the game. One of them stopped to rummage in her bag, while the others chattered on. A tall willowy blonde turned towards the straggler.

"Move it, will you? I'm jonesing for Starbucks."

Dawn Delaney had been a skinny, bossy twelve-year-old, and she was no less imperious now. Her expression bore that jaded look of haughty nonchalance common to rouged dowagers at the tables in Monte Carlo, and the teenage children of the affluent in Los Angeles. She stood with one hand on her hip, sighing with exasperation. Her straight sun-streaked hair was pulled back loosely in a ponytail; her face glowed from her exertions on the field. She tapped her foot impatiently. The long socks and high shorts of her soccer uniform revealed long lean legs.

"Coming," said the straggler, a dark-haired girl whose face was hidden from me as she searched her bag.

"I don't know if I can go to Starbucks. My Dante paper's due tomorrow," said a third girl. I recognized Heather O'Connor, whom I remembered as an intense redhead whose mother liked to dress her in plaid. She had grown into a tawny strawberry blonde with pale eyelashes and hazel eyes. She made a face. "*The Inferno*. Ugh." Then, "Hannah, come on."

If I hadn't heard the name, I never would have recognized the dark-haired beauty who found what she'd been looking for—a pack of cigarettes—and now shook one out and lit it. Hannah Rosen had been a chubby little girl with tight curly hair and glasses; I remembered how cute she looked in her karate class white outfit, roly-poly and serious. Now she was slender and shapely. Her tight curls had grown into a wild nimbus of dark hair; her eyes, no longer hidden by glasses, were long-lashed, dark and soulful. She inhaled the cigarette then blew the smoke out in a long plume.

"Heather. Hannah. Dawn."

They didn't recognize me. Dawn's initial reaction was wary and suspicious, whereas Heather's smile of curiosity was open and gracious.

"Brett Tanager. I used to live with Julia Weissman's dad."

Dawn's distrust did not relax even as she placed me, but Heather and Hannah broke into smiles.

"You created *Murder Will Out*. You took us all on the set for Julia's birthday." Heather remembered what even I'd forgotten.

"Is that show still on the air?" asked Hannah.

"No," said Dawn, always the expert. "Kate McKenzie's on *Dallas Central* now. Well of course, it's still on cable in the mornings. I watch it if I'm home sick. The clothes are a riot. You can't believe the way they used to dress."

The show had been created six years ago, lasted five seasons, and been off the air a year. But I guess to a sixteen-year-old, that was a generation ago.

"Cool," said Heather. "What are you working on now?"

The eternal show biz question, even from kids.

"Taking a breather. The show wore me out."

"My dad says things are the worst he's ever seen," Dawn declared. "I mean, if you get an eleven share, you're lucky. And you can forget about a back end. That's why he and Jonathan went to Poseidon when they bought Trident. It was the only way they could keep their points."

"Well, it's reality. You can't get points in reality; you can't even get Guild minimum. That's why Amy's dad couldn't keep her in school; they don't need writers for reality."

"Reality's not going away. The numbers on reality are just too good."

"If they could just figure out how to monetize content on the Internet."

"Listen," I interrupted. Savvy as these girls might be, and much as they could relaunch my career with a word to the right person, that's not why I had come. "Is Julia around? She came to see me yesterday, and we started a conversation we never got to finish. Have you seen her?"

They looked from one to another with a look that was easy to read: Don't tell her anything, she's a grown-up.

"I'm not here to get anyone into trouble, I promise," I added. "Was she in school today?"

Dawn's look said, "Executive privilege, get a subpoena."

We were surrounded by parents and nannies, coming to collect their kids.

"Look, is there somewhere we can talk more privately? Isn't there a Starbucks nearby?" Maybe I could play on her caffeine needs. I could use some myself. Mike said "don't take the first drug," but based on what I'd seen at the clubhouse, I knew caffeine didn't count. I was feeling sweaty and shaky; maybe coffee might help.

"Across Sunset. We usually go there after practice."

"Let me buy you a Frappuccino."

Dawn looked me up and down. I was still wearing the clothes I'd put on to go down to Mike's yesterday: jeans, sneakers, a white t-shirt, and a suede jacket I'd bought in Florence that never went out of style. My palms were sweating, and my hands were jammed into my pockets because I thought they were probably trembling. My five foot eight frame was cadaverous; I hadn't bothered to eat much lately. Still, being thin has never been a liability in this town, and evidently, I fell within the range of Dawn's standards.

"Sure," she said with a toss of the head, "Why not." We walked to Sunset and crossed at the intersection to a Starbucks in a mini-mall across the street, catching up on who was how old now, and what we remembered about times we'd shared when I lived with Jonathan and Julia. They remembered the stories I told them at bedtime; I remembered the shows they put on in our living room. The delight I'd felt watching them seemed now as unrecoverable as the eight-year-olds within those teenage girls. I wondered if any of them were doing what Julia had spoken of.

The police had been to school that day, interviewing kids about Caleigh, but I wanted to wait until we were seated before asking them harder questions.

The store had put a few plastic tables and chairs on the side-walk. It faced Sunset Boulevard, which was heavy with traffic in both directions, and the odor of exhaust fumes was an unpleasant accompaniment to our coffees. But it was private, in the way that sitting on a public street in a neighborhood where nobody walks can be.

We ordered our drinks and settled at a table outside, so that Hannah could smoke. The other two derided her habit but indulged it.

"Was Julia in school at all today?"

They exchanged furtive glances and shook their heads no.

"Do you have any idea where she is? I saw her yesterday. She came to see me at the beach," I added.

"Did you call her?" Heather was already taking out her cell phone and punching in Julia's speed dial. She listened for a bit then said, "Hey, it's me, we're at Starbucks. Your step-mom's here, she's looking for you." I was signaling for her to leave my number. Instead, she handed me her phone. I spoke into it. "Julia?" It was her voice mail. "Look, call me on my cell." And I left the number.

I handed the phone back to Heather.

"Julia came to see me because she was worried about Caleigh. And now that the Nussbaums have reported Caleigh missing, I'm worried too. Do you have any idea where Caleigh is?"

"On another planet?" Dawn shook several packets of artificial sweetener into her already sweet Soy Chai Frozen Latte.

"Caleigh's sort of in her own world," said Heather. "She acts like she's better than everybody because of her dad, and a lot of kids humor her because they want to get into the business. But nobody really likes her."

"Julia does." Hannah's voice was soft even when disagreeing. Shimmering beneath the surface, like the reflection of a tree in a pond, I could see traces of the little ninja dumpling in the beauty she'd become.

"Well, right, Julia, because she's loyal. She's always sticking up for Caleigh. But nobody else likes her. She's kind of a bitch."

"Kind of?" Dawn was dismissive. "She's worse than her mother."

Heather laughed. "Caleigh would shit a brick if she heard you say she was like her mother." She turned to me. "Caleigh hates her mother."

"How come?

Dawn slurped her drink. "Do you know her mother?"

"Anyway," said Heather, "the police were here earlier asking about Caleigh. They talked to all of us. I told them I hadn't seen her since Monday and have no idea where she is."

She looked to the others; they all agreed that's what they had said too.

"Did you tell them about 'enjo kosai'?"

Hannah startled as if a car had backfired. She and Heather exchanged uneasy glances before Hannah looked away. Dawn stared down into her latte, slurping loudly, but not looking at anyone.

"What did Julia tell you?" asked Heather softly.

"She said 'enjo kosai' was something Caleigh was into. She called it 'paid dating.' She said someone had told Caleigh that it was a fad in Japan but that Caleigh had gotten some kids from Eastman into it."

"Did she say who?" asked Heather.

I watched Hannah's hands tremble as she stubbed out one cigarette and lit another. I knew she was listening for my answer.

"No. But she thought it might have something to do with what's happened to Caleigh."

"That is so lame," said Dawn. "Caleigh makes up these stories. I don't believe any of it."

"She talked about it," said Heather. "She said it was a way we could make money. But I don't think anyone actually did it."

"Like Caleigh showed up at school one day waving a thousand dollar bill around and bragging about how she got it? Like it's so hard for Caleigh to come up with a thousand dollar bill? Give me a break. She probably just took it from her dad's wallet."

"Did she say who had given it to her?"

"Caleigh lies about everything. Nobody would believe anything she'd say anyway."

"I've got to go," said Hannah, standing. "I've got my Dante paper due tomorrow."

Dawn looked at her watch, and Heather drained her latte, crumpled her napkin, and stood, looking for a place to throw them.

"Wait a minute," I said. "Before you go." I dug into my bag to get my notebook and a pen. "Let me get Julia's phone number. And give you mine." I started to write my number down on a piece of paper. That just goes to show how laughably retro I am.

"I'll bump it to you," said Heather.

Noticing my clueless expression, Heather took my phone away from me, held it in the other hand from hers, bumped the two together, and handed mine back. Julia's name, number, and photo showed up on my cell phone. And mine on hers.

"How'd you do that?" I asked, marveling.

"It's easy." Heather used her phone to take my picture and attach it to my number. She showed it around, and they all laughed at the expression of bewilderment on my face.

"Can I give mine to each of you? And would you please call me if you hear from Julia or find out anything about Caleigh?"

With some mysterious combination of finger taps and gestures they instantly had my contact, and I theirs, as I stood by helpless in the face of technology that came so easily to them.

"Before you go. Even if you think it was a lie. Who did Caleigh say had given her the thousand dollars?"

"Some movie star wasn't it?" asked Heather.

"Campbell McCauley," Dawn raised her eyes. "Yeah, right. Like Campbell McCauley, only the sexiest man on the planet, who's married to Rosalie Bennett, like the biggest box office star in the world, has nothing better to do than pay Caleigh Nussbaum a thousand dollars to have sex with him. Give me a break."

They tossed their empty cups into the trash, and got ready to leave. I remembered the look of fear in Julia's eyes as she'd turned from watching the runner on the beach. Coincidence?

I wondered if I'd hear from them again.

CHAPTER 7

Still reluctant to go back to Gerry's, I turned off Sunset and went north on Cliffwood, hoping to find Julia at home. It felt strange driving into my old neighborhood. I drove past homes that I remembered as modest and unassuming, recessed from view behind bursts of bougainvillea. Remodeled, they had expanded to twice their size, and now squatted swollen and pretentious, like gluttons who had burst their seams, jostling and competing for space.

Since I'd moved out, *Murder* had gone on without me and had made its lucrative syndication deal. It was still playing, somewhere in the world, any hour of day or night. My points had been net, and what little back end I had was being garnished by the IRS. Jonathan on the other hand had a track record that warranted gross points. He worked for Poseidon now, and the success of *Murder* and other shows he'd developed had resulted in stock options and bonuses exceeding even the producer's share of profits. He was a rich man with a new trophy wife.

I turned into my old driveway. If I'd expected a remodeled monstrosity, what I saw was worse: Nothing had changed. The house was as unpretentious and charming as ever, nothing different except the absence of me.

It hadn't occurred to me that either Jonathan or Lynda would be home this time of day. But the blue BMW in the driveway was the model Jonathan leased new every three years, and I'd bet anything that the pearl grey Jaguar beside it belonged to Lynda. No sign of Julia's Prius.

I went to the door and rang the bell.

A maid in uniform, who appeared to be Hawaiian or Philippine, answered my ring. I didn't recognize her.

"Hi. I'm Brett Tanager. Is Julia home?"

The maid looked uneasily around as if unsure of how to handle the situation. She decided on a simple, "No." But before she could close the door, I heard the sharp staccato of heels on the stone floor, and a woman's voice ask, "Who is it, Maile?" The heels belonged to a pair of sling-backs so minimalist that when you saw them in a store window, you'd ask yourself "who wears shoes like that?" The answer walked towards me: Lynda.

She stopped short when she recognized me. "Brett. What are you doing here?"

Lynda LeWylie, now Lynda LeWylie-Weissman, was a "suit," like Jonathan. The people who actually wrote, directed, and produced the shows spoke disparagingly of the "suits"—executives who didn't have to solve problems, only create them by giving "notes." Lynda's was Armani, natch, with a mini-skirt so high and a plunging cream silk neckline so low they all but met in the middle. Her outfit managed to communicate at one and the same time a willingness to please and the will to command. The large diamond sparkling from her left hand signaled that she had married well.

"I'm looking for Julia," I said, coming into the house as if I'd been invited.

"Why?"

"Research." The lie came easily as I walked past her into the large entry room, which opened onto the living room with its sensational hillside view of the canyon.

The first thing I noticed was that the table was gone: the antique washstand near the door that we'd used as a catchall for mail and keys. And that the floor, which had been Spanish tile, had been replaced by white marble.

"I've been working on a teen thing, and she said she'd help me with some background." Those tiles had been so beautiful. Brilliantly colored, hand-painted, consistent with the Spanish Moorish design of the house. Who could possibly think this white stone was an improvement?

"When?" asked Lynda.

Jonathan came in from the kitchen, a look of concern disturbing his usually sanguine features. "I called the O'Connors and the Rosens and the Delaneys. Nobody knows anything." He stopped short when he saw me standing there.

"Brett. What are you doing here?"

I was unprepared for the bolt of longing that shot through me at the sight of him. Jonathan was tall and well proportioned. The curve of his jaw, the roundness of his cheeks, cleft in his chin, indentation of his lips, even the tendrils of his richly layered hair combined to give his slightly rabbinical features a soft and sensuous intelligence. He wore his muted grey, hand-tailored wool suit as easily as a jogging outfit and moved with a natural grace, his fluid movements calling up images of rocking hips and rumpled sheets. The images were unwelcome.

"I came to see Julia."

"She's not here. You'd better go."

His body and eyes were as closed to me as a locked gate, and he waited for me to leave. I stayed.

"Has something happened?"

Jonathan and Lynda exchanged a look just as the girls had. Her eyes told him "keep quiet." Nonetheless, he allowed, "Julia's off playing hooky somewhere. Nobody knows where she is. She hasn't been to school in two days." An unspoken argument was taking place between Jonathan and Lynda, all in the eyes. Jonathan's confession had been some sort of gauntlet from which Lynda felt she could now retreat.

"I'm leaving," she said.

"I wish you wouldn't."

"Handle it however you want. But I have a 5:30 over the hill, and I'm not going to be late."

She headed for the door, but Jonathan blocked the way.

"The police will want to talk to you."

Lynda blinked in outrage. "The police! If you call the police, this will all be up on Jason Ratt's website before you hang up the phone."

"That's not what I'm worried about."

"I know. But you should be. Don't you see this is just what she wants? I suppose you think this is a coincidence. That of all times, she picks now to do this." Her eyes glinted with the sure knowledge she was right. "If you call the police now, how's that going to look to Alliance?"

"Jonathan, please. Is Julia in trouble?"

I might as well have been an ant crawling along the baseboard for all the attention they paid to me.

"Julia's more important to me than a merger with Alliance. The police are looking for Caleigh; we have to tell them Julia's missing too." Jonathan's voice broke. "They say the trail goes cold in 48 hours."

"Nothing's happened to her. She's a spoiled brat, hell-bent on destroying everything you've worked for, and everyone can see it but you. When she can't get what she wants, she pulls a stunt like this to get negative attention." She elbowed her way past Jonathan. "Well, I for one will not play that game with her. I've got the whole team assembled; I'm not missing this meeting."

"Julia came to see me in Malibu. I saw her yesterday."

Abruptly, they both remembered I was there.

"What time?" asked Jonathan. And then, as an afterthought, "Why?" And then, "You'd better come in."

If I was going to stay and talk to Jonathan, Lynda wasn't going to leave. She took out a cell phone and punched a button. "It's me. Traffic's horrendous. Call everyone and push it back a half hour." She followed us into the living room. "What else?" She murmured as she listened to her messages, grunting slightly at each, until she exclaimed, "Oh, fuck him. Tell him…" she looked at her watch. "Never mind, I'll call him myself. Remind me. There in a jiff." She pressed the off button and tossed the phone back in her bag.

When I lived there, the biggest piece in the living room had been a huge, sectional sofa that Jonathan and I could lie perpendicular to one another, me with my laptop, him with a book or a pile of scripts, a soft chenille throw for each of us. Sometimes it was Julia curled up opposite while Jonathan read in his armchair, feet on an ottoman, staring out at the wonderful view of the canyon. We were a family of readers; there was a pillowed nook by every window. The room had been functional and comfortable, an eclectic mix of antique and contemporary pieces; the Moroccan rug from the last century, the inlaid wood coffee table made last year by a carpenter/actor in Santa Monica.

The only thing left was the view and the fireplace. The furniture that filled the space now was angular, spare, and minimalist; repelling, rather than inviting. Not a pillow out of place, not a newspaper or magazine to give any indication that anyone spent time in this room; nonetheless, it made an imposing impression. It was the perfectly designed set for the successful Hollywood power couple, including silver framed photos of Jonathan and Lynda, gazing starry-eyed at each other in romantic getaways in secluded spots—except, then, who took the picture? It was expensive and beautiful, but generic, as if Lynda or her designer had walked into a showroom and bought everything in it at once.

"I guess it was about eleven a.m. I wasn't thinking about it being a school day. I was so glad to see her. I didn't stop to think."

"No, you never did." Jonathan's words were meant to wound. They succeeded.

"She said you had mentioned to her that I was staying at Gerry Talbot's, so she knew where to find me."

I looked to see the effect it would have on Lynda to know that Jonathan and Julia still talked about me. It registered. I wondered where the rug was now. Or what happened to the case that housed found treasures, like Jonathan's beloved antique toy soldiers. I remembered the excitement I'd felt when I'd spotted a complete set at the flea market. I'd given them to him for his birthday, and I knew he loved them. They were gone.

"Why did she come to see you?"

I hesitated. I didn't want to betray Julia's confidence, but I also didn't want to stand in the way of her getting help if she needed it. "She was worried about Caleigh Nussbaum. She said that Caleigh hadn't been to school, and she was afraid something might have happened to her. This was before the Nussbaums had gone to the police."

Jonathan and Lynda didn't speak, but I could tell that a subtle shift had taken place. No longer arguing, they were now in complete agreement.

"What else did she tell you?"

"Just that she didn't feel the Nussbaums were being completely up-front with her. Have you spoken to them?"

Lynda shot Jonathan a warning look, and he caught it easily. "Brett, you have to go now."

"I don't mind waiting. If you call the police, they may want to talk to me." I decided my promise to Julia did not preclude talking to the cops; if something serious had happened, I couldn't withhold information that might be important.

"This is a family matter. It doesn't concern you."

"But I'd like to help."

Lynda took her place beside Jonathan. "We don't need your help." They were now a united front. She even took his arm.

"But if Julia's in trouble..."

"If Julia's in trouble it's in large part due to the kinds of things she was exposed to when you lived here. You've done her enough harm." He was already walking me towards the door. "Maile, see Brett out."

"Wait a minute," I said. "Do you mind if I just use the restroom before I leave?"

Jonathan gestured for me to go down the hall. I could hear them arguing as I left.

"If you have to call the cops, at least get someone in first who knows how to control the flow of information. Aren't the Nussbaums using Nic Ripetti?"

I slipped into Julia's room.

When I'd left, it had been cluttered with books, comics, and toys: the room of a child in transition to teen. Now the wall color, fabrics, and furniture had the same out-of-the-showroom-and-into-your-house generic quality as the living room. There was nothing of Julia in this room except for the screensaver on the large, flat-panel computer monitor, which showed a horse galloping on the beach. Julia had been wild for horses as a child. Attached to her computer or near it was every gizmo and gadget that could be bought for a child of affluence.

I moved the mouse to wake up her computer, clicked onto her Internet browser, and saw that her friends had been sending her instant messages, trying to find her. At least, that's how I deciphered, "WRU?" I tried to read them, but they were in a language that bore little relation to the English I had always written. I took out my notebook, and jotted down screen names and messages. "OMG. CD9 – P911." "RU doing Sushi?"

I wrote it all down, hoping to make sense of it later.

I rummaged through the notebooks on her desk, looking for scraps of paper, whatever I could find. I rifled through the books on her shelf.

I was gratified to see how many books were in the room, not only on her desk and shelves, but by her bed. Julia read for pleasure, an unusual trait in someone her age—or mine, for that matter.

Also on her bed, leaning against the pillow, was a frayed and tattered Piglet doll. The only remnant of the child I left behind.

I looked through the books stacked by her bed then felt behind the pillows and under the mattress. Success. A notebook was jammed under the box spring. I recognized it as the journal I had given her for her birthday along with a copy of *The Diary of Anne Frank*. I flipped it open now but heard Jonathan's footsteps in the hall coming towards me. I slipped it into my bag along with the notes I'd found in her notebooks. When Jonathan arrived at the door, he found me sitting on her bed, holding the tattered Piglet next to me. His face, angry a moment before, softened slightly.

"Brett, you have to leave."

I put the Piglet back down on the bed. "How are you? Aside from this? I guess there is no aside from this right now, is there."

"No. You?"

What could I say? It was too complicated, and now was not the time.

I could feel Jonathan's and Lynda's eyes on me as I walked back down the hall towards the front door, which Maile was holding open.

A smile flitted across Lynda's face. If she were thirty years younger, she would have stuck out her tongue at me. As it was, all she had to do was slightly arch an eyebrow.

The door closed behind me on a family to which I no longer belonged.

CHAPTER 8

As I drove away from Jonathan's—and Lynda's—I had to
remember that now it was her house too—the sky turned from blue
to a cold grey slate; soon it would be black. A cool mist rolled in from
the ocean, bringing with it a dank cold that brought drops of con-
densation to the windows. I too was enveloped in the fog of all I had
lost. It wasn't only the career, the money, the house, the boyfriend, or
the family. It was the sense when Jonathan and I were together that
there was somewhere I belonged. Now the man who used to love me,
who'd thought I was funny and smart and talented and sexy, froze at
the sight of me, and who could blame him? I'd put his daughter's life
and happiness at risk too many times to count.

Where was she?

I pulled over to the side of the street and stopped the car. I reached
for the journal I'd taken from Julia's bedroom. I'd given it to her for
her 13th birthday, and she'd made sporadic notations in it since then.

My heart contracted at the sight of her handwriting. I recognized
in its roots the mother's day cards and valentines she'd written me as
a child.

I thumbed through its pages. She'd write every day for a couple of days, and then there'd be big gaps until the next burst.

"October 2. We won against Bentley!!!! 2-0 (25-13, 25-22)!!! Megan Gannaway cried when they lost. Next week is Calhoun/Webster. They're first in the league, and they've got Tawna Dunworth, but we were on it! I put away 11 kills. Not bad. Heather keeps bugging her Mom to let her get a nose job.

October 3. Dawn came over to study. She's going to get grounded unless she brings her grades up."

I took out my notebook and made notes of names she mentioned, thinking it would give me clues as to who might know where she had gone.

"Feb. 19. Dad says I should try out for the debating team. I told him I feel so self-conscious in front of people, but he says that's why I should do it. Brett so obnoxious. Trying to get Dad to dance with her and teasing him about how uptight he was, but she was acting like a jerk. I hate it when she gets like that. And if you say anything to her about it, she gets mean."

I closed my eyes, like a child who thinks if he covers his face, he can't be seen, but it did nothing to staunch the flood of remorse. Whatever illusion I'd entertained that my drinking and drug use had hurt nobody but myself—and Rosa Aguilar, of course—evaporated. Thinking of Rosa, I flipped through the notebook quickly, to see if there was anything about the night of…the "accident"…on Coldwater. But I'd given this notebook to Julia for her 13th birthday, and that was after the fact.

I took a deep breath and continued to read.

"March 3. Just finished Silas Marner. Loved it!!! Now I have to write the paper. Brett shit-faced. So obnoxious."

"March 29. Tomorrow is the debate with Calhoun/Webster. I'm going to be awful!!!! I have to argue the case FOR using animals for medical experiments, and I don't believe in it!!! Dad says it will be good practice. Brett says it will teach me to be a television executive. That just gets them started again. They should just make a CD. They always say the same things over and over."

"April 23. Brett left. Dad says I'll still be able to see her, but she won't live with us anymore. At least the fighting will stop."

"May 3. "Caleigh says her Dad wants her to go to the prom with Lance Pearlman because his Dad is the agent for *Space Wizards*."

"May 16. Caleigh went to the prom with Lance, but she gave Tyler a BJ in the parking lot. I'm worried about Caleigh. She seems lost. Lynda's so phony it makes me want to puke. Oh, Heather's bulimic. She stuffs her face and then barfs her brains out. Her trainer told her it was bad for her electrolytes, but she says she'll look like her mom if she doesn't do it. I hate my body. I hate my hair. I hate my eyes. I hate my life. I wish Brett were here…"

"Feb 18. Well, dear Diary, I'm 15! Dad says I look more like my mother every day. He says I'll be beautiful like her as if that makes everything okay, but I know when he looks at me, he sees her, he never sees <u>me</u>. I can't even remember a time when I mattered to anyone…"

✶ ✶ ✶

There wasn't enough air in the car. I rolled down the windows. It didn't help. I gasped for air, strangled by a mixture of grief, loss, and remorse that constricted my throat and made it hard to breathe. There was only one thing I couldn't understand. How could you possibly not drink over pain like this?

I put the car in gear and headed back south.

Chapter 9

Boots Caruthers commandeered me as soon as I walked into the Playa del Sol Alano Club. She was using both hands to carry a giant coffee pot. "Hello, precious. Just in time to make coffee." Her gravelly voice left no room for discussion, and I followed her into the kitchen. She handed me the pot, and I measured out coffee into the strainer.

"Have you seen Mike?"

"Drummond?" She looked around. "He's a popular guy. You're the second person tonight who's asked for him."

"Who else?"

"Some redhead," Boots said, adding with a laugh and a confidential nudge, "I should talk. That's one bottle I'll never give up."

I must have looked as wretched as I felt because her eyes softened. "How much time do you have, sugar?"

"It's my second day," I said.

"Oh, baby," she said, "It's going to get better."

A concave young man with a goatee, wispy hair, and Elvis Costello glasses came into the kitchen in search of coffee. "We were hoping some big, strong, good-looking young man would come along, and here you are. Would you get that down from there, precious?" She pointed to a box on a shelf over the sink where the meeting kept its supplies.

The young man looked around to see whom she was addressing. He had sallow skin and newcomer eyes, a look that managed to say "help me!" and "fuck you!" at the same time.

"What's your name?" she asked, as he reached for the box.

He put it on the counter. "Greg."

"How long have you been with us, Greg?"

He ran his hand through his thinning wisps, beads of sweat forming on his upper lip. "Twelve days."

"Twelve days!" Boots shook her head with a look of wonder you'd expect had her grandchild dressed himself for the first time. "Well, Greg, come meet Brett. She's got even less time than you. You can tell her how it works."

I was filling the pot with water from a faucet at the sink, but I stopped to wipe my hands on my jeans, and offer one of them to Greg. I don't know which of us felt more foolish. Or whose hands were sweating more. Neither of us made eye contact.

"It gets better," Greg mumbled, but neither of us believed it.

Boots told Greg to bring the box of supplies into the meeting room and set them out. "When you're done, come back, and I'll give you something else to do."

"Who is she? The woman asking for Mike?"

"I've never seen her here before. I thought she might be new. But she said no, she was just looking for Mike and knew he came here every Wednesday."

"What did she look like?" I asked, surprised at the twinge of jealousy I felt. People were starting to amble into the meeting room, saving seats for themselves by putting down car keys and business cards, before mingling.

"Scared," answered Boots, "but then, who isn't?"

Greg and I set out the donuts and cookies while the coffee brewed. The room was beginning to fill. There was a hum of conversation, laughter, hugs. Greg and I hovered by the imaginary shelter of the coffee table. A few people remembered me from yesterday, and greeted me warmly. I introduced them to Greg. "He's got twelve days." Greg was welcomed with grins, handshakes, and hugs. Even though Greg's hands were sweaty and still shaky, he started to loosen up under the onslaught of bonhomie. When the coffee was ready, I poured myself a cup, added sugar, and cast my eyes around the room for Mike.

He wasn't hard to miss when he arrived. I remembered now his penchant for loud Hawaiian shirts. The one he wore tonight sported hula girls in grass skirts swaying under palm trees. Mike entered like a hero, shaking hands and hugging almost all who came in his path.

I took my coffee and crossed the room.

"Brett!" Ruth S., the secretary, waylaid me midway. "You're new, aren't you? Would you lead the meeting?"

"Sorry," I said. "I can't." I tried to push past her to Mike, but she blocked my way.

"Please? The leader just called from her car; she's stuck in traffic. It's not hard. You just read from the format."

I tried to catch Mike's eye, half-hoping he would get me out of this, though I knew he wouldn't. A woman entered the room, and I was sure she was the one Boots had mentioned. She not only had red hair; she wore a red dress with a plunging neckline and red high heeled shoes. She scanned the room. Boots was right; she did look scared.

The secretary tried to maneuver me towards the podium, but I pulled away and went towards Mike. The red-headed red-dress woman got to him first and whispered urgently in his ear. He frowned, glanced at his watch. She seemed upset, almost on the verge of tears. He followed her out of the meeting.

The secretary caught up to me and showed me the loose-leaf notebook with the script I was to read introducing readers and speakers. She took out laminated copies of the steps, traditions, and promises, excerpts from AA's "Big Book" and told me to ask for volunteers to read them.

"I told you, I can't," I said, pulling away.

"It's how we stay sober," she said kind, but firm.

Mike and the woman had gone.

I reluctantly agreed. Not knowing anyone, I went up to people at random and asked if they'd read the handouts. Everyone said yes and thanked me.

It was still ten minutes before the meeting started, so I went outside to look for Mike.

I'd left my jacket on my seat, and the ocean air was damp and cold on my bare arms. The sun had set, and the night was dark. A bare sliver of moon was pale and low in the sky. Somewhere nearby, a drummer was practicing, playing the same riff over and over.

The parking lot was full. Cars arriving this late had to turn around and look for places on the street. People hurried into the meeting. I walked through the parking lot onto the street and looked in both directions.

I didn't see them until I'd walked almost two blocks down from the meeting. Mike and the woman in the red dress were deep in conversation. I started to walk towards them, but their body language shouted "private." The woman was agitated, rubbing her arms and pacing as she spoke, anguish in her features. Mike spoke soothingly and calmly, but she kept interrupting him. Her manner registered not social anxiety but fear of a different magnitude.

Her red dress was cut in a long "v" that revealed the tops of her breasts, and her high heels sunk into the ground like golf cleats. Mike said something to her softly; she whirled around to spit out an angry reply, the only words I could hear.

"What if he finds out it was you? He'll kill you!"

Her heel stuck and her ankle twisted, and she stumbled. Mike caught her and stopped her fall. He took her in his arms, and she burrowed into his powerful embrace; the tears she'd been holding back finally spilled. Her shoulders shook with sobs. Mike held her as she rocked against him. A tall man, he looked over her head, to see who might be watching. Instinctively, I stepped back into the shadows. He seemed furtive, anxious, a man who does not want to be seen. He took her by the arm and led her away.

I looked at my watch. 8 o'clock, time to start the meeting.

CHAPTER 10

"Jan 3. Caleigh doing sushi."

"Jan. 15. Hannah did sushi. PC took them to a party, and she did it with—you won't believe this—Paolo Navarro!!!!! Am I crazy for saying no?"

* * *

Mike never came back to the meeting. I knew I had to go back to Gerry's eventually, and I thought it might as well be now. Needing help was not my strong suit; one of the things I prided myself on was how little I asked of anyone. I drove back, made myself a cup of tea, and flipped through the pages of Julia's journal. I copied every name I read into my notebook.

It had begun to rain. Fat drops slashed against the window and trickled down the glass. Even in the dark, the ocean outside was dotted with white flecks of foam, crests of waves roiled by the winter storm.

The sporadic entries spanned the years to the present; the entries I was reading now were from just last month.

"Jan. 31. "OMG!!!!! Finally decided to do sushi with Caleigh and Hannah. PC set it up. Said it was up to me if I hooked up or not, all I'd have to do is go and have a good time, but if I hooked up, $$$$. Got to party and who was there!!!! Clinton!!!! OMG I wanted to die. Soooooooooo embarrassed, but he was totally cool about it. But now he knows…"

"Feb. 11. Was doing sushi and ran into Brett!!!! Could she tell? She was so out of it, she probably won't even remember, but OMG I thought I would die!!! What if she tells my dad????"

What? Feb. 11? That was just a few days ago. When had she come to see me? Was it really just yesterday? I checked the calendar on my phone. So that was the look I'd seen in her eyes when she came to see me on the beach. I'd seen her just a few days before and hadn't remembered. Where? Who was she with?

I wracked my memory, but it was blank. I remembered being at the Topaz Lounge, knocking back shots of 151 proof rum, feeling invulnerable because of the cocaine. I was with a group of people. Who were they? How had I gotten there? Then I remember coming to behind the wheel of Gerry Talbot's Range Rover, doing 85 on the freeway, terrified of what I might have done and not even known about. I'd been having more and more of these blackouts, but that didn't make them any easier. Mike had said that was a symptom of alcoholism. But to see Julia? In danger? And not even know? What kind of a monster had I become? I closed my notebook and looked out the window into the darkness. Julia! What happened to that adorable girl, so guileless and good-spirited? The answer was unavoidable. I was the closest thing to a mother she'd had, and I'd failed her. Even before I left, I wasn't there.

I'd told myself I was so toxic, she was better off without me. But without a mother to guide her, she'd gotten lost. She was throwing herself away, as I had. How could it have been different if all she had was me?

But what if I'd stayed? What kind of a mother could I have been if all I'd had as a model was my own? She had retreated so far behind a veil of pills and alcohol she might as well not have been there at all. In fact, I wished she hadn't been there because her occasional attempts to rise to the occasion were so ill-timed and inappropriate she caused more harm than good.

Exactly how Julia felt about me.

I'd always thought I hated my mother. I realized I'd become her.

Like a curtain descending, exhaustion overtook me. I decided to try to get some sleep and deal with this in the morning.

* * *

Gerry Talbot had a built-in entertainment system. As I got ready for bed, I flipped on the TV, and it played in the background as I brushed my teeth.

I was only half listening, but a word here and there told me that the body of a teenage girl had been found, believed to have been murdered. My hand froze mid-brush, my mouth filled with toothpaste foam. I walked back into the bedroom.

On the screen, a series of shots taken earlier that day showed a crime scene in a wilderness area of the mountains, marked by yellow tape. Police cars barricaded the road, blocking traffic, allowing only cars from the Mobile Crime Unit and the Medical Examiner's Office. A team of forensic investigators blanketed the mountain. A stretcher was loaded into the van of the medical examiner. A jogger hopped from foot to foot with a dog by his side, which he held by its collar while a plainclothes policeman asked him questions and made notes of his answers.

I watched, frozen in fear, and gradually learned the details. The jogger running with his dog in the Angeles National Forrest had found what had turned out to be the body of a young woman who had subsequently been identified as Caleigh Nussbaum, daughter of Erika and Marty Nussbaum, chairman and CEO of Poseidon Entertainment, one of the largest media conglomerates in the world.

I went back to the bathroom and spit out the toothpaste, rinsing my mouth and coming back to watch as the footage switched to a live shot of a reporter, in rain gear, at night at the same scene, empty now of personnel, telling viewers that work had been suspended. The team had worked into the night, to try to collect as much physical evidence as they could before the rain started, as it would destroy footprints, tire tracks, and the like. In the background, we could see that the last police cars had left; only the media trucks remained, as well as a news helicopter, which hovered in the background, taking footage of the mountain wilderness.

I called Jonathan immediately, but it went to voicemail. The momentary relief I had felt at the realization that the body was not Julia's had been supplanted by sadness for Caleigh and fear. I wondered if Julia had yet come home, and I continued to try Jonathan as I watched the rest of the story.

The anchor recapped as he showed the footage I'd seen earlier that day of the Nussbaum's public announcement of their daughter's disappearance with its toll-free hotline. Ironically, almost simultaneously, the jogger had stumbled upon the body. Caleigh's father had identified Caleigh at the morgue; her parents were now in seclusion.

There followed a montage of file footage of Marty and Erika at premiers, Caleigh as a child cutting the ribbon at the first of Poseidon's theme parks, and clips of some of Poseidon's highest grossing films and TV shows as the reporters speculated on the effect this might have on the pending merger between Poseidon and Alliance, a deal that was valued at several billion dollars.

I finally got through to Jonathan. He was cool and distant, telling me only that they had not yet heard from Julia, and my participation in this family drama was not welcome.

I called Mike, but got no answer. I left word for him to call me. I said it was urgent.

There was no alternative to being alone with these feelings.

Maybe just a nightcap to help me fall asleep.

Oh, right. I don't drink anymore.

Gerry had a fully stocked bar downstairs. I shouldn't be alone with it. I should pour that stuff out.

I knew if I even went near it I would drink.

The bathroom off the upstairs master bedroom had a recessed whirlpool tub next to the slanted picture window on the ocean side. I ran a hot bath and poured in a dollop of freesia-scented oil. Easing myself in, I watched the rain slash against the window, listened to the crash of the waves, massaged by the pulse of the whirlpool bath. I thought back to a night when Jonathan, Julia, and I were on vacation in Hawaii in the beginning, when it was still all good. Jonathan and Julia had gone to Volcano National Park while I had stayed at the hotel, writing. Later, Julia came into our room, frightened by a nightmare she'd had about Pele, the Goddess of the Volcanoes. Taking her back, I got into bed with her and made up a story. I told her that I had magic powers. At night, I could turn into a bird and fly all around the world, looking into people's windows and finding out their secrets. That's how I got my stories; that's what made me a good writer. I told her that if she went to sleep, I'd turn myself into a bird and fly to Pele and make her promise not to make any volcanoes erupt while we were in Hawaii but to wait until we were back home. Only thing, I couldn't turn myself into a bird until she fell asleep. She did, in my arms.

How I wished that story were true, that I could fly around Los Angeles, peering into every window until I found Julia, so I could keep her safe.

Somehow, I got out of the tub, into bed, and under the covers without taking a drink or a drug.

Day 2.

CHAPTER 11

When a poor black or Chicana girl is killed, ho-hum. When a rich white girl is killed, stop the presses. But when the daughter of one of the world's richest men is murdered, a media magnate whose company owned a good percentage of the gross national product, it took precedence over anything else. The murder of Caleigh Nussbaum was the lead story in every media outlet, in every part of the globe that Poseidon reached, which was everywhere in the world.

The next day, every news station was broadcasting all-Caleigh, all-the-time, hastily edited "tributes" summarizing the highpoints of her life and death. They went over again and again the details of her disappearance and the discovery of the body, giving particular emphasis to the location.

Rattlesnake Canyon had previously gained notoriety as the spot where Richard Percy, a serial murderer who raped and strangled prostitutes, had dumped his victims, earning him the nickname of the Rattlesnake Killer. Percy was on death row and had been for three years, so he was ruled out as a suspect. DNA testing had tied him irrefutably to the crimes for which he was sentenced; there was no question of having the wrong person in jail. But for the seven years of his killing spree, and even more after he had been captured, he had become a media celebrity. His sultry good looks, soulful eyes, and long lashes had drawn a cadre of lonely women to his trial, and he had gotten more than one marriage proposal after his sentence to death row. The fear was that a copy-cat wannabe was walking in his footsteps.

An additional irony was that, after the Rattlesnake Killer had been caught and convicted, a TV movie had been made about him, his victims, and the women who loved him. The fact that this exercise in exploitation had been made by Poseidon, the company run by Caleigh Nussbaum's father, was discussed endlessly by various media pundits.

Pundits also discussed the impact of Caleigh's death on the proposed merger between Poseidon and Alliance, but nobody could guess the outcome. Poseidon and Alliance each owned media outlets in every major city. Combining their assets might require fresh interpretation of anti-trust regulation, or require congress to revise laws determining how many stations one company could own, but that wasn't expected to be a problem given the influence of corporate money on elections. Public interest groups were lobbying congress to crack down on this expansion of influence, saying that it threatened competition and stifled independent voices. The anchor added that, in fairness, it should be disclosed that this station was owned by Poseidon.

I switched to another all-news station, but it was owned by Alliance, and the news they gave out was identical. Mike finally called. He said he'd heard about Caleigh and wanted to make sure I was okay. I told him how worried I was about Julia. She had either run away or disappeared but, in any case, was now missing. Just as Caleigh had been, until her body was found. I was frantic to find out where Julia was and asked him for help. He was silent for a moment.

"Brett, I don't want to seem unkind, but this isn't any of your business. Don't you have enough on your hands right now?"

"I can't just sit around in meetings while Julia might be in danger."

"Why not? What can you possibly do that could be of more help to her than get sober?"

I looked out at the expanse of sand, pockmarked from last night's rain. The ocean was gunmetal grey, flecked with white; the sky one big dark cloud.

"Julia came to me for help. I was virtually her mother for six years. Call it amends. Isn't that one of the twelve steps?"

I remembered the fear in her eye as she scanned the beach empty of all but sandpipers. Where do birds go in the rain? They were nowhere in sight now.

"It's number nine. The steps are numbered for a reason. Nine comes after the other eight. From what I can see, you're still working on the first."

The first step was the one about admitting I was powerless, and he was right. I knew I'd fucked up. But "powerless" seemed overstating it. Worse, it seemed like shirking responsibility for the terrible things I'd done.

"I saw her. Four days ago. She was with someone, and I can't remember who, because I was in a blackout. It could be important; it could have something to do with what happened to Caleigh." I thought about telling Mike about the diary I'd taken from Julia's room and the names it had mentioned. But I was embarrassed by what it revealed about me. So I said only, "Julia and a bunch of her friends have been sleeping with very powerful men for money. And now Caleigh's dead, and Julia's missing."

If I had to show him the diary, okay. But he interrupted. "Look, I'll call some cops I know and nose around. I'll make sure they get in touch with you; you can tell them whatever you know. But in the meanwhile—first things first. Okay?"

He went over with me what I would do that day, what I would eat, what meetings I would go to, and when I should next check back in with him.

I hung up and sipped my coffee. The things I'd read about myself in Julia's diary sent me spiraling down a sewer of shame. All the things I'd done and pretended I hadn't; moments of degradation, betrayal and deceit I'd tried to obliterate with drugs and booze regurgitated back to consciousness, like refuse that would not decompose.

From the slough, rising like a bloated corpse, came Rosa Aguilar. The woman from whom I had run but who followed me now, like a spurned but faithful lover.

CHAPTER 12

"We're not supposed to talk about it. Ever. To anyone."

Hannah sat shivering in my car. School was closed because of Caleigh, and I'd phoned her at home. She'd been initially reluctant to speak to me, but when I told her that I knew about "sushi" and the party she'd been to with Paulo Navarro, she agreed to meet me. She said she could sneak out of her house and meet me at the Starbucks across from school, but then we'd have to go somewhere we couldn't be seen. I'd driven up Mandeville Canyon and turned onto Sullivan Canyon, a trail used by dog walkers and mountain bikers. I turned off the ignition. The wipers stopped, and the rain trickled down the windshield.

"Who told you not to talk to anyone?"

Hannah burrowed into her bag and found a cigarette and matches. Her hands trembled as she lit her cigarette then lowered the window just enough to blow a plume of smoke out of it. All this took time, and she said nothing while she did it.

"Honey, I know this must be hard. And if the stakes were any lower, I'd let it go. But Caleigh was killed. Julia's missing. I don't want anything to happen to you. I need to know about "sushi," how it worked, and who was involved, and you're the only one who can tell me."

Hannah blinked back tears as best she could, but they came anyway.

"Hannah, believe me, whatever you've done, I've done worse. There isn't anything you can say that will shock me. I just need to understand."

"It's not that. It's just…I'm so scared."

I wished I could promise her nothing bad would happen. But all I could do was say, "I know. Me too."

We sat in quiet, as the rain fell against the windshield.

"Do you have any idea where Julia is?"

"No."

"When Julia came to see me, she mentioned "enjo kosai." Is that "sushi"?

A whisper. "Yes."

"Do you think that has anything to do with what happened to Caleigh? Or where Julia is now?"

"I don't know. Maybe." She bit her inside lip. "Probably."

She took a drag from her cigarette and blew the smoke out the window, attempting to mask her fear. But her brow, so young and free of blemish or line, was furrowed with anxiety, pinching her features askew.

"Who's PC? The one who set it up and brought you to the parties?"

She looked at me in surprise but didn't question my knowledge.

"Patrick. Patrick Caiman."

It was my turn to be surprised. Even I, banished to the outskirts of the business, knew who Patrick Caiman was. He and Marty used to run Poseidon together. Patrick was known as the creative partner, whereas Marty was the business shark. Patrick was known for his outsized ego—an impressive accomplishment in this town—and also for the spectacular fall he took when Marty ousted him. I tried to remember the reason. All I could remember was Patrick going down in very public flames: fired by the board of directors at the peak of his career. Something about charging drugs and hookers to the budget of Poseidon films. And now that I thought of it, wasn't there also some scandal involving an underage actress?

"Caleigh ran into him at a premiere. He'd just gotten back from Japan. He told her it was a fad there, and he asked her if she'd be interested. I think at first she just did it to stick it to her father because she knows how much he hates Patrick. But she did it a few times and made a lot of money. Patrick told her that if she could find other girls who'd do it, he could find the guys. He said they'd all be like cool guys in the business, no creeps, like guys you'd want to do it with anyway, well, maybe older, but—anyway, you'd get a thousand dollars to do it. There was no downside."

The short beige pleated skirt of her school uniform fell mid-thigh on her bare legs. Her small, taut breasts sprouted up beneath her white polo shirt, and her clear skin was smooth as a pond. She must have seemed fresh indeed, to men jaded by Botox and silicone. It made me wonder about the price of innocence. A thousand dollars?

She took a deep breath and spoke quickly, as if trying to get her story over with as soon as possible.

"I mean, lots of people get paid to go to parties, if you're like a celebrity or something, and this was kind of like that. You know, they just like to have girls like us at their parties because of the way we dress and the way we look. So it was almost like that, except we got paid more if we, well, hooked up. I mean, it's not like we were virgins or anything. And money's money."

Yes. Isn't it.

"Caleigh used this car service to pick us up, and we all went to this house on Mulholland. There was a party with a DJ and some really awesome people and a deck with a view of the Valley. Caleigh introduced us to the woman giving the party, and she asked if we were cool with this because if we weren't we should tell her. She said there was no pressure, we didn't have to do anything, but if we wanted to hook up, she'd make sure it was safe. But we had to promise not to tell anyone. Parents, friends..." She looked at me, realizing she was violating this promise. "...Anyone."

She looked for a place to put out her cigarette. The car had no ashtray.

"But Caleigh's dead. And Julia's missing. That changes the equation."

She squashed her cigarette out in the cup holder, dropping the butt there. "So first we're just hanging out, and then Toby says, why don't we get comfortable and go in the hot tub."

"Toby?"

"The woman giving the party. She shows us where we can change, and she gives us robes, and we go in the hot tub. It's outside, on the deck, overlooking the Valley. So we're drinking champagne, and someone comes over to me and hands me a joint, and it's Paulo Navarro." She giggled, unable to conceal her childish glee in attracting such a prize. Paulo Navarro was a hot young television star, whose presence in a teen-themed night-time soap had made it the most watched show in the prized 13-22 demographic. His hairless bare chest often graced the covers of tween fan magazines, his sensitive eyes and protruding lips seemed to seek a soulful connection with a girl—maybe the one buying the magazine. The one sitting next to me had not only had sex with him; she'd been paid a thousand dollars to do it. Only in LA.

"We were fooling around in the hot tub, and then we went down the hall to a room, and…we did it."

I thought back to my own high school days. Funny how things change. A hand job in a Chevy seemed as quaint as a quilting bee.

"Afterwards, the car came back and picked us up and took us home. The driver gave us each the money in an envelope."

The cuticle she'd been poking at started to bleed. She put it into her mouth and sucked it, almost as a child would suck her thumb except that she seemed so frightened.

"Did Julia hook up that night too?"

"I think so. But I don't know with who. In the car, after, she wouldn't talk about it. She was crying." After a moment, she said, "I decided to tell Caleigh that I didn't want to do it anymore. But I never saw her again."

I sat there absorbing all that she'd said. The rain trickled down the windows. We were completely alone. Nobody was going to hike or jog or bike in this weather.

"Who's Clinton?"

"Clinton Cole. He's a dealer. He comes to our parties sometimes and brings the drugs. Some of the kids buy from him. Julia liked him."

"Was he at the party that night?"

"Yes. Julia was talking to him.

"Do you know where he lives? Or how I could talk to him?"

"No."

"Maybe one of the kids who buys from him would have a number for him. Can you ask around? And let me know?"

"I guess so." The sky was one big dark cloud, obscuring any sunset. When daylight ended, it became suddenly dark.

CHAPTER 13

Caleigh's funeral was held at Bayside Memorial Chapel, a large mortuary visible from the San Diego freeway. It was the final resting place of some major stars, a frequent stop on bus tours of the dead and famous. The funeral was by invitation only.

I'd called Marty Nussbaum's office and told the secretary that I'd been Julia Weissman's stepmother and had known Caleigh as a child. She took down my name and said she'd get back to me. I was glad I could give Gerry Talbot's Broad Beach Road address in Malibu; it carried more clout than my recent lack of credits. I received a hand-delivered invitation by special messenger a few hours later.

The day of the funeral was cruelly beautiful. The rain had stopped, and a bright winter sun shone on a day clear of smog; a few white clouds formed puffy shapes against a deep blue sky; the grass and trees fairly glistened in the sunlight. Outside, news trucks with satellite dishes were parked around the perimeter of the chapel, providing live feed as the stars made their entrances. Caleigh's funeral was covered as completely as the Golden Globes. Industry players, dressed for the world-wide exposure they knew they'd receive, pulled up in limos and paused on their way to the chapel, as reporters asked them for comments.

Those of us who didn't have drivers parked and walked to the chapel. I made my way past throngs of roped off fans jockeying for position, calling out names, and thrusting autograph books as if they were at a premiere.

There were as many stars of the political sphere as there were from the entertainment business. Both political parties were represented, reflecting Marty's bet-hedging contributions across the spectrum. Our charismatic Governor was there, along with our charismatic Mayor, the Chief of Police, District Attorney, and members of the City Council.

The DA and Police Chief were both pulled aside for interviews. Neither of them would offer any comment on the ongoing investigation, but each of them promised to use every resource to find and prosecute Caleigh Nussbaum's killer. I would have liked to ask some questions myself, but I couldn't get close enough. Somebody called my name.

"Brett Tanager?" He said it as if it were a wild guess in a game of Trivial Pursuit. Brad Castleman, our network executive on *Murder*, came towards me with an incredulous look on his face. "My God, it's been a hundred years!"

He air kissed me quickly, stepping back so he could see what shape I was in. His beady eyes behind his large glasses took quick inventory: Gained weight? Lost weight? Had any work done? I was four days sober, still sweating, but so was everybody out here in the sun, and at least I was no longer shaking. Ordinarily, Brad wore jeans and silk t-shirts, clothes that proclaimed that, though he was a "suit," he was creative, and nobody owned him. But for this occasion, Brad wore wool.

"What are you working on?" Like a chicken scratching for feed, Brad reflexively hunted for morsels of information that would give him an advantage, although he immediately realized how unproductive asking me would be.

Not walking into the ocean, I thought. But what I said was, "Oh, just noodling around on a spec thing. Sort of *Murder* in High School."

His eyes showed a flicker of interest. Like cellophane, they told me he was thinking, "Why didn't I think of that? If I rip it off, who can I get to do it?" What he said was, "Do you have pages?" He added, since I hadn't mentioned it, "I don't know if you heard, I'm head of programming now."

Suddenly a gasp went up, and the crowd surged forward and us with it as if caught in a tide. Campbell McCauley and his wife, Rosalie Bennett, had just emerged from their limousine and waved, smiling in spite of the occasion, to the throngs of fans who screamed their names. McCauley and Bennett were about as well-known as any couple on earth. There wasn't a month when their pictures, alone or together, didn't grace the covers of magazines in the checkout lines of supermarkets. As well known for their philanthropy as their films, they were photographed endlessly traipsing the globe bringing attention to the plight of poor and orphaned children. They sponsored a foundation that raised money to send doctors and medication to children infected with AIDS and had used their star power to host telethons that had raised hundreds of millions. For his efforts, Campbell had recently been appointed by the President to be an honorary ambassador for UNICEF. He was blonde, with high chiseled cheek bones and the soulful eyes of a puppy in the middle of a perfectly proportioned face. His wife Rosalie was a dark-haired beauty famous for her violet eyes, husky voice, and a tempestuous nature that didn't shy away from calling industrial nations to task for their callous indifference towards the suffering of the poor.

They stopped for a brief interview on their way to the chapel. Reporters asked if they had known Caleigh Nussbaum. Campbell said that both he and his wife knew Caleigh slightly, as their production company was housed at Poseidon, and they had a business relationship with her father. They'd been to social events at the Nussbaums and had seen her there recently. But nothing had prepared them for this tragic, untimely, and brutal end. A reporter asked him to comment on the irony of such tragedy befalling someone of Caleigh's privilege. Campbell mumbled something about the importance of every one of God's creatures while his wife, Rosalie, said that, every day, thousands of women and girls were brutally murdered, and it would be nice if attention were paid to them as well. It did not diminish one's compassion for the Nussbaums in their time of loss to be mindful that poor mothers also experienced grief when their children died.

"My God, look at that boob job. She used to have a chest you could pour syrup on and serve at IHOP and just look at that rack now."

The man beside me took out his tiny digital camera and snapped photos of the radiant couple.

"You know Jason Ratt, don't you?" Brad introduced me to the speaker, an intense young man in a fedora with three gold earrings in one ear. He wore a vintage zoot suit jacket over jeans and a t-shirt. His eyes were fierce as an eagle's under a pronounced overhanging brow. "He's got that website, 'your-biz-my-biz.com.' Brett used to be the show runner on *Murder Will Out* before Sally Robinson took over."

Jason nodded vaguely, uninterested, snapping as many photos as he could of Campbell and Rosalie and anyone who might be of interest to his readers. That did not include either Brad or me.

"Brad, I do have pages, and actually, I'd like to talk to you about them. There are a few people I'd like to show them to, maybe you could introduce me."

Brad held his hand to the side of his face, his thumb pointing up, his pinkie down, and mouthed "Call me" before following Jason into the chapel.

I went in and took a seat in the back. Unlike the others here, I was more interested in seeing than being seen.

* * *

I recognized many of the executives who took the front rows, although I couldn't always match a name to a face. I certainly couldn't match them to their jobs. In the recent orgy of mergers and acquisitions, as companies folded into one another before splitting off and merging with others like paramecia in a Petri dish, it was impossible to follow the musical chairs of who landed where. There was a joke that you could work for five different companies in two years and never leave your desk.

I might have stopped keeping score, but the same couldn't be said of the other guests. As people came in and found seats, all necks were craned to see who was sitting where and next to whom. People jumped out of their seats to greet, kiss, hug, and console before looking around to see who else was there. This may have been a time for somber reflection, but it was still a room that could be worked like few others.

Jonathan and Lynda came down the aisle together. Jonathan's rimless glasses did nothing to hide the dark circles beneath his puffy eyes. His cherubic dimples looked like hollow crags. Lynda shook hands, kissed, and greeted as she walked down the aisle to a front row. She wore an expression of solemnity that accessorized her dark suit as well as her scarf.

Dawn and Heather each came with her parents but, when they saw each other, ran into each other's arms. Hannah was there with her mother. When she saw me, she looked away, avoiding my eyes. Other Eastman kids and their parents huddled together in circles of grief, bonded by shock and the shared realization that if this could happen to Caleigh, it could happen to any of them.

After everyone was seated, Marty and Erika entered from the front and took their places in the first row. Marty's jaw was clenched tight beneath his jowls as he steered Erika to their seats. Even in his sorrow, his bearing transformed into authority what in another would be considered fat.

Erika was a tiny woman, a pinky to her husband's fist. She teetered on high heels, unsteady on her feet without Marty's hand to guide her. She wore a heavily brocaded black knit suit, black hose, and a black hat with a veil over it, the dotted tulle covering her eyes. She seemed sedated, like someone who had been able to appear in public only with the aid of a doctor.

"A young person with every advantage life could possibly offer. Barely out of childhood, poised on the brink of womanhood, with all of her life ahead of her. A young woman who will never graduate from college or even high school, never marry, never have children, never give her parents grandchildren. How can we explain this? How can we reconcile this with a loving God?"

A rabbi in a business suit, yarmulke, and prayer shawl spoke from his deep barrel chest with a voice rich in Jewish cadences.

"These questions—why is life so unfair? Why is there suffering? If God is good, how could this happen? These questions are as old as the book of Job."

I scanned the faces of the listeners nodding as the Rabbi spoke, looking for the men whose names I'd read in Julia's diary.

Campbell McCauley sat close by his wife, his somber expression doing nothing to diminish the star power that exuded from him in seemingly effortless magnetism. What must it be like to live life on such a big stage? Anyone who went through a checkout line at a supermarket knew—or thought they knew—intimate details about their marriage. What were the consequences of having your private life dished up for public consumption?

On the other side of the aisle sat Paulo Navarro, the teen idol with whom Hannah had "sushi." He fidgeted nervously, looking at his fingernails, the restless energy of youth making it hard for him to sit still.

I scanned the room for Patrick Caiman, but if he was there, I didn't see him.

"Who can blame us for having these feelings? What, then, do we do with them? Do we lie to God and say, oh, all right, God, whatever you say, you know best, when in our heart of hearts, we think 'you bastard'?"

There was an uneasy shifting in seats, a few murmurs from the crowd. Was the Rabbi doing *shtick*? Campbell McCauley, sitting close by his wife, chuckled slightly, never seeming anything but poised and at ease.

"Perhaps when we say to God 'you bastard,' it is the most honest prayer we could say because it is our truth. And what could God want from us more than the truth?"

Jason Ratt held his cell phone just at pew level, and while he kept a look of mournful solemnity on his face, I could see him using it to capture the rabbi and attendees on video that would be posted momentarily on his website.

The rabbi looked directly at Marty and Erika. "To the parents, there is not one of us who could presume to say 'we know how you feel.' How could we possibly know what it feels like to lose your only child?"

Jonathan had tears in his eyes. Lynda squeezed his hand.

"But we can say 'let us share your grief.' This room is filled with people to whom you are family."

He looked out at the hall, raising his arms to encompass us all.

"And I would say the same to everyone here. In times like these, when our hearts are shattered, let us gather together to find comfort with each other. Even if we cannot find answers, we will know we are not alone. I think if Caleigh were here—and I believe that she is—this is what she would have wanted."

People reached for hands to clasp and wiped away tears.

Afterwards, we moved to the adjoining cemetery where we watched silently as the rabbi intoned the blessing. The February sun was white and relentless. Caleigh's casket of polished mahogany was lowered into the ground. The air was still. A few birds were chirping, some people sobbed. The only other sound was the shovelfuls of dirt landing on Caleigh's coffin.

CHAPTER 14

The reception was held at the Nussbaum mansion. After giving my name to the guard at the gate, I drove up to the house.

The enormous living room held hundreds of people comfortably. A Steinway Grand stood off to the side, and a pianist played a medley that segued from "The Way We Were" to "Tiny Dancer' as servers circulated among the guests with canapés and drinks. The mantles and side tables overflowed with cut crystal, Faberge eggs, and other dazzling bric-a-brac, as well as photographs of Marty with notables ranging from Ronald Reagan to Nelson Mandela to Koby, the Poseidon Koala.

A server offered me a tray with glasses of white wine and mineral water. I grabbed a water and chugged it, as if it would help.

I recognized Gavin Parker, my former agent. He was standing alone, drink in hand, his eyes scanning the group. I moved over to him and said hello.

"Brett Tanager! My god, it's been a hundred years!"

Like primitive tribes who had no word for numbers larger than the twenty they could count on their fingers and toes, people in television had no way of describing time between three seasons ago and "a hundred years." Gavin glanced around nervously to see who might be watching us. Failure is regarded as a contagious disease in this town, and Gavin knew I had a bad case. But Gavin is an agent, attuned to fluctuations of the business in the way Native Americans could read the currents of a river to know where to find fish. If I had value, he needed to know, so he smiled as if the last conversation between us had never happened. The one in which he'd told me that I had become an unacceptable risk, was basically unemployable, and the agency could no longer represent me.

"What are you up to these days?"

"Actually, I've got a project I'd like to talk to you about. Does your agency represent Paulo Navarro?"

Before he could answer, he was accosted by a large woman with ferret eyes.

"Gavin. Have you seen Patrick Caiman?" Her gravelly voice was distinctive; I remembered her name was Hope Newton.

She wore a necklace of Tibetan prayer bells, a bracelet of chunky pieces of petrified amber, and dangling earrings of Hopi fetishes, all designed to draw attention from her dark-clad commodious girth.

"No. Is he here?"

"That's what everybody's asking. Nobody's seen him!"

They had angled themselves away from me in a way that did not include or even acknowledge my presence. Hope Newton was a lawyer with Windsor, Newton, Goldman Brown, King: a firm Gavin's agency often did business with.

"That's not surprising," said Gavin, "given all the bad blood between him and Marty."

"I heard they were making up. Patrick optioned *Space Wizards*, and Marty wanted it enough to let bygones be bygones. Someone saw them at the Peninsula the other day. Oh, darling, speaking of the Peninsula, I had lunch there with a client who needs a director-show-runner for another C. S. I. spin-off, and I want him to see your B-list."

Gavin and Hope walked away, leaving me behind. Gavin called over his shoulder, "Call me. We'll have lunch."

Right.

Mike had spoken about the benefit of admitting one was powerless, but I couldn't see what was so great about it. This whole house was about power. Everyone here seemed to be doing just fine, not by admitting they were powerless, but proclaiming, exulting in power. What was power, after all, but the ability to get other people to do what you want? What was wrong with that? If I'd been drinking, I'd have been able to ask the right questions, elicit the information I wanted. Sober, I felt as tongue-tied as a Bosnian refugee with a note pinned to my jacket.

On a coffee table, I saw a crystal box with cigarettes. I reached in and took one. If I couldn't drink, at least I could smoke. I looked for matches or a lighter, moving through the throng into another room in search of one.

"Brett!"

The voice sounded happy to see me, and I looked up expectantly. I froze when I saw Zeke, my old dealer.

His hand-tooled leather jacket fell loosely on his thin, lanky frame, his hair was short and fashionably moussed and tousled. His face was deeply lined, but his smile was relaxed and ironic, unperturbed and slightly superior:; a man above the fray. Zeke was known not only for the quality but also the diversity of his drugs. Like a purveyor of fine coffees or teas, he knew where and how they were grown and cultivated. He also dealt in pharmaceuticals, priding himself on the specificity of their effects. Like a painter with a multicolored palette, he could find the right chemical for every occasion which would take you up or down or in or out, depending on your need or desire. He had obviously chosen well to fortify himself for this event. Whatever he was on worked. He seemed easy-going and comfortable. Only his eyes were dead.

"Hey, stranger. Where've you been keeping yourself?"

Before I'd moved to Gerry Talbot's, I'd been sleeping on Zeke's couch, and being around him had hastened my descent. When Gerry threw me the lifeline of his house-sit, I'd left Zeke's and not contacted him since.

"Did you know Caleigh?" I managed to stammer out.

"Something like this happens, it affects the whole community. I mean, we're all family, right? Hey, is everything okay between you and me?"

Zeke was continuing the illusion we both subscribed to: that we were friends, that when I went over to his house it was to see him, rather than to get drugs.

"I'm clean, Zeke. Clean and sober." I didn't mention that this was only my fourth day, and there hadn't been a moment when I didn't want to drink or use.

The lines on his face fell into a smile. "Hey, that's great. Everyone should clean up now and then. I do it myself. Spas, colonics, juice fast. The body is a temple; you got to keep it clean. Too easy to burn out otherwise." He took a sip of his drink. "It makes the high so much better when you come back."

"I go to meetings. I'm done." I was? Had I really said that?

"Hey, fantastic. I go myself every now and then. I love the God stuff." His dull eyes took on a slight glint. "I've got something you're going to love. It's from South America. It would be great for you because it's not a drug; it's a plant. The shamans use it for healing. You literally see God. And it isn't addictive, so you'd be okay. I mean, Bill Wilson took LSD."

I knew I should leave, but I was mesmerized. I was probably drooling.

"You get these visions…I learned more about myself in one night than in ten years of therapy. It completely changed my relationship with my father. And talk about beauty? Man…" His eyes stared into the distance.

Maybe if I took it, it would lead me to Julia. Maybe I'd be able to figure out what had happened to Caleigh. Bill Wilson was the founder of AA. If he took LSD, maybe Zeke was right, and it didn't count.

"There you are. I need to talk to you."

It was Jason Ratt, negotiating his way through the clusters of people to find me.

"Call me." Zeke handed me his card. "It's my new number."

"You know Julia Weissman, don't you?" Jason Ratt grabbed my arm and led me away to a corner of the room to talk privately. "I just put two and two together and realized who you were. Did Julia Weissman say anything to you recently about Caleigh?"

"Why?"

He looked around confidentially. "I already told the cops this. Caleigh called me a week ago. She said she had a scoop for me that would knock my socks off, something that would blow the town wide open, but she didn't say what it was. And now this. I'm creaming to know what it is. I know that she and Julia Weissman are buds. Did Julia say anything to you about what it could have been?"

Across the room, I saw Paolo Navarro involved in a quiet conversation with Marty Nussbaum, murmuring what I could only guess were condolences. Marty took him in his arms and embraced him. The two men held the hug, and Paolo whispered in Marty's ear.

"What do you think Marty and Paolo Navarro are talking about?" I asked Jason.

"His contract, probably. Paolo was threatening not to re-up. Looks like they might have worked things out." Marty released Paolo from his embrace. He walked away, but wherever he went, people reached out to him, and murmured sympathies to him. He stopped and accepted each condolence with gruff graciousness, before continuing out of the room. Jason continued. "Did Julia say anything to you about what Caleigh might have meant?"

I said I hadn't spoken to either of them for a while and couldn't help him.

I continued my search for a lighter, eventually finding myself in front of the library. The door was open. Marty was pacing angrily in a way I was only too familiar with speaking to a woman, whose back was towards me, in the voice that had always made me cringe.

"I'm going to tear you a new fucking asshole. What do I pay you for?"

The woman's hands trembled as she went through some papers on the desk.

"It's all right here. Nothing is lost; everything's backed up…"

The woman found the papers and handed them to Marty, who scanned them quickly. When she turned, I knew she looked familiar, but I couldn't say from where. All I knew was that when I saw her,

I felt uneasy. I held back by the side of the door and didn't go in. Marty threw the papers down on the floor in disgust.

"Not these, you idiot. Jesus Fucking Christ. Get Ripetti in here." And then, "Pick those up."

The woman bent down to pick up the papers he'd thrown and hurried out of the room. He stopped her before she left.

"Wait a minute. Don't take those out there, give them to me." And then, as she handed them to him, more conversationally, "Is Patrick out there? I didn't see him at the chapel."

"I haven't seen him."

"That little prick. I swear, if he tries to back out of this, I'll have his ass in court so fucking fast he'll still be shitting when he gets there. We've got the contracts, don't we? Alliance wants to see them."

"They're in the files. I'll get Ripetti and show them to you when I get back."

"And find Patrick and tell him we're going forward with him or without him. And re-schedule the press conference."

She hurried out of the library. As she passed me, the mixture of panic and despair on her face jolted me into a realization of where I'd seen her before. Now wearing black, she was the woman in the red dress I'd seen with Mike at the Alano Club. I followed her through the house, but she moved faster than I did. In the foyer, I bumped into Jonathan.

"Who is that woman?" I asked him.

"Susanna Terrell? She's Marty's assistant."

"She seems upset."

His helpless look said "who isn't?" and was a poignant reminder of the reason we were all at this A-list party to begin with. I asked him if he'd had any news, crumpling my still unlit cigarette and dumping it an ashtray. He shook his head mournfully. "It's like she dropped off the face of the earth. We're watching her credit cards, cell phone—she hasn't used either of them. Brett, I just don't think I could bear it…"

I touched his arm. A moment of sympathy passed between us, thick with echoes of the past:; tumbling in loving laughter, sweaty bellies slapping, hands reaching, eyes shining. And sobs, bellows of rage, silence. What happens to love when it dies? Does it cease to exist? Or, like the soul, transition to another form?

As if our closeness had blipped some internal radar that Lynda carried, she was there in an instant, beaming and enthusiastic as she stepped between us and took Jonathan's arm.

"We've got *Space Wizards*! If this doesn't make Alliance cream their pants, I don't know what will. Oh, hello." She gave me a dismissive look and returned to Jonathan. "Do you realize what *Space Wizards* can do for this company? We're starting a whole new marketing campaign. Koby Koala can retire to the Motion Picture home. We can rebrand Poseidon. Soon to be Poseidon/Alliance, thank you very much."

She tossed her head back like a champion racehorse at the starting line. I had never seen such unbridled delight at a funeral.

"Not only that!" she exulted. "As if that weren't enough. Paolo Navarro's back in the fold. Taking his deal, and backing off the lawsuit. So we can use his show to market the be-Jesus out of it…"

"Call me," said Jonathan.

As his eyes met mine, they seemed to send me a signal. Was it embarrassment? Apology? A warning? There was a time when it seemed we could read each other perfectly. But that time had gone.

CHAPTER 15

Erika sat in a large upholstered chair in the living room, holding herself in a regal position as she accepted condolences. She kept her hat on, and its veil successfully blocked her eyes from view. She wore a white camisole under her black brocade suit. Several diamond rings adorned each hand, gold and jewel-encrusted bracelets on each arm, pearl earrings, more jewels on her brooch, as if she couldn't find enough places on her body to showcase the gifts her husband had lavished on her over the course of their long and fabled marriage.

I waited in line as a procession of guests approached her, pressed her hand, and kissed her cheek, murmuring condolences at her loss. A strange, almost eerie smile floated over the part of her face not covered by the veil; the receiving line smile, as if she were so long accustomed to disguising her feelings that she couldn't stop, even now that her daughter had been killed.

I waited as Jason Ratt kneeled beside her, her hand in his, speaking softly of his sadness. He whispered something in her ear, and she smiled that eerie smile. He kissed her on the cheek, stood, and walked past me.

"Erika, I don't know if you remember me. I'm Brett Tanager. I wrote *Murder Will Out*, and I used to live with Jonathan Weissman when Caleigh and Julia were kids. I wanted to tell you how very sorry I am."

Her eyes made a weak attempt to swim up from the depths of her grief to take me in, but the effort required more energy than she had, and they sank down again.

"Thank you for coming."

She took my hand with a flaccid grasp. Then she turned her attention away from me to whoever was next in line. But I stayed.

"I'm sure this is an awful time for you, but I need to speak to you about Caleigh and Julia. It's urgent."

"Yes," she said in a way that made me unsure she had heard what I'd said.

"Julia came to see me Tuesday because she was worried about Caleigh and didn't know where she was. Now Julia's missing too. Could we talk for a moment? I'd like to ask you some questions.

Her face was a mask. Other people came over, gave their hands, and murmured condolences. The ghastly smile of perpetual greeting never left her face.

"Thank you," she said to each person who spoke to her.

"As I said, I know this is a bad time. But if there's any way you could give me a few minutes, if not now, then perhaps soon…"

Her eyes focused momentarily on something across the room. I followed her gaze and saw her husband in an urgent, private conversation with a security man in a black suit. At first their backs were to us, but then the security man turned towards us and— was I being paranoid?—gestured towards me with his chin. Marty frowned. Their conversation continued as the man spoke softly in his ear.

"Come with me," said Erika. "We can talk upstairs."

She stood, swaying slightly. I reached an arm out to steady her.

"Are you sure? There are people here who want to speak to you."

"They're here to see my husband," she said, and in fact, nobody seemed to notice as we left the room. I followed her upstairs and down a hall to her private suite. Erika was well-known for her daily forays into Beverly Hills on shopping sprees, and had a separate wing to house all her purchases. One room was filled with packages that had yet to be opened. Others were museum-like in their display of expensive furniture and accessories; others were basically room-sized closets. It was rumored that the mansion's enormous size—over 60,000 square feet—was to accommodate the harvest of Erika's compulsive shopping.

She brought me into a sitting room done in muted pastels, the subtle harmonies of its color scheme bearing the mark of a tasteful decorator with a good eye and unlimited funds. As I entered, a creepy feeling came over me, as if I were being watched. I used to feel like this when I worked at Poseidon, before I'd been fired. I'd become obsessed with the idea that I was being followed. At the time, I'd told myself I was paranoid, but I couldn't shake the idea that I was under surveillance and believed the cops were spying on me, just waiting for me to make an incriminating move. Why should I feel that now? It was only as I took in the whole room that I realized that the walls were lined with cases of dolls. I was being watched by a thousand pairs of eyes.

The collection was as wide-ranging as it was enormous. There were antique dolls, handmade dolls, porcelain and rag dolls, Nancy Reagan, Barbie, and Britney Spears. Most were in cases; some were hung on stands.

I was speechless.

Erika saw my amazement and came over to proudly point out the gems in her collection.

"This one was made in Paris, France, in 1887," she said of an antique doll on a stand under glass. "Those are the original clothes. Under her dress, she's wearing real lace undies." She giggled and covered her mouth with her hand, eyes sparkling as if she'd said something wicked. Then she looked back at the doll and her expression softened. "Can't you just get lost in those eyes?"

"Extraordinary."

"Isn't she? I just love her." She moved down the row and pointed out a similar doll, also under glass. "This is her sister. They'd been separated for over a hundred years, until I found her on eBay. See, her dress is made from the same silk, and the lace pattern on her shawl is exactly the same. And now they're together again."

I tried to imagine the time and money—and interest—it would take to amass a collection like this. Unless, of course, she had a staff do it for her, which wouldn't surprise me. Except that, as she explained the details and origins of each doll, her face, so anesthetized a moment ago, came to life.

"It's an amazing collection," I offered.

"I didn't grow up with money," she sighed, "to say the least. As a child, I spent many years in an orphanage. The only person I could trust was my doll. When they took her away from me..." Even the veil that shielded her face could not conceal the stab of grief that overtook her. "...I made a promise, to her and to myself, that one day I'd find her again." She looked at the vast collection: all the dolls that money could buy. "Maybe I never found her, but I've found others. I like to think I've given them all a good home."

She went to her sofa, which also had dolls reclining on it, and sat down. She still had not removed her hat. Her bearing was erect, regal, gracious, a queen granting an audience, as she gestured for me to sit opposite. She picked up one of her dolls and held it in her lap as we spoke.

"Tell me how I can help."

"When Julia came to see me, she was afraid something awful had happened to Caleigh. Now we know she was right, and she's disappeared also. I know how hard this must be for you. But if you could tell me what you know about where Caleigh might have been before she was killed, it might help to find Julia."

"I'm not sure what help I could be. Caleigh didn't confide in me very much." Erika stroked the doll she held in her lap. "This was one of Caleigh's dolls when she was younger." Her face softened as she gazed into the doll's eyes. "Caleigh told her everything…You know, in a way, I think the most intimate relationship there is is between a girl and her doll, don't you?" She stared into the eyes of the doll, a wistful sadness passing over her otherwise motionless face. "Did Caleigh tell you where she was going?" she asked the doll. She held the doll's mouth up to her ear, but evidently, the doll said nothing because she looked at me and smiled helplessly.

"Would you like a drink?" It was only when she picked up the phone and punched a button that I noticed the tremor in her hand.

"A chilled bottle of Pouilly, please. We're upstairs."

"Just mineral water for me, please.

"And some Perrier."

"Did Caleigh ever mention "enjo kosai" to you? Or tell you about the men she'd been seeing?"

If Erika was shocked by my question, she didn't show it. Perhaps a quick flash of surprise, subsiding into that flaccid, deadened face.

"Caleigh didn't tell me very much about what she was up to. She was closer to her father, really, than me. And lately, she always seemed so angry. I can't imagine why. Marty gives us absolutely everything we could possibly want." She straightened her skirt and glanced at the door.

"When was the last time you saw her?"

"The police asked me the same thing. And I've tried to remember. I think it was the day of the Thalians dinner."

Again, that eerie hostess smile.

A smartly dressed woman in a suit and low heels brought in a tray, with a chilled bottle of white wine, opened, a bottle of mineral water, and glasses for both of us. She set it down on a table beside Erika's sofa. Erika introduced her to me as Caroline, her assistant. "Caroline could probably help you more than I can. When was that Thalians dinner?"

Caroline poured the white wine into a glass for Erika.

"Last Thursday, the 10th."

Erika took the glass of wine in both trembling hands and drank from it. Almost instantly, the tension she'd held in her body relaxed.

"I'm trying to piece together where Caleigh was and what she was doing before she was killed," I explained to Caroline.

"Are you with the police? I've already spoken to them"

"It's all right, Caroline; she's a friend of the family." To me, she said, "Caroline keeps things running smoothly around here. I don't know what we would do without her."

Caroline poured my water.

"Wasn't that the last time I saw Caleigh?" asked Erika, as if her assistant had a better grasp on her memory than she did. "The night of the Thalians? I was getting one of my migraines. The trainer had just finished working Caleigh out in our gym, and she was going back to her room to shower and change. We spoke briefly—I think she said she was going out that night. I took a Fiorinal and went to bed. Marty went without me. The next day, I was asleep when she went off to school. I never saw her again." How anesthetized she must have been, for her face showed little expression as she added, "If I'd known it was going to be the last time I saw her, I would have…I don't know…paid closer attention."

She smiled.

"Will there be anything else?" Caroline said.

Erika asked if I'd like Caroline to print out Caleigh's schedule to show me. I said I would, very much, and perhaps Caroline and I could speak later. Caroline agreed and left as efficiently and unobtrusively as she'd entered.

Erika took another sip of her wine. The trembling in her fingers had stopped.

"What did Julia say to you?" she asked.

"She told me the girls had been playing some game, that involved going out with men and getting paid for it. Men who enjoyed being with teenage girls. They called it 'enjo kosai' because it was a fad in Japan. Julia told me that Patrick Caiman had suggested it first to Caleigh."

For the first time, Erika responded with real surprise.

"Patrick Caiman! No, that couldn't be. Julia must have gotten that part wrong."

"Why do you say that?"

"Well, all that bad blood between him and Marty. It almost broke Marty's heart when he had to fire Patrick; they'd been close as brothers. But after all that Patrick had been doing behind Marty's back, he had no choice. Running up budgets by charging his…well, his bad habits…to the pictures he was supposed to be overseeing. And then, that business with Caleigh. No, I'm sure Caleigh wouldn't have been running around with Patrick. She'd know it would break her father's heart." She picked up the doll again and asked, while fingering its clothes, "What else did Julia say?"

"What business with Caleigh?" I asked instead.

She took a long sigh and stared into her drink before answering. "We kept it quiet, of course, to protect Caleigh. But Marty had a pretty good idea that Patrick had been…" she took a long pause before continuing, "going into Caleigh's room and…let's just say behaving inappropriately."

"When was this? How old was Caleigh at the time?"

"Eleven? Twelve? Ten? I'm not sure. I just know that once Marty found out, there was no way he could continue working with Patrick; it was all I could do to keep him from killing him. Marty made up some cover story and made sure he was let go and not allowed anywhere near this family again."

"I'd heard they're making a deal together. At least, that's the buzz downstairs."

She seemed surprised to hear it.

"Patrick has the option on a project Marty wants. They've decided to let bygones be bygones."

"Maybe. I wouldn't know. I don't keep track of the business side of things. But even if they are, I'm sure Caleigh would not have anything to do with Patrick Caiman. She was the one who told us what he'd been doing to her."

She picked up the doll and nuzzled its nose. "Daddy doesn't always tell us everything, does he baby." She resumed her adult voice. "Would you like to see Caleigh's room?"

I said I would, very much. She brought the doll with her as she led me down the hall.

Caleigh's room was in another wing of the mansion, a designer's tribute to a typical teenage girl—if the girl happened to be an empress. There was a large canopy bed with pillows, bolsters, shams, and skirting, all in Egyptian cotton. The wall featured a display case for pictures of rock, movie, and TV stars; all the pictures were autographed to Caleigh and could be rotated electronically, replaced easily. Bookshelves held school textbooks, some romance paperbacks, and advanced publication copies of new books. Her desk had an insert for a recessed computer screen and keyboard, but her computer had been removed.

"The police already took a lot of things."

"Did she have a phone?"

"Yes. The police were looking for it, but I don't think they found it."

"It wasn't on her when she was found?"

The wince of pain that crossed her face reminded me that Caleigh's body had been naked when found.

For a vanity, Caleigh had a professional makeup table, with a mirror with lights around it, and enough hair products and cosmetics for a movie star. When I remarked on it, Erika told me that Marty occasionally sent someone over from the studio to do Caleigh's hair and makeup, particularly if they were going somewhere where they would be photographed as a family. "The camera adds ten pounds, and Caleigh was very self-conscious about her weight. You know, her father is constantly surrounded by some of the most beautiful women in the world. It's hard for Caleigh to compete."

"Have the police returned any of the things they took?

I didn't wait for an answer before rifling through the books on the shelves. I opened the desk drawer, rummaging among the discarded cosmetics, but saw nothing.

I went into Caleigh's walk-in closet. I've lived in apartments that were smaller. I pressed a button, and the clothes moved on automated racks, like the ones at the dry cleaners. They were arranged meticulously. All the skirts were together, all the shirts, pants, jackets, suits, and within each category, her clothes were arranged by color. For a child who went to a school which insisted on uniforms. Perhaps this was why.

I wandered through the closet like Alice in Wonderland. What would it be like to be sixteen and have so many clothes? I tried to put myself in Caleigh's place, but I really couldn't imagine it. When the jackets came towards me, I felt in their pockets. I'd written a scene for Jinx Magruder where she found an important clue this way.

"People are wondering where you are." Marty Nussbaum came into the room. Noticing the drink in his wife's hand, he said, "For Christ's sake, is it too much to ask you to stay awake at least until the guests leave? You took your Xanax, didn't you? You know what the combination does to you."

If there had been any notes in any of these pockets, the police would have found them. And from what I had seen of these girls, they didn't write notes anymore, just texted each other on their cell phones.

I came out of the closet and extended my hand to Marty Nussbaum.

"Marty, I'm so very sorry. Caleigh was a wonderful child. What an awful loss. I can't even imagine."

He looked at me blankly without taking my hand. The muscles in his jaw clenched and unclenched as he took in the fact that I was in Caleigh's room.

"Brett Tanager," I reminded him, "I used to…"

"I know very well who you are," he said, "I remember every dime you ever cost me."

"Nobody knows where Julia is," interjected Erika, explaining my presence to her husband. "They're afraid that whoever…" she could barely speak "…did this to Caleigh…" She sat down heavily on Caleigh's vanity, for someplace to sit. At the sight of herself in the mirror, she reflexively straightened a wisp of her hair and made a quick face of disapproval at her reflection.

"I know all about it," he said. "My investigator told me."

"Would you happen to know if Caleigh's cell phone was recovered along with her body? By any chance was it retuned to you with her effects?"

Marty sat down heavily on the bed, as if unable to support his own weight. His eyes blazed with anger, and he opened his mouth to speak. But instead of the bellow of rage I expected, a sound emerged unlike any I'd ever heard from him. It took me a moment to realize it was a sob. He turned away and buried his face in his hands.

Erika went over to him and touched his heaving shoulders.

He clasped her around the legs and held her, sobbing uncontrollably.

A security man appeared in the doorway. He was heavy-set, wore a black suit and tie, white shirt, a wireless earpiece. Marty nodded in my direction. The man came towards me, to usher me out. I made it easier for him and left on my own.

CHAPTER 16

As I drove along the canyon road leading down from the Nussbaum's mountaintop mansion, I realized why Erika had so often reminded me of my mother. The vacant stares, the headaches, the afternoons spent "resting" were as familiar to me as the address of my childhood home. I remembered the tension in the jaw of my former beauty queen mother; the effort it cost her to keep her features properly arranged on her face. And I remembered the moments when the effort was too much; the jaw slackened, the words slurred, and the lady became a drunk. I remembered my dread of bringing people home for fear of what they might see. If I were lucky, she'd be passed out in her bedroom, and I only had to worry that she might empty one bottle and have to shuffle through the living room to the bar for another. But other times—and you never knew when it might be— her temper would flare, and we'd all be held hostage as her fiery rage scorched the landscape leaving nothing alive in its wake.

I thought of how rarely Julia went to visit Caleigh, how often Caleigh came to us. I felt a surge of sympathy for Caleigh. I remembered only too well what it was like growing up in a household where the same behavior might get praise in the morning and rage at night.

Was that what it was like for Julia growing up with me?

I realized why Jonathan and I had lived together and not married. I'd been playing house, like a child dressing up and pretending. I hadn't known the first thing about being a wife, a mother, a grown-up. I was as immature and ill-prepared for life as Julia, without her excuse of actually being a child.

I'd known these things about myself when I was drinking, but I'd been able to blur their sharp edges. With sobriety came awareness. That's why I hated it.

I thought about Jonathan and the moment we'd shared this afternoon, connected now, as then, by Julia. But it was more than that. Jonathan and I worked well together creatively, as well as sexually and romantically. We'd created the show as a team and laughed a lot as we'd done it. We could finish each other's sentences or be so in tune that finishing the sentence wasn't necessary. After the accident, I retreated to a dark place deep inside, imprisoned by fear, unable to let anyone in. No longer partners or lovers, Jonathan and I lost the ability even to be friends. Then I sensed, from the lifting of his spirits and his own furtive glances, that he had begun to see someone else.

I remembered being with Jonathan at a corporate retreat, after Poseidon had bought our network and our show. Poseidon owned a ranch in the canyons of the "big wild" of the Santa Monica Mountains north of Malibu, a huge wilderness area often used as a location for westerns. Poseidon had built a lodge on the property, and we all gathered there to hear motivational speakers, attend seminars, and socialize with the rest of the Poseidon "family." It was the first time I'd met Lynda. She gave a presentation at the banquet on "corporate branding." She suggested ways that an entertainment company, by using Jungian archetypes, could create an association in the public imagination with a loving, nurturing parent and thus invest the products they advertised with magical powers that filled deep psychic needs.

I'd looked over at Jonathan, confident he would share my view that this was baloney, but realized from the look on his face that she was the One. I'd been knocking back drinks all night. When I jumped to my feet to ask a question, I staggered. I asked if it wasn't the role of drama, forget about art, to stir people up, frighten them, and, yes, make them angry. Whatever she answered seemed condescending and pat. I went off on a riff about artistic integrity and good old-fashioned storytelling, but whatever I said was marred by the way that I said it, which was drunk, rude, and belligerent. When Jonathan tried to silence me, I shoved him aside. My speech was slurred, and I wobbled as I tried to make the point that basically I was right and everybody else was wrong. I don't remember too much of what I said, but I do remember shouting that Jonathan had no right to shut me up because "You just want to fuck her." In retaliation, I staggered out of the room, found someone equally drunk, went down by the artificial trout stream, and fucked him.

What was his name? Who was he? I couldn't remember.

In the morning, I was lying on the floor, the coolness of the tile the only balm against the stabbing in my head. I had thrown my insides up and out, still I couldn't stop heaving. There wasn't a cell in me that didn't ache. My eyes were swollen, my throat parched. It hurt to hear. Worse than the physical torment was the mental anguish of realizing that one more time, I had done the very worst thing I could have done, guaranteed to achieve the opposite of what I longed for.

"I'm sick" was all I could say.

"I know," said Jonathan. "Why don't you just die."

Now, seeing only the past before me, I found that without realizing what I was doing, I had driven to Coldwater Canyon, the scene of…I always called it "the accident," but the more accurate term was "crime." A street I hadn't allowed myself to drive on since. Now, neither drunk nor high as I had been then, I drove down the twisting canyon. I saw the bend in the road where Rosa Aguilar had been changing her tire. There were no markers, flowers, or notes of remembrance as I'd seen at other sites of traffic fatalities, but I knew the spot, familiar as a dream. I pulled over to the side of the road and got out of my car.

It was twilight. The sun, so blinding and white earlier, now blazed orange as it dipped low in the west, casting a pink glow on the clouds low in the sky; in the east, a pale white sliver of a moon rose in the sky. I stood at the spot where Rosa Aguilar had changed her tire.

I knelt, as she had, my back to the road, and imagined what it must have been like for her. A car, out of control, careening around the bend, taking it too wide, speeding past, and striking her. Had she stood up when she heard another car on this deserted street at two in the morning and tried to flag it down to ask for help? Or could she tell from the roar of the engine and the squeal of the tires that the person behind the wheel of this car could only harm, bringing nothing to her but death.

A car whizzed past as I knelt, and I jumped back. Instinctively, I turned and hid, facing away from traffic, not wanting to be seen here nor recognized. I stood next to a ficus tree, which gave off an earthy, slightly rotting odor. My heart beat loudly, as it had that night.

I got back in my car but continued to sit at the spot. I put my arms on my steering wheel and rested my head against them, trying to breathe. No way of being with myself, knowing what I knew, without something to diminish the pain. I reached into my pocket and found Zeke's card.

I kept my hand in my pocket, holding the card against me, not taking it out. I kept my eyes closed and tried to bring myself back to earth.

Not daring to take the card out of my pocket, instead, I reached into my bag for my notebook and pen.

I began jotting down everything I could remember about who I'd seen and what I'd heard at the party that might have any bearing on where to look for Julia.

CHAPTER *17*

The next day, after going to an early morning meeting in Malibu, I sat out on the deck at Gerry's, drinking coffee and looking over my notes, comparing what I'd written to Julia's diary, looking for commonalities. I called Hannah to see if she'd gotten a number for Clinton Cole but got no answer, left a message.

Before I'd been a TV writer, I'd been a reporter in San Diego. I'd worked the metro desk, covering local news. Every once in a while, I'd catch a good crime case, which I'd milk and massage into headline grabbing news. They had provided a lot of the stories for the first year of *Murder* and had been a selling point when Jonathan pitched me to the network. In my time there, I'd gotten to know a lot of cops. It was one of them, Earl Roemer, whom I called now.

"Hey, Brett, how are things in Tinsel Town?" he asked, after I'd identified myself. Evidently the story of my descent had not reached San Diego.

"Sparkling, as always."

"They got you running the studio yet? Did you call because you're looking for someone to play a sexy young cop who always gets the girl?" I'd long since learned that any conversation with cops includes a ritual foreplay of banter.

"No, but when I am, I'll be sure to call and ask for your partner."

He laughed. "What can I do you for, Bunkie?"

"I'm trying to find a kid; he's a dealer. Clinton Cole. My stepdaughter's run away, and he might know where she is."

He whistled. "You working with anyone on this?"

"Yeah, sort of. She's a friend of Caleigh Nussbaum. It's just that everyone up here is so caught up in that they're not giving this a high priority. I want to talk to him, but I don't have an address or phone number. "

"Any idea of his DOB?"

"He's a kid. Not older than 20. I don't know his birthday."

I heard him tapping on his computer. "Yeah, I got him. Hey, Brett, you might want to get some back up. This guy has a rap sheet." He read from his computer. "Did time as a juvenile…one arrest, no conviction, assault with a deadly weapon. He could be dangerous. I'd be careful if I were you." I assured him I would be, and he gave me the address.

* * *

I needed to use my Thomas Guide to find the apartment. Solano Avenue was in a neighborhood I'd never been to, deep in the San Fernando Valley. Built as a planned community for the workers in a nearby tire factory, the plans had long since gone awry, the factory closed, the populace swollen with an influx of ethnicities the planners couldn't have imagined. The day was arid and dull, the sky the color of underwear in a hamper. Clinton's street was lined with palm trees, but they were seedy and cheerless, choked by the smoggy air. Shaggy bark and dried fronds clogged the gutters and littered the street. Tejano music blared from open windows. A gutted out Camaro sat on cinderblocks, stripped for parts.

I found the address. My heart leapt when I saw a Prius parked outside. Ubiquitous on the west side, they were rare here, and I hoped it might be Julia's. The building had two long lines of apartments, one of top of the other. "El Encantador" was written on the side in elegant script, but one corroded and rusted metal letter was missing.

I looked at the row of mailboxes. There were few names. None of them was Clinton Cole.

The manager's apartment was on the first floor. When I rang the bell, a little dog barked in high pitched frenzy.

"Roxie! Quiet!"

The dog yapped anyway. A woman in a muumuu opened the door to an apartment that smelled of kitty litter, mentholated cigarettes, and gin. She eyed me suspiciously from under a tangled mess of bleached blonde hair. Dark eyebrows on her scowling face were furrowed in permanent mistrust.

"Yes?" she asked, although "no" was imbedded in her use of the word.

"Can you tell me which apartment is Clinton Cole's?"

"You a cop?" She looked me up and down.

"No. I'm looking for a friend." In the background, the television was on to a daytime talk show. The announcer promised stories that would teach you how to add spice to your marriage and protect yourself from consumer fraud, after these messages. "I see my friend's car outside, so I know she's here, but I don't know which apartment it is."

"207, upstairs." She pointed to the second level and closed the door behind her before I could finish saying, "Thank you."

Outside 207, a few dead plants drooped in pots of dry dirt. A take-out menu from a local pizza joint hung from the doorknob. Heavy curtains concealed the interior from view, but I could hear music coming from inside—raucous angry rock, turned down low. I knocked on the door. I heard some brief scuffling then saw an eye come to the eyepiece and stare at me.

"I'm looking for Clinton Cole or Julia Weissman. I'm a friend of Julia's."

The eye disappeared. I heard some muffled conversation. Then nothing. Just the music. I knocked again.

I heard a series of dead bolt locks turning, but the young man who answered kept the chain lock on, peering at me through a narrow crack. His eyes were as open and welcoming as the chain-locked door.

"My name is Brett Tanager," I said. "Julia came to see me the other day. I need to talk to her. Is she here, or do you know where I can find her?"

He closed the door before I'd finished speaking, and I heard again the sound of the deadbolt lock. I waited, wondering what to do next, since this was turning into a dead end. I knocked again.

This time, the door opened just wide enough to let me in. The thin young man peered around to see if anyone was with me before shutting the door behind me and locking it again.

The apartment was so dark it took a while before I could see anything, coming as I did from the bright sun outside. The young man couldn't have been any older than twenty, but the hard cast of his face and his eyes empty of trust made him appear older. Rail thin, he wore jeans and a rock band's promotional t-shirt that clung to his concave torso. He held a gun by his side.

The air was close; the smell of cigarettes, stale beer, and burned cocaine was trapped inside curtained windows that were never opened. A television played music videos in the background with the sound turned low. The living room, kitchen, and the counter between them were cluttered with pizza boxes, crumpled beer cans, cigarettes spilling over the ashtrays. The bedroom door opened on an unmade bed, clothes littered the floor. The sofa facing the coffee table had cigarette burns in its nubby fabric.

And then I saw her, standing in the doorway between living room and kitchen. She was wearing one of his t-shirts over a pair of jeans; her body seemed fragile as a wren. Her skin was mottled and pale. Her lids drooped; her jaw was slack; her face sagged under the weight of the drugs she was using. Faint bubbles of teen acne poked through unwashed make-up that left dark circles smudged around unfocused eyes that managed to look both frightened and deadened, like a flare blanketed by fog.

My relief at seeing her alive overrode my distress at seeing her loaded. Nevertheless, the difference between the girl I saw now and the one who'd come to see me only five days before made it hard for me to speak.

"Caleigh's dead." Julia spoke in a voice so quiet it might have been a whisper.

"I know. I was at the funeral. Your father is worried sick about you. We all are."

Her eyes darted over to Clinton, as if for help knowing what to say or do.

"She's fine. Everything's under control."

He came away from the door and sat down on a large armchair of faded plaid, resting the gun beneath the chair. Julia followed him with her eyes, rubbing her arms.

"Is she cool?" He asked Julia, gesturing me with his head.

Julia's doped eyes softened. "Yeah. Totally."

Our eyes held a look that told me the connection between us remained.

Clinton rummaged through a large bowl in the middle of the coffee table, overflowing with prescription bottles, baggies, vials, and various drug paraphernalia. This was a dealer's apartment. I knew these surroundings like I knew my mother's womb. As comforting and as threatening as that former abode, it was a place my life depended on leaving.

But not without Julia.

"Come on, sweetie. Let me take you home."

Julia backed away.

"Nobody's angry; nobody's going to make trouble for you. But you need to let your father know you're okay."

"I can't."

Clinton found what he was looking for: a glass pipe with a clear low bottom belly that made what went through it transparent. He reached for a wire hanger and a packet of Brillo.

"Why not?"

It was as if she wanted to answer, but what she needed to say was unspeakable. She felt in her pocket for something but never took her eyes off Clinton.

"Because of Caleigh?"

She gave a tiny nod. She took her phone out of her pocket and glanced at it, fingering it as a child would a security blanket.

"Why? Do you know who killed her?"

She didn't answer but looked at Clinton, who had found a small film can which he opened, spilling out clusters of small rocks onto a paper plate. As if I were in an airplane that took a sudden dive, my stomach lurched, and I broke out in beads of cold sweat. Julia cast a quick look at me that said she knew I'd understand and sat in the chair next him, giving him her full attention.

"Julia. You asked me for help, you have to tell me. Was it because of 'enjo kosai'?"

"We called it 'sushi.'"

"Hooking's hooking, in any language," snorted Clinton, using the film can to break the rocks into smaller pieces. "Don't have to call it a Japanese word. She's a whore."

"She is not!"

"She's fucking guys for money, Julia. That's called a whore."

Julia said nothing, and I thought of her admission to me that she too had given "enjo kosai" a try.

"Did Patrick Caiman set Caleigh up with her last date? He wasn't at the funeral."

Clinton fitted a piece of Brillo into the mouth of the pipe with a wire hanger.

"He's such a perv," said Clinton. "And he hated Caleigh's dad almost as much as Caleigh did. The whole thing was just one big fuck you to Marty." He placed one the rocks on the steel wool and found a butane lighter.

And offered the lighter and pipe to me.

For a moment I had the wild thought, *I should do it to be polite, so they trust me.* I had never done crack. But I sure had done coke, and the lining of my nose burned at the memory; the muscles of my body clenched in anticipation. My mouth felt dry; I could taste that bitter drip at the back of my throat as if I had just taken a hit. My head was shaking side to side indicating no. I couldn't speak.

Clinton shrugged and handed the pipe and lighter to Julia.

A memory: I'm at my dressing table, doing my make-up before going out to a party. I lay out a line of coke on the table and snort it up through my nose using a little straw I keep in the drawer. In the mirror behind me, I see little Julia in her nightie staring at me. She's come in to say goodnight. I rub my nose, turn to her, spread out my arms for her to run to, embrace, and kiss her good-night. Now I'm with her in a dealer's apartment, watching her put a crack pipe to her lips. The slice through my heart was swift and clean but not painless.

"Come on. I'm taking you home."

I grabbed the pipe away from her.

"I thought you said she was cool!" protested Clinton.

"Brett…I can't…" She was terrified.

We all heard a sharp knock on the door. Clinton froze. So did Julia. So did I.

Clinton gestured for us not to move. He put down the pipe, reached under his chair for the gun, a semi-automatic pistol. He moved to the wall, flattened himself at the side of the curtained window, and peered behind it towards the door.

He put his finger to his lips, silencing any protests we might have made, and gestured with the gun for us to move into the bedroom. Julia went without question, but I stood between them. I started to say something, but Clinton shushed me.

"Stay with her."

I didn't move. I felt that I should stay in control. "What's happening?"

He shook his head and used the gun to shepherd us into the bedroom. Once we were in, he closed the door.

The bed was unmade, the sheets twisted. Julia could tell I had surmised that she and Clinton had been in bed together before I got there. She smiled shyly at the secret we shared.

"Are you going to tell my parents?"

"Julia, you have to talk to the police. Tell them what you know."

"It won't do any good."

"Why not?"

"Clinton doesn't trust the police."

"Of course he doesn't trust the police, he's a dealer."

She fingered the phone she'd brought with her.

"Honey…When I saw you before you came to Malibu—who were you with?"

"Brett—there's video…"

A sudden clunk in the next room sounded like a body falling to the floor. Clinton hurried into the bedroom, carrying the gun. He grabbed Julia by the arm and pulled her towards the living room.

"Hurry!"

I followed after them. A man lay sprawled on the floor, facing the living room. It looked as if Clinton had hit him with the gun as soon as he'd entered. Clinton led Julia through the living room towards the kitchen.

The man moaned and stumbled to his feet. He too had a gun; he reached for it and raised it.

The gunman stumbled towards Clinton who was shoving Julia out the back door. I ran after Clinton and Julia.

A loud crack. An explosion of light. The smell of smoke.

I fell to the floor, and everything went dark.

CHAPTER 18

I remember blood; I remember fear. I remember pain, darkness. Liquids seeping out of my body, gulping air that seemed to go right through me without becoming breath.

And a man's face, gazing down at me as if I were on the bottom of a well. I couldn't discern his features. He seemed kind. He seemed concerned but not afraid; confident and assured. His presence was comforting.

He asked if I could hear him. His voice sounded slow and distorted, as if spoken through a tube. I tried to speak but heard only the sound of the ocean in my ears. He told me to hold on. He knelt by my side. I thought I saw my blood on his clothes. He called me by my name.

Suddenly the room bustled with paramedics. They snapped on latex gloves. As if I were watching from the ceiling, I saw them swab and bind my wounds. One of them fit a mask over my face, and it helped me breathe. I watched rather than felt them prick my arm and run an IV. I saw them lift me onto a stretcher.

They carried me out the door and down the stairs. A small crowd had formed. Gawkers peered over each other's shoulders to catch a glimpse of me, murmuring rumors among themselves. I was lifted into the ambulance. I felt a lurch and heard its wail. I remember feeling embarrassed.

I was wheeled into Emergency, and the stranger ran beside me, explaining that I'd been shot. He filled out the forms that got me admitted. He knew my name. He knew I was a member of the Writers Guild and knew where to find my insurance card. He knew my address at Gerry Talbot's. I remember wondering how.

I was wheeled into X-ray and then out again and back into a bay in the Emergency Room. The stranger sat with me as I lay shivering with pain and fear. If we spoke, I don't remember. But I do remember his presence. He never left my side.

I remember wondering if I was dying and realizing that I probably was. I'd wasted my one and only life. I had squandered the gifts I'd been given. I'd ripped through life like a hurricane, leaving only damage in my wake. I'd hurt the people I loved, if I loved anyone at all. Suddenly a great fear rose up within me as I thought about Rosa Aguilar and realized that I could be going to hell, for all eternity. I struggled against losing consciousness, thrashing wildly on the gurney in a futile attempt to escape.

Then the surgeon came in and explained that a bullet had gone through my chest and lodged in a muscle in my back but didn't appear to have hit the lung or the spine. I was a lucky woman. He patted my hand and said the anesthesiologist would be into see me soon.

Anesthesiologist?

He said that due to the location of the bullet they'd have to use a general anesthetic. But not to worry, they would give me a mild sedative first, and I wouldn't be aware of anything until I was in the recovery room.

Sedatives! Anesthesia! A neon EXIT sign at the end of a dark tunnel. Elation replaced fear. Blessed oblivion was soon to be mine—and it wasn't my fault! Nobody could call it a slip, not if an anesthesiologist gave you a drug in the hospital! And then there'd be pain meds. Vicodin! I could take Vicodin! Just the idea of it billowed in like a cloud, lifting me into a dreamy floating loveliness. Sobriety, with its relentless torment of consciousness, would be vanquished. Soon I'd be taking that downy slide down a tumbling river of grace, soothed and solaced, languid and luscious, caressed by the ease of careless abandon.

"Brett!" Julia's voice cut through the dream, along with the last image I'd seen before I'd lost consciousness—Julia's arms reaching out to me as Clinton dragged her from the apartment and out onto the porch and down the stairs, followed by the assailant crawling on the floor, his gun still in his hands.

"Call Mike," I managed to say. I gave the stranger Mike's phone number.

Then the anesthesiologist came in, hung his bag on the IV, and found a vein.

* * *

"Some people will do anything to get drugs."

Mike was waiting for me as I was wheeled into a room after spending a few hours in recovery.

I tried to speak, but felt pressure in my chest, woozy from the drugs, and disconnected from my body.

"Julia?" was all I could manage.

"You were alone."

I tried to sit up, but even encased in bandages and floating on the residue of the anesthesia, the pressure in my chest stopped me. I gasped and lay back down.

"Julia…" I said again. The only thing I knew for sure was that she was in trouble, and I had to find her.

"Don't worry, kiddo. I'm going to help you find her. You don't have to do this on your own anymore."

"No. You've got us both on your team now."

It was only then that I noticed a man standing off to the side of Mike. As large as Mike but younger and trimmer, his thick black hair, slicked back from a widow's peak, gave him an appearance that was both tough and sleek.

"Nic Ripetti," he said, hints of New York in his sandpaper voice. It was the man who'd found me the night before and brought me in. "Julia's parents hired me to look for her. You beat me to it. Let that get around, there goes my street cred." He raised one eyebrow slightly, containing a smile.

"Hired you?"

"I'm a P.I. Like him," he gestured to Mike with a nod of his head.

I knew nothing except that he'd saved my life. Tears of relief sprang to my eyes. I might have died but hadn't, thanks to him. A deep sense of gratitude gave rise to a surge of joy at being alive. This is why I love drugs. I was on Demerol.

"Thank you."

He shrugged modestly. I noticed he hadn't shaved and realized he'd been here with me all night.

"They say you're going to be fine. Bullet missed your heart by a mile."

"Too small a target." I was flirting, half-dead though I was.

"I do security work for Marty Nussbaum. He's asked me to keep on top of the police investigation to make sure everything possible is being done to find their daughter's killer. Mrs. Nussbaum asked me to look for Julia too. She thinks the two cases are related.

"Yes," I said, "I'm sure of it."

Mike stepped between us. "He's been hired by the Nussbaums. I've been hired by you." He would not hear of an objection. "We'll work out the details later. We're both going to help you find Julia, kiddo." There were uneasy looks between them. "We know each other. From when we were both cops."

"He taught me everything I know," said Ripetti good-naturedly. Mike had about ten years on him, at least.

"Not quite," said Mike, an edge to his voice. They seemed as comfortable with each other as estranged brothers at a funeral. "In any case, we all have the same goal: find Julia and bring her back home. It's important that we all stay on the same page. Pool our information." Mike regarded Ripetti with suspicion. "Whatever one of us knows, we all know."

"Sure. I have no problem with that," were the words that came out of Ripetti's mouth, but the look on his face said, "Tag along if you like, but there's no question of who'll get the job done." They each seemed to be jockeying for the space at my bedside, an unspoken turf war as to who had my confidence. It had been a while since I had men vying for me; maybe it was the drugs, but I enjoyed it.

"How's the patient?"

A young doctor in a white coat with a dark face stepped into view. His nameplate identified him as Dr. Darshani. He went to the end of my bed, picked up my chart, glanced at it quickly, then came over to the bedside. He peered at my face and held my wrist to check my pulse. His brown eyes glinted like jewels offset by clear white.

He asked me how I was feeling, and I said okay. He asked Mike and Ripetti to excuse us for a moment, and he whisked the curtain around my bed, shielding me from view.

He pressed the bed pedal to lift me into a seated position. He untied my hospital gown and let it fall. My chest was taped and bound, with bandages on front and back. Darshani cut through the tape, and lifted the bandages, his manner professional and disinterested. I pulled my head back like a turtle to see the wound, on the side of my left breast. It was a purple and yellow splotch, with spindly tentacles reaching out in all directions. The stitches were neat but uneven, like an elementary school sewing project. "Very nice," he said, admiring the wound and his work. He put the buds of his stethoscope in his ears, and listened to me breathe. "Excellent," he said, patting my shoulder. "Two centimeters difference and this could have pierced your lung. You're very lucky. But you lost a lot of blood; I'd advise taking it easy for a while." He said the bullet had cut through some muscle. They'd keep me here today to keep an eye on things, but he expected I'd be able to leave tomorrow. I'd need to come back to get checked, and eventually, he'd prescribe physical therapy.

"What about pain meds?" That was Mike. Darshani said he'd prescribe something for me to go home with, along with antibiotics.

"What kind?" I asked, perking up. I heard Mike cough. I stammered to Darshani that I'd had some problems in the past with substance abuse. I heard Mike snort a laugh. I told Darshani I was an addict and probably should be wary of taking narcotics.

Darshani frowned. "You're going to need something. The body won't heal if it's in pain."

"She can stay with me, and I'll dole 'em out to her," said Mike.

I hated the idea of being dependent upon Mike. "It's okay. I'll be fine."

Darshani re-bandaged the wound, tied my gown back, and opened the curtain.

"You need to take them, and I don't want you alone with a bottle of Vicodin," said Mike, shooting a one-up look at Ripetti. "It's just for a few days." He brushed his hand over my hand, in a sort of affectionate pat.

"I'll be fine." I pulled my hand away. I didn't want Ripetti to misunderstand the nature of my relationship with Mike; I didn't understand it myself. "And Gerry Talbot is paying me to house-sit for him."

"I'll have my guys check in on things. It's just for a few days."

I knew I was only one of Mike's many reclamation projects. Over the years, he'd helped countless drunks get sober, taking them through the "steps," serving along the way as sponsor/father/brother/confidant. If he occasionally asked a favor in return, most were glad to do it for him. These were the guys he'd ask.

"What about it, Doc? Isn't she better off resting on a sofa and having someone cook for her?"

"I'd take him up on the offer before he changes his mind." He advised me to get some rest. I didn't have much choice. I was exhausted and drifted back to sleep.

CHAPTER *19*

I woke to find two detectives in my room who introduced themselves and asked me if I were up to answering a few questions. I tried to sit up before realizing I couldn't. Instead, I found the switch that raised the bed.

Detective Luke Norton was a stocky man built in a rectangle, with a strong broad chest and a wide stance. He wore thick black rubber soled shoes and an off-the-rack navy blue suit that looked a little too tight to be comfortable. His hair was so blond it appeared white; he wore it short, brushed forward, with no part. His jaw was square and his eyes brown and serious. Although he seemed about my age, he spoke to me with a respect that made me feel older. His partner, Theresa Martinez, wore a blue blazer with grey slacks and a white shirt. The one dash of color she allowed herself was on her ears: studs of red that matched a ring she wore on her right hand.

Norton asked the questions while Martinez took notes. His voice was low and gruff, his manner dogged, as he got me to go over the scene in detail, dredging up from memory everything I could remember about my assailant. I said he'd been sprawled face down on the floor when I first saw him. He wore black jeans, a tight black t-shirt, and black high top boots. As he scrambled to his feet, it seemed to me that he was Japanese, or Eskimo, or Native American; difficult to say. His eyes were covered by wraparound aviator sunglasses. But he had a high, wide forehead and pronounced cheekbones, straight black hair. He gave the impression of an ethnicity other than Caucasian, but I couldn't say which. He was slender, good-looking.

"Which hand did he use to lift the gun?"

I closed my eyes and tried to recreate the scene in my mind. I remembered the sneer of hatred on his face as he was trying to stand, the peculiar grace of his movements even as he stumbled forward in chase. My attention had been careening from him to Clinton and Julia fleeing out the back. I recalled him holding the gun in both hands, but it seemed that his right hand was on the trigger, his left steadying.

"Right. And he had a scar, here." I gestured towards my cheek, surprised at the detail I'd just remembered.

"Did you hear anyone say his name?"

"No. Clinton peered at him from behind the curtain, and I'm pretty sure he knew who he was. He pushed us into the bedroom. They had a conversation in the other room, but I couldn't hear the words; I was talking to Julia in the bedroom. I think Clinton hit him on the head with his gun and then came into the bedroom to get us. I didn't hear any conversation."

"But you think Clinton knew who it was?"

"I'm sure of it."

"What were you doing there?"

I thought before answering. Julia had confided in me, and I put a high value on not betraying confidences. But Caleigh's murder had changed things, and it seemed to me that Julia was in too much trouble to hold back. I had promised Julia I wouldn't tell Jonathan about "enjo kosai." But if it was relevant to where she was, or why she was so frightened, how could I keep it to myself?

All this was going through my mind as I answered. "I was looking for Julia. She had come to see me because she was worried about Caleigh Nussbaum. They were best friends. Then Caleigh's body was found, and Julia ran away."

Martinez wrote it down.

"I knew that Julia was infatuated with Clinton; that's why I went there. He's a dealer who sells drugs to high school kids. He's dangerous. He's got a gun, a record, and they're scared. Do you think you can find them? I think she's with him."

"What did you say was the nature of your relationship exactly? Are you her mother?"

"No. Step-mother. Ex-step-mother. Sort of. I used to live with her and her father."

"Friend of the family?" Martinez suggested, writing it down.

How could I explain what Julia was to me in conventional terms? "Extended family. The point is, I think Julia knew something about Caleigh Nussbaum's murder, and that's why she was scared, and that's why she went to Clinton's, and it could be that the guy who came in with a gun was coming after her. And if he's still out there, she's in danger."

"What do you think she knew?"

I took a deep breath. "Caleigh Nussbaum was playing a game they called 'enjo kosai.' She was sleeping with men and getting paid for it. You know, like some girls play house? Caleigh was playing hooker."

Martinez wrote down everything I said.

"It was all set in motion by a former business partner of her father's, Patrick Caiman. Marty had fired him, and Patrick was paying him back by corrupting his daughter. And not for the first time. Caleigh's mother told me they'd found out he'd been molesting Caleigh when she was younger. The men Patrick Caiman was setting Caleigh up with were all fairly prominent, and I think they were all in business with her father. I can give you the names I know. After Caleigh disappeared, Julia became afraid for her life. That's why she went to see Clinton Cole. She thought he could protect her."

"Clinton Cole's a drug dealer."

"But she knew him from school, and he knew what they'd been doing. She'd seen him at one of the parties."

"How do you know the gunman wasn't coming after him?" Norton asked.

"I don't. But Julia's in danger as long as she's with Clinton whoever the gunman is."

Martinez checked her notes. "You said she went to see Clinton on her own. And that there was a romantic involvement between them."

"Yes, but she's underage. He isn't."

"Have her parents reported her missing?"

"I don't know. They must have. They hired a private detective."

Martinez made a note, saying, "That's not the same thing."

"She's a material witness," Norton said. "We'll do all we can to find her. Does she have a cell phone?"

"She's bonded to it. It's her link to the world."

"We'll talk to her parents and monitor her phone and credit cards. In the meanwhile, we have to treat this as an attempted homicide. We've taken the bullet they removed from you into evidence. We're going to see if we get a match with similar assaults. Clinton Cole is a drug dealer, and he recognized the assailant; we have to explore the possibility that this is drug related. But I'll call the people from Robbery-Homicide who are working on the Caleigh Nussbaum murder and tell them what you've told me. I'm sure they'll want to talk to you. So get some rest, and as soon as you're able, I'd like you to come down and look at photos. I'd like to see if you can ID your assailant."

After they left, I rang for the nurse to bring my belongings. I was surprised at how little interest the police had showed in the "enjo kosai" angle. I'd been worrying about whether or not to turn over Julia's diary to them; now I was glad I hadn't. Still, I wanted to talk to Mike and Ripetti about what I knew, and I wanted to go through it again, now that I'd spoken to Julia and Hannah and had a better idea of how to interpret what was in it.

When the nurse returned, she brought with her a plastic bag of my belongings. I found my purse in it and my wallet, with nothing missing. But Julia's diary and my notebook were gone.

CHAPTER 20

When I left the hospital, Mike drove me back to his house in one of his beloved Woodies; this one, a lime green 1946 Mercury, its polished chrome grills and walnut varnished slats as lovingly restored as a Stradivarius. Two of the guys he sponsored brought my car to his house and went to Gerry's to pick up some of my things, offering to watch the house until I returned. My arm was sore; I shouldn't drive. I had to take antibiotics and Vicodin every four hours, always with food.

Mike's house, three houses down from the beachfront walk on a side street, was an old craftsman bungalow with a long sloping roof and oak pillars that were heavy, square, and simple. The house was solid and comforting, like Mike. Although it didn't face the ocean, it was still close enough that the rhythmic ebb and flow of the tide was the subtle undercurrent to all the other sounds of his home. The house was always suffused with the aroma of good strong coffee; it was the perfume I associated with Mike.

The last time I'd stayed here, I was too sick to be interested, or, I imagine, interesting. Now I wasn't so sure.

When we'd arrived, I watched as one more time he made up the bed in the spare room for me and lent me a pair of his pajamas. He'd also unrolled a sleeping bag on the leather sofa in the living room, so I could curl up and watch TV. The shirt I'd worn to the hospital was blood-soaked, and my own clothes irritated the bandage, so he offered me a pair of sweats and one of his Hawaiian shirts to wear around the house.

I was aware, as we passed each other in the hall, of a current that ran between us. I thought about him when I was standing naked in the shower, and I knew that he was thinking similar thoughts about me. I had never thought of Mike sexually before, but he was behaving towards me with so much love, I had no other way of interpreting it.

Now I lay on his sofa, curled up in his sleeping bag, buoyed by his coffee, and soothed by the Vicodin. I watched him in the kitchen make me soup and a grilled cheese sandwich.

Mike was older than me by at least fifteen years, but he had the well-muscled body of an athlete. He surfed every morning as assiduously as a monk. He told me that when AA suggested he find a "power greater than himself" he'd picked the ocean. Surfing was his way of being in its presence. Finding the balance between effort and surrender necessary to stand and ride its waves, he said, taught him all he needed to know of life.

It also had given him a body that was supple as well as strong, that moved, I was noticing for the first time, with masculine grace. I imagined burrowing into the safety of those gentle and powerful arms, losing myself in his embrace. Imagining it gave me the same lush and languid abandon as the Vicodin

He called me into the kitchen for lunch. He showed me a little pad, and explained that every time I took a pill I was to make note of it.

When he turned back for my sandwich, I went up behind him and put my arms around him, leaning my cheek against his shoulder, from behind. I heard him sigh, almost a groan, and then he turned to me, taking me into his arms. I relaxed into the comforting mass of him.

Desire rose within me like embers catching fire. As we held each other, our bodies communicated without words. I felt his longing as well as my own, in the quickness of his breath, the urgency of his touch. I tipped my head, searching for his mouth with mine. Instead of kissing me, he suddenly released me, almost flinging me away from him.

"No, Brett. You have to get sober first."

He busied himself with things in the kitchen. I came towards him, but he pulled away.

"Get a different sponsor. A woman. Someone you can talk to."

"I can talk to you." I knew I was lying, that I would never talk to anyone, woman or man, about the truths at the heart of me.

"It's too complicated. Believe me, Brett, I know what I'm talking about. You don't know the first thing about getting sober." His voice was gruff. "We've got a lot of work to do. Finish your sandwich and meet me in the office."

* * *

His office was in one of the bedrooms on the same side of the house as mine. The windows looked out only at the side of the house next door. They were curtained, but the curtains were open. Files and reports were stacked on his desk, along with old phone books for various cities. Filing cabinets lined the walls, but his desk also contained readily accessible "hot files" for current cases. Environmental impact reports, deposition transcripts and other papers were stacked on his desk and coffee table. His bookcase overflowed with reference books of all kinds. The computer at his desk was connected to a printer, fax, and various external drives.

Mike invited me to stand behind him at his computer. He entered his user name and password to access special databases available only to licensed investigators and law enforcement. The day was cold and foggy, the sun yet to appear. Mike entered Clinton's name and address, and with a few clicks, he had a report that listed all of Clinton's known addresses and the address and phone numbers of neighbors, friends, relatives, and associates his path had crossed. He knew where he was born, what his mother's name was, and that he'd dropped out in 10th grade.

"Do you know why she went to see him?"

"He could be involved in this 'enjo kosai' thing. He was at one of the parties. Now she's sleeping with him."

I noticed how broad Mike's shoulders were, how muscular his upper arms, from paddling into the waves. And yet how long and slender his forearms were, his fingers almost delicate. I thought about the moment that had passed between us in the kitchen, and wondered why I didn't feel rejected. Truthfully, I was almost relieved. I wasn't sure if what I'd felt wasn't simply longing for escape. Sobriety was relentless.

Within minutes, Mike had a profile of Clinton that included his driving record, credit history, car registration, and the bank who held the loan. His complete criminal history, including all his arrests, his time at the California Youth Authority, who his parole officer had been, and who he had lived with when he first got out. He even found out that as a kid, he'd once been the recipient of a scholarship to a camp for underprivileged children a newspaper had underwritten.

"I'll talk to some cops I know, see if I can put a tap on his mom's phone. Then I'll go see his parole officer and some of these associates. Should be able to get a lead on where he might have taken her."

"What about the names in the diary?"

"I thought you said the diary was missing."

"Yes, but I remember some of the names."

He thought a minute. "Let's make that phase two. First thing to do is find Clinton Cole and see if she's still with him."

The sun was attempting to come through the fog; dappled rays of light shone through the curtains. Somewhere nearby, a drummer was playing the same riff over and over, underscoring our conversation.

"Why didn't you tell me you know Marty Nussbaum's assistant?"

Mike put down what he was doing, partly offended, partly defended, completely surprised.

"What?"

"All this time I've been talking to you about Julia and Caleigh Nussbaum. You never mentioned that you knew Marty Nussbaum's assistant. I saw you with her the night of the meeting."

The look that crossed his face was similar to the one I'd seen that night: the furtive glance of a man with something to hide.

"She's a client." Mike returned his attention to his computer.

I remembered the way he'd held her, the shelter she'd sought and found in his arms, just as I had, moments before. The skeptical look on my face must have showed.

"Brett, my relationships with my clients are confidential. I don't owe you any explanations." He hit print. His computer spewed out the profile he'd compiled. "It's got nothing to do with you," he added.

I thought how lucky it was that our relationship had not become intimate. I resolved to go home as soon as possible.

"How do you know Ripetti?"

"We were cops together."

"But you don't trust him"

"No and neither should you." After a beat, he added, "He took a bullet for me. When I was fucked up. So, in a way, I owe him my life. It's complicated."

The few shafts of light that had managed to come into the window vanished back into shade as the sun pulled behind a cloud.

"You said at the hospital the two of you would be working together."

"Nic Ripetti is the go-to investigator for the stars. He's working for Julia's parents and the Nussbaums. If he's looking for Julia, there's a good chance he'll find her. I'd just feel better if we stay on top of things."

He turned off his computer. "This gives me a lot to go on." He looked at his watch. "When'd you take your last pill?"

I reached for the pad he'd given me to write such things down.

"Almost an hour ago."

He took the bottle from his pocket, shook out two more, and handed them to me.

"In three hours, take these. I'll be back before you'll need any more."

He left the room. I listened as drawers and doors were opened and closed in the bedroom, trying to hear where he might be putting that bottle of pills.

I followed him. He was changing his clothes, getting ready to leave.

"Will you be okay?" he asked me.

"Of course."

He went back to his office, opened and closed a few more drawers, before coming back to me.

"You have my cell. Call me if you need anything, and call me for sure when you take your next pills."

I put the pills in the pocket of his pajamas and promised.

CHAPTER 21

But. Two Vicodin weren't enough. I knew that with the kind of tolerance I'd built up over the years, I'd need more. I couldn't expect Mike to understand, but I knew I had the metabolism to handle it. Besides, I was enjoying this floaty feeling and didn't want it to end. I settled into Mike's sofa, watching Fred Astaire croon to Ginger Rogers that he was in heaven dancing cheek to cheek with her. I thought that with a few more Vicodin, I could be too. I got up to check the medicine cabinet in Mike's bedroom, to see if I could find the bottle. Just to know where they were.

Talk about the medicine chest of a sober man! There was Tiger Balm, Ben-Gay, some shaving things, aspirin, Tums, dental floss, and zip!

I went into his bedroom. On his nightstand were books by Elmore Leonard and James Ellroy, along with a biography of J. Edgar Hoover, and a large book about some FBI agents in Boston who had worked for the mob. I opened the drawer by his bed. I saw condoms, more dental floss, some keys, some clutter—and a meeting directory that at first I assumed was for AA, but when I looked closer, saw was for something called "Sex and Love Addicts Anonymous." He had a whole bunch of pamphlets and literature from a twelve-step program for "sexual addiction." Hmmmm. He'd never mentioned that one. There was also a photograph of Mike with the redheaded woman, Susanna Terrell, Marty's assistant. They were at a table in a restaurant. She beamed at him with love in her eyes. He laughed with delighted surprise, as if she had just moved her hand up his leg. A client? Sure.

His closet held his collection of Hawaiian shirts. He must have had close to a hundred. Many were classics, vintage and rare. None were dull. I checked the pockets of them all. And his pants. Nothing. His closet housed running shoes, sandals, and flip-flops. Only one pair of leather shoes. I rifled through them all quickly.

No pills.

I remembered he'd gone back to his office, so I went there to look through those drawers.

One drawer was locked. Convinced this was where he'd hidden the pills from me, I pulled at it hard, trying to jar it loose. It didn't open. I searched for the key but couldn't find it.

I fingered the two Vicodin he'd left me with and almost took them. But I wanted to make sure I had more before I did. I called Dr. Geller, someone I knew to be generous with prescriptions and refills. He wasn't available. I told the receptionist I'd had a reoccurrence of my old back injury and needed some pain meds. She said the doctor would have to call me back. I left my name, Mike's number, and my cell phone number.

While waiting for Dr. Geller to return my call, I remembered seeing keys in the clutter of Mike's nightstand and wondered if they might open this desk drawer. Worth a try. I went back to get them and brought them back to the office.

I tried the key without a moment's hesitation. Would I want someone doing this to me? No. Did I even think about the wisdom or karmic consequences of doing it to someone else? No again.

The key worked, and the drawer opened. In it, I did not find the pills.

What I found instead was my notebook and Julia's diary.

It must have been a good five minutes before my heartbeat returned to normal. It was as if I'd been picked up by a cyclone that whirled me in a spiral of betrayal, outrage, and fear before landing me back at his desk, trying to adjust to this new reality. What were my things doing in Mike's locked drawer? Julia's diary? My notebook? It couldn't have been 30 minutes ago that we were talking about them, and he'd never mentioned that he knew where they were, let alone that he'd taken them and hidden them away. Mike had lied to me. He could not be trusted.

Okay. Why should that surprise me? Before house-sitting for Gerry, I'd been living with a dealer, and before that, hanging out with addicts. I knew very well that nobody could be trusted, least of all and especially me. Why should Mike be any different?

Because. He'd seemed so different.

Well, kiddo, welcome back to the real world.

I went to the kitchen for some water and quickly took the two Vicodin he'd given me. For all I knew, he was lying about his sobriety too. He probably had some secret stash of booze. I knew I'd better find some more pills before these wore off.

I went back to his office to call another doctor but noticed his computer still on that website available only to law enforcement and private investigators, although his session was over. Using the password I'd noticed him typing in earlier, I logged on as him. I clicked on his recent history and saw all the information he'd just run on Clinton. I printed it out.

On a lark, I typed in my own name, DOB, and Social, and got an eyeful. I saw my entire employment history, going back to my first summer job as a file clerk in the office of a friend of my father's when I was fifteen, in Roanoke, Va. It included the newspaper I'd worked for in San Diego before going to work for Jonathan and all the incarnations of the company Jonathan had worked for before and after it had been acquired by Poseidon.

I saw every address I'd ever lived at, including Jonathan's, and the names of all my neighbors. Jonathan and Julia were listed, as was Lynda LeWylie-Weissman. All the money I owed. No outstanding tickets, no arrest warrants. As far as the law was concerned, I was a deadbeat, but I was clean.

I typed in a name that was never far from the surface of my consciousness—Rosa Aguilar.

I held my breath then pressed submit. In a few seconds, I got a read-out about Rosa similar to the ones I'd just seen on Clinton and myself. I found out where she'd lived the night of the accident and the names of her two children, Enrique and Yolanda. No husband. I also had a list of her neighbors. I saw the name of the family she was working for the night she'd been killed.

I hit print and typed in the names of her children to see what would come up. The doorbell rang. I froze, as if a hand had clapped me on the shoulder. I sat there quietly, ignoring the bell, as the printer shot out its damning evidence. The doorbell rang again. I thought it might be the police. To help Julia? Or capture me? I scooped up the pages and turned off the computer, pulse racing. I hurried to my room, shoved the pages into the side pocket of my duffel, and then lumbered to the door as the bell rang one more time.

It was the first time I'd seen him when I wasn't bleeding to death or under anesthesia. My dark angel, my own Lone Ranger, the man who'd magically appeared when I needed him and vanished when I didn't. He was a large man, tall but not lean, muscular in a way that suggested discipline rather than genetics. He wore a leather jacket over dark trousers and a t-shirt showing beneath a merino wool polo shirt. His chin was softer than his strapping body would lead you to expect, with a hint of jowl, as if beyond the reach of his exercise regimen. He wore aviator sunglasses.

"Come in," I said, my voice shaky.

He ducked slightly as he came in the door. He took off his sunglasses, folded them, and stuck one of its shafts into the neck of his t-shirt.

"You know, in Japan they say that when you save somebody's life, they become your responsibility from then on." The slight lift of his brow made the statement sound sly, intimate, as if we already shared a secret. The hairs on my arms tingled, the air suddenly electric with static, like the sky before a summer storm.

"Don't worry about it. You're off the hook." I felt suddenly self-conscious. It was one thing for Mike to see me lying around in pajamas; this was different. I wished I were dressed. I found myself straightening up the newspapers magazines and books that lay scattered around the sofa like fallen leaves.

Nic Ripetti looked around the room, seeming to take in every aspect of his surroundings, like a surveillance camera, in constantly shifting angles. On the television, Fred Astaire was leaping over furniture with fluid grace. I turned it off. The elegance of Fred jarred with the energy Ripetti's presence brought to the room. I sat on the leather sofa and tucked my feet under me, gathering my sleeping bag around me, as much to hide my pajamas as for warmth or comfort.

He sat down across from me and stretched his legs out, leaning back in the chair. He owned the space he occupied. His jacket fell open slightly, and I noticed he wore a shoulder holster and gun.

"So. What did Julia tell you when you saw her at Clinton Cole's?"

I stared at the well-worn Navajo rug beneath the coffee table between my sofa and his chair. I remembered Mike's warning not to trust him. But now I knew I couldn't trust Mike. And when I'd lain bleeding, floating between life and death, this man's presence by my side had anchored me.

He shifted slightly. Not with his body, but with his eyes. It reminded me of the switch an optometrist might make, testing a different lens.

"We're on the same side. The Weissman's hired me to find her. I found you instead."

I was sorry I had taken the Vicodin. I couldn't think straight.

"What's the story between you and Mike?" I asked him.

"What did he say?"

"That you took a bullet for him when he was fucked up, and he owes you his life."

He got up and strode into the kitchen as if it were his own. Without asking, he dumped the coffee from this morning still in the pot on the stove and opened the cupboards to look for filter papers to make fresh coffee as if he were the host and I the guest.

"He ever tell you why he stopped drinking?"

"I can do that."

Mike was very particular about his coffee. He made a special blend of French Roast from beans he kept in the freezer and ground himself. Ripetti gestured me to sit where I was, finding for himself the beans and grinder and putting fresh water on to boil.

"Really. I'm curious. What did he tell you?"

"Something about blowing a murder case. A girl got killed, and the killer got off because of him."

"Well, that's one way of putting it." He spooned out coffee grinds into filter paper though Mike made his in a French Press. "He tell you he was a suspect himself? And all the evidence conveniently disappeared? Along with a material witness, who died using drugs he'd given to her? But that he claimed to be in…" he wiggled his fingers to indicate quotation marks he thought little of "…an 'alcoholic blackout' so he remembered nothing?"

I heard little of whatever Ripetti said next as my mind raced to process this new information and what bearing it might have on my own situation. I'd had blackouts, where I'd come to with no memory of where I'd been or what I'd been doing, so I knew it was possible. Could Mike have a secret as dark as mine? Why not?

Ripetti must have used a different bean or made the coffee a different way; it didn't have the same aroma as Mike's. It reminded me of one male dog peeing on another one's spot, to eradicate its scent.

"What happened?"

"No evidence, and without it, no case, so he only lost his job. But hey. I hear he's turned his life around, so I'm happy for him. And if he's with you, that speaks well for him too. You take milk or sugar?"

"We're not together; I'm just staying here for now."

He fixed my cup of coffee and kept one for himself, bringing mine over to me in the living room. "Whatever. The point is we're all on the same team."

His smile was open and ingratiating, and yet, he seemed to be studying me. His eyes took everything in but gave very little out. I watched the dust particles dance in the late morning sunlight that streamed through the windows. Beyond the window was the porch with Mike's surfboard leaning against the screen.

"What's with the gun?"

"Part of the image. Clients like it."

"Do you ever use it?"

He touched it. "You don't have to use it when people know you've got it."

Maybe. But seeing it did not make me feel safe, just the opposite. There was the threat of danger, a hint of potential violence. Was it the gun? The conflict between him and Mike? Or that old male-female thing, with its promise of pleasure and probability of pain? I'd felt it earlier with Mike, and now, only moments later, again with this other man. Was it them? Or me? He turned those X-ray eyes on me, and I felt a shiver of anticipation; a bowling pin before the strike.

"Did you give Mike the diary?"

"What diary?"

"When you brought me to the hospital, I had two notebooks: one of mine and one of Julia's. What did you do with them?"

"I just scooped up your bag and brought it in the ambulance. It had your insurance card in your wallet. I didn't see any notebooks."

That meant he was lying too. Those notebooks were there; he'd have to have seen them. Did that mean he had given them to Mike? Was the rivalry between them an act?

"Julia's diary?" His curiosity seemed genuine. "Did you read it? What did she say? Anything that could help us find her now?"

I sipped my sweet milky coffee, my knees tucked under me, and considered him. What if I told him Mike had the diaries? He and I could go through them together and figure out how their contents could lead us to Julia. Something stopped me. I didn't trust Mike, and I didn't trust Ripetti either. Since I didn't trust myself, it was a perfect trifecta. The Vicodin didn't help.

"Did she say anything about Patrick Caiman?"

The drummer who'd been practicing down the street stopped, and the room went suddenly quiet. I picked up one of the pillows beside me and hugged it close.

"What do you know about that?"

"I know what he and Caleigh were up to. And I know he got Julia into it too."

"Do you know with who?"

"Not yet. I will."

"I saw her with somebody, but I'm not sure who it was."

"Where?"

I ransacked my memory. "Maybe the Topaz Lounge?" I rubbed my head, willing it to spew forth memories that were locked behind an alcoholic shroud. "What was Mike supposed to have done in a blackout? What made him a suspect?"

Ripetti shook his head. "I think you'd better ask him that. Right now let's find Julia. Tell me everything you remember. What Julia said to you, or what she wrote in the diary."

"Mike thinks she's with Clinton."

Ripetti sat for a long time, looking at me but not really seeing, as if he were working out a puzzle in his mind. He stood up.

"Well. Maybe he's right, and that was just a drug guy coming after Clinton, like the cops think."

He went back into the kitchen, threw his coffee out, rinsed the cup, and put it away.

"Call me if you think of anything I should know."

He put his sunglasses on.

"Where are you going?" I asked.

"To the crime scene, for a start. I think whoever killed Caleigh has Julia now. Haven't you written that scene a million times? The detective goes to the crime scene to put himself in the mind of the killer? I want to get out there before it gets dark."

I was already off the sofa and headed towards my guest bedroom.

"Wait a minute," I heard myself say. "I'll go with you."

"Are you sure you're up to it?"

I moved my shoulder. Maybe it was the extra Vicodin, but I felt no pain at all. "I'm fine. I'll be fine."

I saw a slight flicker of a smile on his face. I said I would just be a minute, I'd change my clothes.

CHAPTER 22

Rattlesnake Canyon was in the San Gabriel Mountains, northeast of Pasadena, in the Angeles National Forest. It was a long ways from Mike's, and traffic was slow. The sun played hide-and-seek as we drove through a series of beach neighborhoods, occasional patches of brightness alternating with longer stretches of gloom.

The long drive gave us time to talk. Ripetti already knew everything the girls had done, so I told him what I knew, including Patrick's desire to get back at Marty for firing him, and Marty's need to make up with Patrick in order to get the rights to *Space Wizards*. I also told him about Julia's reaction to seeing Campbell McCauley running on the beach, and that he might be one of the men who slept with Caleigh. Ripetti knew about Hannah and Paolo Navarro, but he wouldn't say how he knew.

We drove past a motel. A young woman walked the street in front, another stood at the corner. One wore hot pants, the other, a mini-skirt. Both wore fishnet hose and platform shoes. They looked barely older than Julia or Caleigh.

"What kind of a man goes to hookers?" I asked.

"Men who wear pants?"

"No, really."

He raised an eyebrow. "You've had good relationships with men."

I laughed. As if. But even so. I couldn't imagine paying a man to have sex with me. Were men that different from women? What kind of man would buy a blowjob from a sixteen-year-old? Didn't any of them have daughters?

Ripetti interrupted my train of thought. "Did you ever ask Mike that question?"

"No. Why?"

We had reached the freeway onramp.

"No reason. Just based on the guy I knew before he became a saint." He swung his SUV into the flow of traffic. "Let's just say if you're wondering how a guy could pay for sex, you might ask your roommate."

* * *

To reach Rattlesnake Canyon, we needed to drive up a winding two-lane highway that rose out of the foothills into the Angeles National Forest. The road cut through folds of mountain, sloping down in a deep drop off to the right and rising in sheets of rock on the left. We passed first one, then another reservoir:; large pools of water formed by constructs of concrete damming off the San Gabriel River. But as we rose, we went beyond the hydro-electric manipulation of nature and into a raw, rock-ribbed enclave of rugged canyons, rising into and even above the clouds.

"There's a shooting range near here," said Ripetti, "off the East Fork Road. They take cops to do practice maneuvers there." He shook his head. "Hell of a place to dump a body. Near a cop shooting range."

A scattering of big cone spruce and other conifers began to dot the elfin forest of chaparral that clung to the hillside. A red-tailed hawk circled overhead, searching for prey.

Ripetti turned onto a fire road that was barricaded by a gate with a "No Trespassing" sign, and a large chain lock. He parked, got out of his car, pushed his sunglasses up and examined the lock. He got a tool kit out the back, and selected an instrument that looked like a small screwdriver, and a long, thin pick. He inserted the first, turning gently one way and another, before inserting the pick.

"How does that work?" I asked, coming out of the car to stand by his side and watch.

He gestured for me to be still, as he maneuvered the pick gently. He worked slowly, methodically, with a concentration that excluded all but his intent. It took him several minutes, but he was able to free the lock.

"How did you do that?"

"You listen, and feel, for when you've touched just the right spot."

His look took in my whole body, a tiny smile at the corners of his mouth, as if he could easily do the same to me. Involuntarily, an image rose in my mind, of having sex with him. My body responded as if it were about to happen; like salivating while reading a menu. I pushed the image away, unwelcome and ill-timed. I remembered it wasn't more than a few hours ago I'd been imagining the same thing with Mike.

"What about the killer? How did he get through, if the gate was locked?"

Ripetti looked at the lock and chain. "I don't know. This is a new lock. Maybe he cut it? Or used a crow-bar?" He opened the gate, and gestured me into the car before getting back into the driver's seat. "Or maybe he did what I did, and picked it. It's not that hard to do."

We drove down the paved but unmaintained road, filled with pot holes, and ruptures. We descended into the canyon, twisting deep into the bowels of the wilderness. Eventually, the road paralleled a running stream several feet off to the side. We drove until we saw fragments of the yellow crime scene tape marking where the body had been found.

Ripetti parked just ahead of the place where yellow tape, no longer strung up to protect the spot, flapped in the wind.

The stream was about fifty feet down a hillside, at the bottom of a ravine. The land between the road and the stream had been excavated thoroughly. Metal pins marked evidence collection spots. A few stakes remained, with planks of wood between them; the remains of a makeshift stairway that had been built into the hillside, and taken down again.

Ripetti pushed up his sunglasses and squatted, looking closely at the ground. He walked slowly, studying the road and its markings, the indentations and prints, its pits and crevices.

"Hasn't the site been completely contaminated by now?" I asked. "The cops have been all through here and who knows who else. Also, it's rained several times since."

"We're not here to collect evidence."

He seemed to absorb the landscape, taking in every detail of the sun and the wind, the earth and sky. Either we were above the clouds or the air was just cleaner and brighter. I felt a cool wind on my arms and face and heard the buzz of insects and smelled the air with its noticeable absence of smog. Nothing I observed told me anything of what had happened in the past.

My shoulder hurt, and I thought it was probably time to take my next Vicodin. But I'd already taken them and didn't have any more. How could I get some? I dismissed the thought. I was too interested in what was going on to be bothered, and the pain kept me alert.

"The body was found down there." He took out copies of the crime scene photos and handed them to me. They showed in stark severity the body of a young woman sprawled on her back beside a tree, which I could see from where we stood. It was far enough away from the stream that the body was dry, although it lay in a muddy bed of dead leaves and lichen. She was lying on her back, her legs slightly bent, her arms outstretched in a pose that, even in rigor mortis, looked like a grotesque caricature of a come-on.

In the harsh crime scene photo there was nothing sensual in her nudity. Her flesh had taken on a greenish-black color, with splotches of dark purple on her left side and on her cheek. Liquid seeped from her nose and mouth. Her skin was blistered, her face bloated, her eyes and tongue protruding. Parts of her flesh had been eaten away by animals; there were black marks where insects had bitten.

A horizontal line furrowed her neck, black and bruised. Her eyes were open, with small streaks in the whites. They seemed frozen in a moment of shock. Liquid seeped out of the sockets.

"See those purple splotches on her left side? That's the lividity that comes from stagnant blood pooling where gravity pulls it. That shows she was lying on her side for a while shortly after she was killed. She wasn't killed here; she was killed somewhere else and brought here.

"Those streaks in her eyes come from blood leaking from capillaries ruptured from pressure on the neck. She was strangled.

That horizontal line suggests it was with a ligature. There were no bruises or prints from fingertips or padding on the thumb."

He stood beside me, looking from the crime photos to the scene and back.

"Also, look, she wasn't dumped; she was placed. I mean, he could have just thrown her from the car, but he carried her—and she was dead weight—he'd have had to have been a strong man—all the way down there and placed her, just so. And it was soon enough after she died that rigor mortis had not yet set in; he could still manipulate the body. There's symbolism in the way the body is left."

I examined the photo again. "She looks like a Playboy centerfold. Except dead." There was nothing remotely sexy about the picture of Caleigh's corpse. "Was she nude when she was killed?"

"No," he said. "There were trace fibers of her clothes in her wounds. Someone cut her clothes off after she died."

"Can't the lividity on the body give an indication of where she was killed?" I remember writing an episode of *Murder* where the body had been transported in a car that had a license plate in the trunk. The killer had taken the plates off his car to hide his identity. The blood of the corpse had pooled around the plate, revealing the distinct imprint of the license plate, including its identifying letters and numbers. "Or the kind of car that transported her here?" This killer had not been so obliging as to carry Caleigh on a license plate.

"I'm not sure what these markings indicate. I'll be getting the ME report as soon as it's completed."

"What did the Rattlesnake Killer do? And where did he leave his victims?"

"Same place. But he brought them here in his van and then raped them and killed them. Our guy killed her somewhere else but carried her all the way down there."

Ripetti took a step down the hill and held out his arm to me. "Want to come?"

The thought crossed my mind that a man I'd been told not to trust was leading me down to the spot where other women had been raped, strangled, and killed. It probably wasn't a good idea. Perhaps someone who took better care of herself would be more cautious. I gave him my hand, and he led me down.

We followed the path laid by the crime scene investigators. The soil was damp from recent rains. I could see the pins in the spots where the earth had been dug up when police had taken foot impressions. We made our way down to the tree where Caleigh had been placed.

Here too, the ground had been dug up and marked. I watched a brown beetle crawl slowly over the exposed roots and wondered if it was one for whom she'd been food in this harsh and desperate land.

"It wasn't easy to bring her down here. He did that for a reason too." He looked around the spot, as if the location could speak to him of the killer's mindset. "He's trying to communicate something."

"Like what?"

"I don't know. It can't have been easy. She was dead weight."

He stared at me, as if he were trying to gauge my weight and height and imagine what it would be like to carry me. "Caring? Like he's looking for a lovely spot to leave her."

His expression softened, as if he were seeing me for the first time. I looked away quickly. I did not want to be seen.

I examined the ground where Caleigh's body had been. The police had gone over the scene thoroughly, and anything the killer might have left behind would already have been collected. But it was still chilling to be here. In spite of the rain and collection of evidence, I could still see the imprint her body had made on the grasses by the stream. I fingered the space with my hand, as if I could channel the information it contained, but of course, I couldn't. I stood and walked slowly upstream, eyes on the ground, then on the trees, looking for any trace of fabric, anything at all that might have been left behind. But all I saw were the big clumps left from the spots where footprints had been lifted. Any clues pointing to the killer had already been taken by the police.

Ripetti came up behind me and touched me lightly.

"How's your shoulder?"

I jumped at his touch, and he smiled softly, understanding my fear and signaling he meant me no harm.

My shoulder throbbed with pain, but rather than minding, I found the rhythm of the waves of pain almost comforting. "Fine."

"If you like, when you're feeling better, I can bring you back here and teach you to shoot. Might keep you from getting hurt the next time."

I knew it probably wouldn't be good for my stitches, but I caressed my shoulder, asking it to hold on a little while longer.

"What's wrong with now?"

CHAPTER 23

"Gun fights are like Christmas," said Ripetti. "It's better to give than receive."

The Oak Spring Canyon shooting range was no more than few miles from the crime scene. Now, instead of chaparral, we saw cactus and yucca, even tumbleweeds among the scrub oak and manzanita.

"I've spent a lot of time here," Ripetti said as he pulled into the parking lot.

He rented a Colt .45 semi-automatic for me from the wooden ammo shack in the middle of a large gravel center surrounded by an arid desert parking lot and a ring of port-a-potties at the side. A large woman in a muumuu sat next to a small electric fan, an open bottle of Coca-Cola and overflowing ashtray beside her. Posters for the NRA lined the walls along with a bumper sticker that said, "My wife, sure, my dog, maybe, my gun, never." In exchange for my driver's license and a small deposit, I got my gun. Ripetti bought a few boxes of ammo. She handed us large, earphone-like protectors. Ripetti's own gun was holstered beneath his leather jacket, as always.

He carried my gun and the ammo over to the shooting range. A line of wooden picnic tables stood under a long lean-to roof that offered protection against the sun. Ahead lay the rocky desert floor. A painted line of fire carried warning signs not to step over it. About fifty feet beyond were the targets: straw men with concentric circles painted on the torso, the bull's eye at the heart.

Ripetti loaded a round of ammo into my gun and handed it to me.

Jinx Magruder never used a gun. I'd taken a self-defense course for women while writing the show, and I preferred, when she was in a physical confrontation with killers, for her to use the techniques I'd learned in my class. The truth is I was afraid of guns and prejudiced against them. I thought there were too damn many on the streets in this country, and I didn't want to glamorize their use. Now, as I held the gun in my hand, I was surprised at the rush of excitement it brought.

That's when he gave me his little maxim about Christmas.

First, he showed me how to hold the gun. "Use both hands," he said. "Finger to finger, palm to palm, thumb to thumb."

I held the gun in front of me stiffly.

"Relax," he said. "Don't tense up. How's your shoulder? Okay?"

"Okay." My left arm, where I was bandaged, was weaker than my right, but I held the gun with both hands. The awareness that I held a lethal weapon in my hands gave me the same knot of uneasiness I'd felt every time in the last eight days I'd been around booze.

Ripetti stood behind me and positioned my body into a "weaver stance."

"Like a boxer," he said. "Bend your knees…just a little…keep it loose. Feet hip wide, right leg slightly back." He put his arms around me from behind, adjusting my body.

"You sure you're okay? Okay. Lean forward. Be aggressive. Be assertive."

I held the gun in front of me, balancing the weight of my arms with the weight of my legs.

"That's right. Stabilize your center. Right arm straight and pushing, left arm bent and pulling. Atta girl. Now, line up your site."

The gun had a front and rear site. I peered between them, aligning them in a straight shot at my target's chest.

"Okay. Go for it. Shoot."

"Shoot?"

"Go on. Shoot."

I took a breath, squinted, aimed, and squeezed the trigger.

OW! The recoil knocked me back as if I'd been pushed, and my shoulder shrieked at being shoved. Even with ear protection, the sound had struck my whole body like a gong. The smell of gunpowder was acrid in my nostrils.

I lowered the gun, shaking.

"Suck it in! I want you to leave here with the ten toes you came with." Ripetti showed me how to pull my elbows in and hold the gun at my waist. "You okay? Maybe we should do this another day."

I waited for the throbbing in my shoulder to subside. "I'm fine."

Ripetti squinted at me, unsure whether he should let me continue, but I was determined. I enjoyed the feel of a gun in my hand, and I didn't want to stop. I lifted the gun and took the stance he had showed me. He stepped behind me.

"Aim for his belt, so you can see his hands. Then, when you're ready to shoot, raise it to his chest. He's coming at you. Stop him."

I tried again. My aim was awful. The recoil pushed me back and made my bullet stray far from the straw man, let alone its heart. And the pain in my shoulder demanded to be taken seriously.

"I'm fine," I said, knowing I must be pale-faced.

"You're letting the recoil scare you," he said. "It's nothing. Look. Get into position." I waited a moment, taking deep breaths, overriding the pain in my shoulder. Then I took my stance. He stood next to me, angled slightly in front. "It's no more than this." He pushed me back gently, making sure to stay away from my bandaged shoulder. I recoiled, but I came right back. "See? It's nothing. Get right back in position, and keep your aim."

"But the recoil has already knocked the gun out of position."

"Who cares? The bullet's already left. The point of aim is the point of impact. Come on. Try it again."

I lifted the gun, favoring my shoulder, but holding the gun up nonetheless. I squinted at the target and took aim at the waist of the straw man before me.

BAM!

Ouch.

"You're thinking too much. When you think, you get in trouble. See the motherfucker, shoot the motherfucker."

I raised the gun.

"He's coming towards you. He's got a gun. It's him or you. Which one is it going to be?"

BAM!

Got the motherfucker!

I turned to Ripetti, laughing with the purest pleasure I'd felt in years.

I couldn't see his eyes through his wraparound shades. But it seemed to me that the tiny smile that played around his mouth was one of recognition, as if he saw right through me and was saying, "Gotcha!"

I felt myself blush, a rush of shame at being seen.

"Reload."

"How?"

"Like this."

He took the gun, emptied it, put bullets in the new mag, shoved it in my pistol, and racked the slide. Then he handed it back to me.

"Now you do it."

I imitated what he'd done, although it took three times as long.

"You up for some more?"

I nodded. He stepped back. I lifted the gun and took aim. I took aim at my shame.

BAM!

Whoever had Julia.

BAM!

Whoever killed Caleigh.

BAM!

The network, for gutting the show. Marty Nussbaum, for his sexist notes. Jonathan, for leaving me; Mike, for stealing my journal. Every goddamn motherfucker who had ever stood in my way.

BAM! BAM! BAM!

Powerless?

Watch me!

CHAPTER 24

Ripetti dropped me off at Mike's without coming in. Mike was waiting for me, furious. Telling him where I'd been and what I was doing did nothing to deflect his rage.

"For Christ's sake, Brett, I leave you alone with a couple of Vicodin and ask you to call me, and I don't hear from you all day, and when I come back you're gone, and I can't reach you on your cell phone…"

"I was out of range, up there in Azusa Canyon."

"How do I know that? Couldn't you have called and let me know what you were doing?"

He paced back and forth, his breath almost a snort.

"I told you, I tried, but I couldn't get a signal! Why did you take my journal and Julia's diary and hide them from me?" Outraged all over again at this betrayal, all the more grievous for the way he'd seemed to be my friend.

"What??"

"I found them in your drawer."

"That drawer was locked! How did you get into it?"

"What difference does it make? You lied to me. Stole from me and lied to me!"

I was just as angry as him, furious.

He sat down heavily in his leather chair and swiveled it towards the living room. Outside his window, a small sliver of moon rose in the sky, above the roofs of his neighbors. Music and the muffled sound of other people's laughter interspersed with the ever present roar of the distant surf. "Okay, look. You're right. I'm sorry. I should have told you I had them. I…it's complicated. I can't really explain right now. I just thought…I thought it could help me help you, and I thought it was important to keep them out of the wrong hands. But I should have told you. I'm sorry."

His apology did nothing to mollify me; on the contrary, it fueled my rage.

"Those were my private things!"

"In my locked desk! What were you doing breaking into my things?"

I thought of the way I was ransacking his drawers and closet, searching for pills. Now that the narcotic was out of my system, it was hard to believe I'd behaved that way. I said nothing, too embarrassed to either admit or defend what I'd done, humiliated, but reluctant to give up my rage. I just stood there blinking.

"You were looking for the pills, weren't you? See, that's how it is with us addicts. Once that stuff is in our system, we're just powerless over it; it takes over."

I thought about what Ripetti had said about Mike, not only about being the prime suspect, but his proclivity for prostitutes. The pamphlets in his nightstand about sexual addiction. The look in his eyes as he'd taken off my blouse and helped me into his pajamas.

"I think I should go back to Gerry's."

I went back to the room I'd been staying in, found my duffle, and began throwing in the few things that had been brought for me. Mike appeared in the doorway.

"Wait until morning."

"I don't need you doling out pills to me. I've gone hours without one, so I must not need them anymore. There's no reason for me to be here."

And yet, as I carried a few shirts on hangers from the closet, I winced with pain. Mike took them from me.

"It's been a long day. You're tired. You just had surgery. Give yourself a break." He added, "I spent the day talking to Clinton's pals. At least let me tell you what I found out."

I let him put the shirts back in the closet.

* * *

Even though it was late, Mike made coffee and filled me in on his day. He'd gone to see Clinton's mother after arranging with the police to put a trace on her phone. He'd told her Clinton was in big trouble knowing that she'd call him as soon as he left, and she had—but it was the cell phone they already had for him, and she'd gotten no answer. She had made several other calls to friends of his. Mike had tracked them all down and spoken to them. He was developing a comprehensive profile on Clinton that he was confident would soon lead to his location. Clinton's mother worked in an orthodontist's office in Brentwood; that's how Clinton had gotten to know a lot of the Eastman kids. He'd sold some grass to an Eastman kid, and they both got caught. The kid got a reprimand; Clinton was sent to the California Youth Authority. He came out a criminal with contacts in the drug world, for whom he became an energetic foot soldier, a well-paid and loyal thug.

"He was at the party at Toby Starr's."

Mike looked at me in surprise. "What do you know about Toby Starr?"

I told him she had arranged the parties where the Eastman girls hooked up with the men who paid them. And that Julia had been surprised to see Clinton there when she went to one of those parties.

"He was probably supplying Toby and her girls with drugs. How did you know about Toby Starr?"

"The diary." It was still a sore spot.

He went into his office, and when he came back, he had Julia's diary and my notebook. He handed them back to me.

'I'm sorry," he said. "I shouldn't have taken them."

I looked through them. They seemed unaltered.

"Let's go through them together and develop a list of people to talk to," he suggested.

"That's okay," I said, hugging them close to me. "I remember all the names she mentioned. Patrick Caiman was the first. He was the one who first told Caleigh it was a fad in Japan. I think he did it with her, and then got her to enlist her friends in doing it with other men. I know Caleigh slept with Campbell McCauley. One of her friends slept with Paolo Navarro."

"Anybody else?" He peered at me over his coffee cup.

Where Ripetti's eyes were opaque, Mike's were clear. Ripetti was barricaded; Mike, open. And yet, I could not help but feel that he too had secrets at his depth, protected by their distance from the surface. He waited for my answer.

"I ran into Julia last week at a club. But I didn't see who she was with." I clasped the warm cup with my hands, aware that I was the one looking away, not wanting to be seen. "I don't remember much of that night." I did look at him when I added, "Ripetti told me about the murder case you blew before you stopped drinking. He said you were partying with a material witness, and that's why there was no case. He said the evidence disappeared while it was in your custody and that for a while you were a suspect yourself. But that you were in a blackout and couldn't remember anything."

A dark cloud of anger crossed Mike's face, his by now familiar reaction to being confronted with information he hadn't chosen to reveal.

"I'm sorry he told you that."

"I asked him what kind of man would go to prostitutes, and he suggested I ask you."

"Brett, I wish you'd do your inventory."

The "inventory" was one of AA's twelve steps. You were supposed to write down all the horrible things you'd done and read it to another person. I had as much intention of doing it as I had of walking to Alaska.

"What does that have to do with anything?"

"Do it, and you'll see. Until then, you'll always be looking at things through a distorted lens. You won't recognize what's right in front of you because you'll spend all your energy hiding from yourself."

"I thought we were talking about you."

"No. We were talking about how I spent my day tracking down Julia as a favor for you. What happened between Ripetti and me in the past has nothing to do with you or anything that concerns you. I'm sorry he said that to you about me. All I can say is nobody's perfect, and at least I'm doing everything I can to clean up the damage I've done in my life. I don't think the same can be said of him. Or you."

I stood, poured the dregs of my coffee in the sink.

"I'm sorry I went off with Ripetti without letting you know."

"Thank you."

"And I'm sorry I went through your things. I wouldn't like someone doing that to me."

"Brett…" Mike grabbed my hand and held it. He looked pained, as if he were struggling within himself. "Work the steps," was all he decided to say.

* * *

The next day I got a call from Detective Luke Norton asking me to come in. They'd developed a list of suspects and had some photos they wanted me to look at. I agreed and said that I also needed to talk to whoever was handling Caleigh's case on Robbery-Homicide. I had information for them. He told me that after we'd spoken at the hospital, he'd been in touch with the people on that case, and they were now treating the two cases as related. He gave me directions to the station, asked me to call when I got there, and he'd come down and walk me in.

Before I left, Mike asked me how I wanted to handle the Vicodin. Did I think I could go without it? My shoulder had hurt last night, but I'd taken Advil, and it had done the job. I was still bruised, stiff, and sore, but I had to admit that the over-the-counter pills worked as well as the Vicodin. I had gone over 24 hours without them, and I thought I could build on that.

Mike came back with the bottle. I don't know where he'd kept them and didn't try to guess.

"If I give you two, just in case, will you promise not to take them without calling me first?"

I stared at the Navajo rug on his floor, with its intricate patterns of crosses and symbols. "I can't. Once I have them, I can't guarantee what I'll do. I don't trust myself with them."

My cheeks flushed with shame at the admission. Mike beamed as if I'd just passed a test I didn't know I was taking.

"Come with me."

I followed him into the bathroom. He lifted the toilet seat, handed me the bottle, and gestured for me to pour them in.

I tipped the bottle, watching the little white pills swirl around in the churning water then disappear forever. I felt the way I had when I watched my father's coffin lowered into the ground.

CHAPTER 25

The guys who'd brought my things to Mike's had also
delivered Gerry's Range Rover. It was the first time I'd driven since
being shot, but the mobility in my shoulder was returning, and the
pain had been subsumed by Advil. As I drove towards the freeway, I
thought about the sorts of things I would have to commit to paper
were I to take his advice and write an AA "inventory." I knew I'd
have to write about "the accident" and wondered if I could do that.
It was never far from my thoughts, like a rotten tooth you can't help
but poke at with your tongue, painful though it is each time you do.
But write about it? Talk about it to somebody? To Mike, an ex-cop?

I drove through his beach neighborhood until I got to the wide
four lane boulevard that led to the freeway. I was deep into thoughts
about the bad old days when I glanced in the rearview mirror and saw
a blue Impala. My heart jumped into my throat. When I'd worked
at Poseidon and was convinced that my phone was tapped and I was
being followed, it was by a car just like this. I hadn't seen it in years.

Could I be imagining it now? Or had that same car been behind me every time I'd glanced in the mirror since leaving Mike's?

With a jolt, I suddenly thought of the car that had whizzed past me when I had stopped on Coldwater after Caleigh's funeral. I hadn't paid attention then, but I suddenly knew it was this same car, the one that was following me now. My heart started beating so quickly, I thought I was having a heart attack. My chest hurt, and I was finding it difficult to breathe.

I changed lanes, and the first chance I got, made a right turn, onto a side street, and pulled over against the curb.

I waited to see if the Impala would turn too. It did, speeding past me. Its driver was a heavy-set man in a black leather jacket, with dark glasses. I made a note of the license plate.

The Impala drove to the end of the block and then turned right, out of sight.

I needed a Zoloft. Or a Paxil. Anything to calm my beating heart. I leaned my head on the steering wheel and concentrated on breathing.

I don't know how long I sat there, waiting for my breathing to return to normal. Long enough to satisfy myself that the car was not coming back and that I was being paranoid. It was only when I thought about the accident that I imagined seeing this car.

I made a U-turn, using the driveway of the house across the street, and headed back in the opposite direction from which I'd come.

I didn't see the Impala again until just before I got onto the freeway. It was parked near the onramp. When I got on, it followed me.

I drove at a comfortable pace, not trying to elude it, just watching to see if it would stick with me. It followed me all the way to the Van

Nuys police station. When I pulled into the parking lot, it simply drove past.

* * *

The police station was a two-story cinder block in a plaza of other municipal buildings. I called Detective Luke Norton. He said to come in, and he'd meet me on the other side of the metal detector.

Norton walked me to an elevator. I did not mention being followed. It would mean opening a whole can of peas I was not willing to get into with the police. Instead, after we exchanged a few pleasantries, I asked him what progress had been made towards finding Julia. He told me that they had spoken to her parents and had put a tracer on her cell phone and credit card. He said that he understood that there were not one but two private investigators trying to find her. Both had asked to be informed if they got a hit. Since Mike and Ripetti were ex-cops, with connections and friends in the department, both had been approved.

Detective Norton's "office" was on the second floor, in a large open room of desks within cubicles. Uniformed police with thick belts of guns and clubs walked past detectives with jackets off, shoulder holsters on. The room thrummed with the murmur of many conversations, keyboards tapping, and printers spewing out pages; it smelled of machine-made coffee left standing too long, sugary treats grown stale. All the desks and chairs were grey metal, the cubicles standard issue particleboard. Somewhere, a woman was crying. Norton walked me through to his cubicle.

An autographed baseball sat on his desk, along with a photograph of him holding a just-caught fish with a boy that looked as if he might be his son by his side. His suit jacket hung on the back of his chair; even in shirtsleeves, he wore a gun in a leather holster.

He punched a few buttons on his phone and told Martinez I was here to look at the six-packs. While we waited for her to bring them, I told him I'd been to the crime scene and was more convinced than ever that Caleigh was killed by someone she'd met through the "enjo kosai" game she'd been playing. I also believed that Julia knew either who it was or how it happened, and that was why she was missing now.

"I took this from her room," I said, handing him Julia's diary. "She never meant anybody to read it but her, so please be discrete." His eyes scanned pages that detailed my descent into drunkenness. "PC is Patrick Caiman. He introduced Caleigh to Toby Starr, and she made the arrangements. She's a Hollywood madam."

Theresa Martinez came in, also wearing a gun holstered beneath her blazer, and carrying a stack of "six-packs"—sheets of six photographs each. Norton asked me to tell her what I'd told him, and I said that after Patrick Caiman talked to her, Caleigh set up a sort of high school prostitution ring, and she and Julia and maybe some others had slept with him, Campbell McCauley, Paolo Navarro, and others I didn't know of. One of them might have killed Caleigh, and I thought Julia ran away because of what she knew.

Martinez listened, her eyes widening in surprise, glancing from me to Norton.

"Who gets to interview Campbell McCauley, you or me?" she asked Norton with a dry smile.

Norton frowned. "I don't get it. Caleigh Nussbaum has all the money in the world. Why would she want to work as a hooker?"

"Campbell McCauley?" suggested Martinez.

"Maybe money means something different to people who have

so much of it," I said. "Maybe she wanted attention; maybe it was a cry for help. Julia said it was because her mother wouldn't let her buy her own clothes. But she did it and got a bunch of her friends to do it too. And now she's dead, and one of them is missing."

"Okay." Norton tossed the baseball from hand to hand. "So Caleigh Nussbaum was working as a prostitute. Maybe she saw one too many of her father's movies. How do you know she wasn't killed by some sicko who picked her up? She's not the first hooker to be found in Rattlesnake Canyon, and she's probably not the last."

"If she'd been killed by some random guy, Julia wouldn't have been so scared."

"Do you think this has something with the guy that shot you?" Martinez seemed dubious.

"I don't know. Maybe."

Norton put the baseball down and indicated the sheets of photos in front of me.

"Well, let's start by seeing if you can identify him. That might help us find another piece of the puzzle."

I examined page after page of mug shots of mean looking men, many of them Hispanic or Asian, based on the physical description I had given them in the hospital. None of them seemed familiar or recognizable, until I got to one which caused a sudden shiver. I looked at the photo closely. My assailant had been wearing sunglasses, and the man in the photo was not. Nonetheless, there was something about the wide forehead, pronounced cheekbones, the line of the lips, the pattern of shave, which made me think that this could be the guy. Norton asked me if I were sure, and I hesitated. It wasn't so much that I recognized his face; it was the way I broke out in a clammy sweat at the sight of him, my muscles involuntarily clenching in fear. My body remembered what my brain hadn't registered.

His name was Joe Nakamura. Norton told me he was believed to be a contract gunman. They knew about him from sources; he was known to hire out to loan sharks who used him to collect on their debts. He'd been a suspect when a crucial witness had either been murdered or disappeared before testifying, but they had not been able to pin anything on him.

"Maybe Clinton was holding out on the gang, and they sent this guy in after him."

Maybe, I thought. *Or maybe not.*

CHAPTER 26

Where was I going? Back to Malibu? I hadn't been to Gerry's since getting shot, and I knew I should go back, but I felt too antsy. Gerry was a successful director, who went from one project to another, which meant he spent more time in Canada than home. He insisted I was doing him a favor, instead of the other way around. But his state-of-the-art entertainment system, designer furniture, and private beach spoke to me only of the distance between me and my last credit. And how could I relax with Julia still missing?

I took the freeway back out of the Valley and took Sunset into West Hollywood. I kept looking for the blue Impala, but I did not see it.

* * *

Patrick Caiman had formed a company named Black Hat, which had its offices in a fourteen-story black glass building at the western end of the Sunset Strip that housed many agencies, production companies, and law offices. I signed in with the guard in the lobby, who sat at a desk that housed monitors that played surveillance coverage of the building's entrances, exits, and stairwells.

Black Hat was on the twelfth floor. I opened the door into a reception area and heard a splashing sound: a Japanese water sculpture rose up out of a Zen pebble garden in the middle of the waiting room. Surrounding it were two sofas perpendicular to one another. The coffee table uniting them featured today's trades as well as *the Wall Street Journal* and recent magazines about the business end of show business. The receptionist's desk was empty, but the company's name and logo were etched in a glass panel behind it.

I walked down the hall, past an empty conference room towards an office with an open door. Inside, a young woman was placing awards on the shelves according to a diagram she held in her hand. A clear and spare Lucite desk was in the farthest corner from the entrance of the room facing the door. The window looked out at a twin office tower across the courtyard. An aquarium with black and blue fish was built into the wall. Once the awards were positioned, she reached down to take a stack of screenplays out of a storage box at her feet.

The woman was in her early 30s and wore jeans, sneakers and a form-fitting t-shirt that showed her gym-buffed body to advantage. I gave my name and said I was looking for Patrick Caiman.

"You and everybody else," she said and asked me what it was regarding, her smile polite and guarded.

"Caleigh Nussbaum."

The smile left her face but not her guardedness. She held the scripts in her arms close to her chest, like a shield.

"Are you with the police? Or Nic Ripetti?"

"Neither." I told her about my relationship to Julia and my attempts to find her. She clucked sympathetically and put the scripts onto the shelves, again consulting her diagram for the correct placement.

"I'm sorry. How can I help you?" She dusted off her hands and brushed them on her shirt before telling me her name, Jenna Wilson.

"Why did you ask me if I were with Nic Ripetti?"

"I know he works for Marty Nussbaum. Does all his 'security work.'" She wiggled two fingers on each hand putting quotes around the words. She looked as if she might say more but thought better of it. She consulted the diagram and moved the scripts slightly, taking two off one pile and putting them on another.

"Patrick hired a feng shui consultant to maximize the positive energy flow in the room. It's very important where things are placed. The desk used to be against this wall, but the consultant suggested the command position was there. This is the view that maximizes the flow of chi. Everything in the office has to balance yin and yang. And it did before the police search. Now I have to remember how to put things back."

She switched the position of the Golden Globe award and the one from the National Association of Theater Owners for biggest box office of the year, almost a decade ago.

"Where is Patrick? Do you know?"

"I have no idea and neither does anybody else, apparently, although a lot of people want to know."

"When was the last time you saw him?"

She didn't have to stop to think. "A week ago Friday." Seeing the look on my face she added, "I know. The last day Caleigh was seen. The police were very clear about that."

She told me that when she'd seen Patrick on Friday, everything seemed normal. When Patrick didn't show up on Monday, she was concerned but not alarmed. Patrick sometimes worked from home.

He liked to party and often slept until mid-afternoon and made his calls from his house. For the last few months he'd been raising the money for *Space Wizards* and was meeting with investors all over the city, at their convenience. It wasn't unusual for him not to come in. He should have called, but still, she hadn't given it much thought.

When he didn't show up for his breakfast meeting on Tuesday, she became alarmed. She had the key to his Benedict Canyon home because her job often required her to pick up mail or water the plants. She went there with her heart in her throat, dreading what she might find. She wasn't the only person afraid that one day he'd be found dead from an overdose.

"Do you know what it's like to watch someone you care about killing themselves?"

I didn't answer.

In any case, when she went to the house, the place was empty. Patrick had cleaned out his closets. Most of his clothes, and his suitcases, were gone.

She'd called the police, but without any evidence of foul play, they wouldn't get involved.

Later that same day, Caleigh's body was found. The police checked her phone records and saw that her last call had been made to Patrick. They went to the house and did complete forensic tests on everything. Jenna didn't know what the results were, but she knew that his car had been found at the airport, and tests had been done on that too. The police had come into his office with a search warrant and had gone through everything—phone logs, files, calendars, bank, and brokerage statements. They'd taken a lot but had returned several boxes worth. Now she was trying to put things back in order.

They discovered that he'd bought a plane ticket to Zurich on Sunday night and had used it on Monday. The airline had a record of Patrick, or someone using his passport, being on the plane Monday.

"You don't think it was him?"

Jenna said she didn't know what to think. Patrick hadn't said anything about leaving town; it came as a shock to her. Things were finally turning around for him. He'd been on the outs ever since being fired from Poseidon, but he'd gotten the rights to *Space Wizards,* and both Alliance and Poseidon wanted them. He was in negotiations with Alliance promising a big payoff that would offset the hit he'd taken when he left Poseidon.

"I heard he sold *Space Wizards* to Marty before he left."

"I know." Jenna said she was puzzled by that; she hadn't expected it. Patrick bore a grudge against Marty and delighted in the chance to gain control of a property Marty was salivating over. He never said anything about selling to Marty. But the police had discovered a contract Patrick had signed giving Poseidon the rights in exchange for a fifteen million dollar payment that was sent to an account in Switzerland. It was only one of the many surprising things she'd found out about Patrick over the last two weeks.

"Like what?"

She didn't seem to want to answer, as if loyalty to her boss precluded her saying anything more. So I prompted her.

"Like what he was doing with Caleigh Nussbaum?"

"I had no idea he even knew her, apart from when she was a kid and he worked for her dad. But now, the sorts of things people are saying…I'm sure you've heard the same rumors I have."

"Do you believe them?"

She straightened the last of the scripts on the shelves.

"Come with me. I'll show you something."

She led me to a back room. Nobody had done feng shui here; it simply held file cabinets along the walls, with no balance of yin and yang. Right now, the floor was littered with boxes in various stages of being put away. Jenna apologized for the mess, saying that she was still putting back things the police had taken. She opened a drawer and handed me two photographs.

"Patrick used to keep these two photos in his desk until the feng shui master told him they nurtured negative vibrations and said to get rid of them. But I keep them in here because to me they sum up the real Patrick Caiman."

One photograph showed a fat boy in glasses wearing a Boy Scout uniform that gaped and pulled on his pudgy little body, its kerchief tied awkwardly around his neck. He was in the country, near a campfire, but he was alone, a stick in his hand, poking his foot into the ground. His expression was surly, with a look that all but said, "Think I care? Shows how much you know, stupid."

The other photograph showed a trim Patrick Caiman in clean-pressed jeans, t-shirt, and cashmere sports jacket, flanked on either side by two beautiful blondes in low cut, form fitting sheaths, gazing at him adoringly. They were in the middle of a football field, a helicopter in the background. This time the shit-eating grin as much as said, "Top this, assholes!"

"Patrick in Boy Scout camp and Patrick at his high school reunion. He chartered a helicopter to drop him off in the middle of the football field, flanked by the beautiful "friends" he hired for the day. He had to show that he had achieved more, was richer than, and better off in every way than the kids who tormented him in high school. Show them? Rub their faces in it. The women were the toys that other men wanted, and he had the most and the best. He arrived by helicopter, so he could control his exit. That's why he likes hookers. He says he doesn't pay them to come, he pays them to leave. Because inside he's still the fat kid nobody would sit with in the cafeteria. Whenever I get mad at him, I come look at these, and they help me let go."

She put the photos back in the file.

"That's very sweet," I said, "but Caleigh was no hooker; she was sixteen. The girls Patrick was turning out were still children. Being a fat lonely kid is no justification."

"I know. Honestly, it doesn't jibe with the Patrick I knew. I don't know how he could have done that. If it's true."

"Could it have been to get back at Marty Nussbaum?"

"Everything Patrick did was to get back at Marty Nussbaum. I still don't think he would have done that. Although…" She hesitated, as if weighing whether or not to say what was on her mind. "Well, it would be pretty ironic." She busied herself with the files. "I don't know why they needed these files. They're just contracts and deal memos and shooting schedules. This is going to take days to sort through."

"Can I help?"

I took a handful of files out of the box and scanned their labels hungrily. My eye fell on a file marked "Phone Logs," and I opened it as casually as I could, casting my eye down the list of people Patrick had made calls to. Few surprises; agents and studio executives. My eye was caught by an address Patrick had scribbled on the top of the phone log: 16593 Angelo Crest Road. It was the street Hannah had said the "sushi" had taken place. I used a mnemonic device, dividing the number into chunks I could remember: 16 for the age of the girls, 59, the age my father was when he died, and 3 for Caleigh, Hannah, and Julia.

"What went down between those two, anyway? Everyone's always talking about the rivalry between them. It seems pretty bitter."

I closed the phone log file and handed it to her, helpfully.

"Patrick was devastated by the way he was fired by Marty; he felt it was a real betrayal. Marty was a mentor and father figure to him."

"Erika told me it was Patrick who betrayed Marty. That he broke Marty's heart."

The files in my hand related to film projects that Patrick had worked on in the course of his career. I looked for files related to *Space Wizards* but saw none.

"As if he had one." She took the files from my hands. "Erika Nussbaum has no idea what goes on under her own roof. Everyone knows that Marty and Erika have no sex life—this fabled romance bullshit is just that—PR bullshit. They lead separate lives. From what anyone can see, Erika's primary erotic relationship is with her credit cards. They say she spends $100,000 a day. All these mergers and acquisitions are just to support her spending habit. Patrick was fired before the last one, when Poseidon was sold to the Japanese. They were each going to get a $170 million dollar pay-off and still run the company. But Patrick got fired, and Marty got all the money himself."

"Erika said that Patrick was using company funds to pay for his bad behavior."

"And Marty wasn't? Sure, there was a lot of talk at the time that Patrick was going to hookers and charging it to the company. That's supposedly the reason he was fired. The Japanese were doing their due diligence and discovered all these phony charges. But according to Patrick, Marty was just as good a customer of Toby Starr as he was, despite his reputation as the patron saint of innocence. Yet, Marty got the company, and Patrick got the boot. Once the Nussbaum PR machine goes into action against you, your own mother wouldn't trust you, and once you're on the Nussbaum shit-list, it's pretty hard to get off.

"Erika said Patrick had been molesting Caleigh."

"Case in point."

"You don't think it's true?"

She took the files out of my hands and put them back in the cabinet.

"I honestly don't know what to think anymore. I'd thought I was beyond being surprised by anything that goes on in this town. I see I was wrong."

I noticed a batch of files in the box that were headed "Rattlesnake Killer" and reached for them. I flipped through them, seeing casting calls, deal memos, publicity contacts.

"Excuse me; did Patrick work on this Rattlesnake Killer TV movie?"

"Yes, when he was at Poseidon. He was in between features, and Marty asked him to oversee it."

I read quickly over the files that gave a history of the production.

"Did they shoot it here in LA?" I was looking for a shooting schedule and also a list of cast and crew; the people who might have had access to the location.

"No. They scouted locations here but decided it made more sense to shoot in Canada."

I asked her if she'd mind if I made copies of some of these pages to take with me. She offered to do it for me.

I followed her into a room with a copier. "What did you mean about it being ironic if Patrick really had been pimping Caleigh Nussbaum?"

She put the pages into the Xerox machine.

"Everyone knows Marty has this thing for innocence. He reveres it. He glorifies it in his films. And, according to Patrick, he loves it so much he'll pay to sleep with it. He said Marty only went for hookers that were underage. Like gourmets who like to eat unborn baby lamb."

I thought back to Hannah, bursting with youthful beauty as natural as a wildflower in spring. She and Julia had mentioned several men, but Caleigh's father had not been one of them.

She handed the pages to me and smiled politely. "I hope this helps. I'm afraid I need to get back to work."

"Of course," I said. I wanted to follow her back to the file room, but she ushered me in the other direction, down the hall back towards the reception area. "Just one more question. If Patrick felt he was fired unjustly, why didn't he make more of a stink about it? Sue for wrongful termination, or at least go public with his accusations?"

Her eyes darted down the empty hall, as if wary of being overheard, though we were the only people in the office. She took a long while to answer.

"He was afraid. He knew that Marty would retaliate."

"How? He already had fired him and smeared him."

"I know." Her look urged me to draw my own conclusions; she didn't want to say more. I didn't budge.

"I don't understand."

"Marty likes to have things on people. Patrick knew that because he'd worked for him and saw how he operates. Patrick didn't want to cross him."

"What do you think Marty had on Patrick?"

"I don't know, but it must have been pretty bad to keep Patrick quiet."

We had arrived at the reception area to the sound of water splashing on the stones of the Zen pebble garden, the surfaces and textures a harmonious balance of yin and yang. Whatever it was, Patrick was certainly quiet now.

CHAPTER 27

"You're not working for one of those reality shows, are you? I mean, I don't want to see my business plastered all over the news."

I don't know what I was expecting, but Toby Starr, with her sun-streaked auburn hair and freckled face, seemed more like a sorority girl than a madam. She wore tight white jeans and a faded blue work shirt, tied at the waist, over a low cut chemise that revealed a bosom both ample and amplified. She was slender but fleshy. Her youthful body already spoke of rich dinners in expensive restaurants and more time on the chaise than in the pool. She stood by a serving table on the patio of a house high up in the Hollywood Hills.

"No. I'm only trying to find my step-daughter, Julia. She and Caleigh Nussbaum were best friends. You know what's happened to Caleigh. Nobody knows where Julia is."

Sunlight glinted off the water of the pool and bathed the alabaster statues of Apollo and Aphrodite on either end in a hot white glare.

Other statues of Greek gods lined the lawn, as befit a house in the section known as Mt. Olympus. Toby squinted, not at the sun but in annoyance. "What makes you think I'd know anything about your step-daughter?" Youthful though she was, the scowl that crossed her face furrowed into already forming frown lines. She seemed uninterested in offering any assistance.

"I know that you and Patrick Caiman were hooking up clients with teenage girls. One of them might be a link between Caleigh and Julia. Was there someone each of them slept with?"

Her laugh was almost a bark. "You do get to the point, don't you?"

She handed me the club soda over ice I'd requested. For herself, she splashed a healthy dose of gin, topping it off with tonic.

"Look, I've already spoken to the cops about this. I don't have anything to do with teenagers. There are enough to choose from without raiding schoolyards."

She brought her drink over to a chaise lounge on the patio and lay back, warming herself like a gecko in the sun.

"Please don't lie to me. I know you were setting these girls up. I'm not interested in getting you into trouble, only what happened to Julia."

The sliding glass doors of the house opened, and a statuesque woman came onto the patio. She wore high heels and a tight white suit, its skirt falling midway on her perfect thighs and pulling across her flat belly. She was beautifully made up and manicured, but her makeup skills were no match for the white sun's glare. She looked caked and powdered and brushed with blush, though she'd probably look better in artificial light. Her lips were puffed and fleshy; large sunglasses covered her eyes. She opened her purse, took out a check, and brought it over to Toby.

"He gave me a check; he said you always took his checks."

Toby took what the woman gave to her, and her eyes lit up with pleasure at the sight of it.

"How many men can write a check for cash for forty thousand dollars? And they've never bounced, not once." She gazed at the check as if at a child recovering from fever, then reached for a bag beside the chaise. She stuck the check into her wallet, then took out a few hundred dollar bills and gave them to the woman, squinting even behind her sunglasses.

"Are you leaving?"

"Lunch at Le Dome, and then…" The woman looked over at me.

Toby remembered I was there.

"Oh, I'm sorry. Desiree, this is…what did you say your name was again?"

"Brett Tanager," I said and offered the woman my hand, which she shook. Desiree looked me up and down, surmising that I was being interviewed to be one of Toby's "girls." She appraised me, as a jeweler would regard a gem, and found me faux.

"Brett used to write *Murder Will Out*, and now she's playing detective herself. She heard a rumor that her stepdaughter worked for me, but I told her, you want kids, go to Hollywood Boulevard, don't come here."

"We're all free, white, and twenty-one," said Desiree with a wink. She leaned over to kiss Toby, who reached her cheek up, but they didn't make contact. Desiree left through the gate that opened onto the driveway, and I saw her get into a Mercedes sports car.

"Who wrote the check?" I asked as she left.

Toby frowned. "Sweetie, keeping secrets is my biggest asset."

"Even if it means protecting a murderer?"

"My clients aren't murderers. If they were, I couldn't stay in business. This is an A-list operation. The men know they're going to get a girl who's clean and safe; the girls know they're going to get a gentleman."

"A gentleman who's paying to fuck her."

"That's right. Like he pays the waitress to take his order or the dry cleaners to clean his clothes. I provide a service. One that's in great demand, I might add. So spare me the sermon. I've heard it, and it's nothing but hypocrisy. If there was anything wrong with what I was doing, I wouldn't be making so much money at it."

"Except that one of the 'girls' you provided is dead. And another one is missing."

A cloud cast a shadow that moved across the pool, darkening the water.

"I had nothing to do with that. You think I would get into pimping Marty Nussbaum's daughter? Are you nuts? You think I want to end up in a ditch somewhere?"

She frowned at the peek-a-boo sun, which dappled the patio in a chiaroscuro pattern, its warmth eluding her. She picked up a Mylar reflector by the side of the chaise and opened it beneath her chin.

"Marty Nussbaum runs this town. I'm interested in staying in business. End of story. Anyway, from what I hear, Caleigh was getting her kicks acting a little whore. She could have been walking the street and gotten picked up by some maniac. She was killed by some sex killer, wasn't she? Believe me, honey, I don't do sex killers."

"But you did have a party that Caleigh and her friends came to, and you made some introductions."

She tipped her reflector to the side and shot me a look. "I gave a party, and some kids crashed. What happened after that is none of my business."

"Except that afterwards, you paid each girl ten one hundred dollar bills."

She put down the reflector. The sun had disappeared anyway. She took off her sunglasses, and her eyes glinted like hard new pennies.

"Where are you getting your information?"

"Did you ever set Marty Nussbaum up with underage girls?"

She swung her legs to the side of the chaise and got up, coming up close to me.

"Hasta la vista, chicklet. Time to go." She ushered me towards the gate leading out to the driveway.

"Then I can take that to mean yes."

"You can take that to mean that you can take your wild fishing expedition elsewhere. I've got nothing more to say to you."

Her nose twitched, giving her the look of an irritated ferret. "Who's giving you your information?" she couldn't help but ask.

"No fair. You won't answer any questions of mine, and then you want answers to yours. But I'll trade you. Who slept with both Caleigh and Julia?"

The sound of traffic was muted and distant high up on this hill; a car revved its engine going by, and the sound stood out in the stillness. The only other sound was the crows calling to one another in sharp piercing caws.

"Nothing happened here that has anything to do with Caleigh Nussbaum. Caleigh was sixteen. In a few months, she could join the army, be sent overseas, and be killed. So she was a working girl. What's the diff?"

I looked her in the eye.

"She was murdered. That's the 'diff.' And if the same thing happens to Julia, that's a big 'diff.' But maybe that's okay with you. Maybe you won't mind knowing that someone is dead because you're too chicken-shit to think about anyone but yourself. Maybe you can live with that every day. And night too because it will haunt your dreams. You can forget about getting a good night's sleep; you'll know you're no better than a murderer. It defines you; nothing about you matters but that someone is dead, and it's all on you."

The phone rang. Toby hurried over to it and answered with a silky, "Hello?" that was so unlike her speaking voice, it was as if a ventriloquist had suddenly taken over.

"Hey, sexy…I was just thinking about you!" Stroke a kitten, hear it purr. "Ummm. Sounds like fun." She looked at her watch. "Perfect. Give me a few minutes. I know just the girl. She'll be crazy for you." A soft laugh. "Don't worry, darling, have I ever disappointed? Get right back to you."

She hung up and from her beach bag took out a loose-leaf phone and appointment book stuffed to overflowing; sticky-notes attached to some of its many pages. With an eye towards me, she took the cordless phone and the book with her into the house as she placed a call, going back to her normal voice.

"Hi, it's me. Can you do a call at the place in about a half hour?" She closed the sliding glass door between us. I couldn't hear all of what she said. But when she hung up and called the client back, I did manage to hear an address: 16593 Angelo Crest Road. The same address I'd seen scribbled on Patrick Caiman's phone log: the one I'd memorized, thinking it might be the house where Julia, Hannah, and Caleigh had "done sushi." She came back, carrying the phone and the book.

I grabbed the book out of her hand.

"Give that back to me." Toby reached for the book, baring her pointy teeth.

I held her off and looked through the book's pages.

"Frank De Blasio…he's at Sony, isn't he? Arnold Davidson… Talbot Daniels…And these are only the 'd's.' Some pretty big names here. I was hoping to get some information from Jason Ratt. This would give me just the leverage I'd need."

"Give me the fucking book." She grabbed for it with pudgy fingers with long red nails. I blocked her reach with my arm. Her nails scratched me, but I lifted my arm with sufficient force to knock her back.

"You don't care about morality? Neither do I. I'll bet I could sell this for more money than you made off the names in it. Or, maybe I'll just turn it over to the IRS. Unless you've reported all your income and won't care about an audit."

I saw Campbell McCauley's phone number, as well as Paolo Navarro. Toby lunged at me, but I managed to keep the book away from her as I got my pen and notebook out of my bag. I scribbled some phone numbers on the cover.

"I'll trade you. This book for one piece of information. That's all. Just one."

"What's that?"

"Who slept with both Caleigh and Julia?"

I could see the abacus in her brain adding and subtracting according to whatever moral calculus she kept.

"Campbell McCauley," she said, reaching for the book. "He was the only one who slept with them both. His unlisted number's in there."

I opened the book and wrote it down. Before handing it back

to her, I went back to the "D's" to make sure that I had really seen the name that I thought I had but had not given any indication of having seen. I saw no reason to let her know my reaction to seeing the name, in her book of customers, of my friend, my sponsor, Mike Drummond.

CHAPTER 28

I sat in my car at the bottom of Toby's street, pulled into a turnout. My heart was racing, my chest tight, my breath short and shallow. Mike's name was in her book. That could mean anything. Maybe she needed his services at one time or another. But I knew it was more likely that he required hers.

He had sex with prostitutes. So what? That didn't mean anything. I'd seen the pamphlets by his bed for sexual addiction. Mike's problems were his business, not mine. We weren't lovers; he owed me nothing. And yet...

Why had he stolen my notebook and Julia's diary? I'd accepted the explanation that he'd been trying to help me. What if he'd been trying to protect himself?

Hadn't I withheld the diary for fear of what it might reveal about me? What if he had the same motive? What if he'd needed to see if his own name was mentioned?

Images came in a quick montage of moments we'd been together, going back to the first time I'd mentioned "enjo kosai" and the fact that Julia and her friends were playing prostitute. I remembered the way Mike had looked up from his carburetor with an expression that had seemed at the time like surprise but in retrospect could also have been fear. Of being discovered? According to Ripetti, Mike had been the prime suspect in a murder case and had stolen evidence that might have implicated him.

Mike often seemed a man at war with himself, always around sexual desire. I knew Mike wanted me; I knew he struggled against it. Mike was a man with secrets.

Why shouldn't he be? Wasn't I keeping secrets from him? Maybe Toby hadn't realized that my tirade about her moral rectitude was more about me than her, but I sure did.

I took out my notebook and quickly jotted down the things I'd heard and seen at Patrick's and Toby's. I looked over the shooting schedules and memo's I'd taken from Patrick's office and tried to compare them to the notes I'd made after the funeral, but I couldn't think straight. The flood of feelings triggered by seeing Mike's name in Toby's book had rendered me incapable of logical thought.

The clouds that had cumulated and darkened the skies began to deliver on their promise of rain, as a few drops splashed on my windshield.

I saw another printout—the one that listed the phone numbers and addresses of neighbors and relatives of Rosa Aguilar.

I sat in my car looking at it, the lump in my throat becoming a knot. Without giving myself time to think about what I would say, I dialed the first number, at the address Rosa had lived when she died.

As the number was ringing, I froze at the sight of the car across the street. The same blue Chevy Impala had followed me from Mike's. Now it was parked on the other side of this street, on Mt. Olympus, facing in the opposite direction from me. A man sat in the car, wearing a black leather jacket and sunglasses. He had a receding hairline and a pasty face like a cream-filled donut, probably from eating so many of them. Beefy arms, leather jacket, he chewed gum like a bored secretary. Our eyes met briefly.

A recording answered that the number had been disconnected and there was no forwarding number. I hung up and pulled away from the curb, keeping an eye on my rear view mirror. Surprisingly, the beefy man put his car in gear, pulled away from the curb, and drove up the hill and out of sight.

It had started to rain, and a cold wind was blowing, whipping the leaves off trees. I turned left onto Mulholland, still watching anxiously. I don't know which was more frightening: the thought that I was being followed or the idea that I was so paranoid that every time I thought about Rosa Aguilar I hallucinated being followed.

Mulholland Drive is a two-lane road that traverses the backbone of the mountain that divides the city in two. One side slopes down a hill dotted with swimming pools, to the valley below, nestled in a pinkish brown haze; to the other side, the Hollywood Hills block the view of the Los Angeles basin to the south. I drove the twists and turns of this scenic route, turning on my wipers, as fat drops splashed rain on my windshield. I kept an eye on my rear view mirror for the blue Impala, but I didn't see it. I turned off Mulholland and made my way through a warren of intersecting residential streets until I got to the Cahuenga Pass. As the rain pelted down, I followed the broad winding road into Hollywood.

CHAPTER 29

Jason Ratt, the Internet gossip maven, worked in his underwear. When he opened the door, he was wearing boxer shorts and a t-shirt, and over them, an untied vintage silk men's dressing gown. Without his fedora, his baldness was striking—all the more so because he had shaved his young head to accentuate it. His forehead was broad, overhanging eyes that were small yet dilated with highly caffeinated energy.

"I have an idea what Caleigh's scoop might have been," I said. "Could I come in and talk to you about it?"

He hesitated, but the bait I'd offered was too enticing to resist He motioned me inside.

Every surface of the living room was stacked with newspapers, magazines, press releases, photos, and promotional CDs and DVDs. The open door to his bedroom revealed the same. A large table took up most of the space; it held his computer, cell phone, fax machine, and printer. He gestured for me to have a seat on the sofa, but it was piled with back issues of the kind of magazines whose cover stories tell how many pounds each star gained or lost this week. As he moved them aside to make room for me, his cell phone rang. The tune was familiar, but I couldn't place it.

"Your-biz-my-biz.com," he answered. His face lit up. "Oh, goody. Did you send it?"

He was already opening a file that had just come in on his laptop.

"My God, she's Claude Rains in *The Invisible Man*!" he shrieked, summoning me over to watch the video that was playing on his screen. The movie star Jenna Lee Brasington, known for her radiant beauty, was almost unrecognizable as she scurried from a building into a waiting car, her face concealed by scarf, sunglasses, and bandages. Jason Ratt was already posting it on his website and typing a blurb under it.

"I'll say she just had her incandescent bulb replaced," he chuckled to the person on the other end. "Mille grazie. The check is in the mail, bambino."

He made a note to himself and gulped from a jumbo can of energy drink as he hung up. "So, what's the scoop?"

"I'll trade you. I think I know what Caleigh was going to tell you, but I want some information from you first."

"Depends on what you want."

The fax machine rang and spewed out a page. He glanced at it, dismissed it, and put it on a pile.

"What do you know about Campbell McCauley?"

"He's rich, he's famous, he's married to a hottie, and there isn't a man, woman, or child who doesn't want to fuck him. Your turn."

"No, I mean the dirt. The stuff that nobody knows but you."

"Why? Is that what Caleigh had for me? Something about Campbell?" His eyes lit up. "Was that bad boy one of her tricks?"

"What makes you say that?"

His eyes glinted with greedy pride. "From what I heard, she had turned into the Heidi Fleiss of high school. The cops thought she was picked up by a sex killer, but now it turns out she might have been charging for the privilege of fucking the daughter of the most powerful man in Hollywood. They're thinking she might have been killed by one of her tricks." He hitched his bathrobe, unable to conceal his delight at relishing the dish. "Was that pretty boy paying to poke her? I guess his wife is too busy sending wheat to Africa to make hay at home. But do you think he could have killed her? I'd heard it was Patrick Caiman—that he offed her and left town."

"Who told you that?"

He shot me the smoldering look of a forties vamp. "I never reveal a source." But then the joy of gossip overrode discretion. "Let's just say it wouldn't be the first time," he teased.

"What do you mean?"

He wagged a finger at me. "No fair. You first. What was Caleigh going to tell me?"

"I'll tell you after you tell me what you know about Campbell McCauley. And Patrick Caiman." I had amended my request; I hoped he hadn't noticed. "What do you mean, 'it wouldn't be the first time'? Did Patrick Caiman kill someone?"

"Tit for tat, bambina."

His cell phone went off again, with its funny little ring. He glanced at it, decided not to pick up, and waited for my answer.

"Okay, yes. Campbell McCauley *was* 'one of her tricks.' He paid her $1,000 to have sex with him."

His eyes sparkled as he rubbed his hands with greedy delight. He was already at his laptop.

"So I'm wondering," I continued, "Campbell McCauley doesn't have to pay for sex; girls would line up to sleep with him. Is he into anything kinky? Something that could have ended in death, accidentally or otherwise?"

His eyes widened as if I'd confided in him that this had actually happened.

"You mean, like, some S&M thing gone wrong? Tie me up, choke me, make me cum? Is that what Caleigh was going to tell me about?"

"I don't know. I just wondered if you'd ever heard anything like that about him." He thought long and hard about what he might have heard, or who might be able to tell him.

"What a tragedy! That a young life could be snuffed out so prematurely, before she could tell all!"

He began typing, as if he'd been given an actual news item to report.

"Okay, Jason. Your turn. What did you mean about Patrick Caiman, that 'it wouldn't be the first time'?"

He finished his post before answering. He hesitated, but then, like a man on a diet presented with a chocolate éclair, he dived in.

"Well, nothing was ever proven. And if you quote me, I'll deny it. But I heard he was involved with the whole Stacey Donovan thing."

The name was vaguely familiar, from some old news story, but I couldn't remember any details.

"Remind me. Who was Stacey Donovan?"

"She was a child actress, or at least her mother wanted her to be. She was auditioning for a Poseidon movie when she disappeared. They never found a body, so nobody was ever charged. But there was a tiny bit of buzz that Patrick Caiman was involved. And that's just when he lost his job."

"I thought he lost his job because he was hiring hookers and charging them to production."

"That could have been the cover story. When the Japanese bought into Poseidon, one minute both Nussbaum and Caiman were going to make a fortune in stock options *and* run the company together. The next minute, Caiman is out and Nussbaum is in, getting all the money for himself. Makes you wonder how Nussbaum pulled that off." He raised an eyebrow and let the question hang for a moment.

"You think it has something to do with Stacey Donovan?"

"Right about that time, Poseidon was making this soft-core trashy art movie about a child prostitute in a brothel in New Orleans. They were auditioning child actresses for the part. One of them, Stacey Donovan, disappeared the day after her audition. She was walking to the bus and was never heard from again. So of course the cops interviewed everyone who might have been at her audition or seen the tape, but they never came up with anything, and after a while it got dropped. But that's when Patrick was let go. I figured Nussbaum must have had something on Caiman, or else, how could he make that happen? Well, there was Stacey Donovan. I put two and two together."

It was the second time that day someone had used that expression about Marty Nussbaum.

"Is that how Marty Nussbaum operates? By 'having' something on people?"

"Darling, Marty Nussbaum runs Poseidon like J. Edgar Hoover ran the FBI. He's got a file on everybody. He knows all your dirty secrets, and if you ever try to cross him, he just happens to have a photograph of a hooker giving you a blow job on Sunset Boulevard—little realizing that one day that hooker would be his daughter." His eyes widened. "I heard McCauley wanted out of his deal with Poseidon, but Alliance won't buy Poseidon without it. Wouldn't that put an interesting spin on the negotiations, if Nussbaum knew McCauley was slipping the sausage to his sweet little sixteen?"

"What did the cops say? About Stacey Donovan?"

"They couldn't bring charges because there was no body. But there was buzz at the time about it being Patrick. Some evidence showed up in his office I think. A locket? That belonged to her? Something like that. He said she'd left it there after the audition, and there was no way of proving anything different." His eyes suddenly widened. "Holy moly, bambina, you may have just given me the scoop of scoops! Tell me—was Campbell McCauley really one of Caleigh Nussbaum's tricks? Is that what she was going to tell me?"

"I can't say for sure, but I think it might have been. Why?"

"Campbell McCauley was *in* that brothel movie. It was his screen debut. He couldn't have been more than twenty at the time. But he could have easily been at Stacey Donovan's audition, or seen the tape, same as Patrick Caiman." He held his hand up, as if reading a headline. "'Haunted by sex and death: the twisted life of Campbell McCauley.'"

He was already at his laptop, tapping out a bulletin as if he'd fact-checked and corroborated the story.

I went to the window, drops of rain pelting against it. The building across the street and the cars parked along the curb shimmered in a watery blur. I wondered if perhaps the Impala had followed me here. My heart registered the answer: It was parked outside.

I stepped away from the window, not wanting Jason to see how frightened I was.

"How does Marty Nussbaum get his information?" I'd assumed I was being paranoid when I worked at Poseidon and thought I was being watched. What if I really was? What if Marty knew what I'd done?

"The same way I do. From sources, people feeding him dirt. But he's also got cops on his payroll. He can do wiretaps, surveillance cameras, whatever it takes."

"Is that what Nic Ripetti does for him? Dig up dirt on his enemies?"

And then, an awful thought: *Mike? Could Mike be watching me? Could this whole AA business just be to get me to confess to what I'd done, so they could use it against me?* His phone rang again with its funny little tune. I used it as an opportunity to excuse myself. As I shut the door behind me, I realized what the distinctive ring tone was. It was the melody of "Hooray for Hollywood."

CHAPTER 30

I came out of the building, prepared to confront the driver and ask him who he was and why he was following me. But he was gone before I got outside.

Rather than drive back to Gerry's, I drove down to Hollywood Boulevard and found a corner mini-mart with a middle-eastern restaurant. The menu featured color photographs of the dishes served; I chose a plate of kabobs. Taking out my notebook, I quickly wrote down everything I'd learned from Jason. I added the license plate of the car that had been following me and the places I'd been when I'd seen it.

I called my cop friend Earl Rohmer, in San Diego, and told him I needed a few more favors. He was in the middle of a case of his own, up to his ears; could it wait? I said sure, and hung up.

If I asked Mike, or Detective Norton, or Nic Ripetti to run down the license plate for me, I'd have to give a reason, and I couldn't; it was too closely connected to Rosa Aguilar. That's when I'd started seeing the car, and now only saw it when I thought of her. I could ask them what they knew about Stacey Donovan, but I was too freaked out; I might blurt out something about being followed, and I couldn't afford that. I decided to nose around on my own. Since I couldn't afford a smartphone, I needed to get home to my laptop before I could do research that needed a computer.

And what did any of this have to do with finding Julia?

I looked through my notes for Zeke's card. Julia had disappeared with a drug dealer; maybe he'd know something. Funny how I didn't feel I could trust the police but felt comfortable calling Zeke.

"Hey, stranger. I was wondering when I'd hear from you."

"I need to talk to you. Can I meet you somewhere?"

He told me he'd be at Nova later, why didn't I meet him there? "If you don't want to slip, stay out of slippery places." I heard Mike's voice in my head as I arranged to meet him in an hour.

The Rosa printout was folded in my notebook. I made a note that the first number I'd called had been disconnected. Wondering why I was doing it, I dialed the next.

"My name is Carrie Pentel," I said, looking at my pen as a heavily accented man said hello. "I'm calling to find out information about Rosa Aguilar."

"Está muerta," said a voice in Spanish and then with a thick accent, "She dead."

"Yes, I know. Do you speak English? I'm a friend of the Engelmanns, the family she was working for when she was killed. They want to do something for her kids. I'm looking for information about what happened to them after she died."

"They have papers. They are legal."

"I'm not from immigration. I don't care about that. The Engelmanns just want to get in touch with her family. Rosa was such a good worker for them; they want to do something for the children."

The waiter set down my kabobs.

"They no live here anymore."

"Do you know where they moved to?"

"Sorry."

"No, wait a minute. Please don't hang up. The Engelmanns really want to find the children. Do you know where they are?"

He said he thought the kids were in foster care, but he didn't know where. Rosa had raised her kids alone and worked two jobs to do it. Their father couldn't be located. The funeral was very sad. Nobody knew what was going to happen to the kids. He and his wife had even considered taking them, but they couldn't. After that, they'd lost touch.

I thanked him and hung up. I stared at my kabobs, my appetite gone. I wished I hadn't thrown away that Vicodin. Then I remembered this wasn't the kind of pain it was for.

* * *

The Nova was a popular industry hangout judging from the line of Porsches, Mercedes, and BMWs lined up behind a team of parking valets. After giving my keys to a spry young man who drove my car away, I walked into the restaurant, hoping that, despite my jeans, my suede jacket would allow me to pass. It didn't. The maître d' frowned as I entered. The restaurant was filled with well-dressed and well fed people dropping hundreds of dollars on their meals. The men wore suits, the women cocktail dresses. I told the maître d' I wouldn't be eating, just meeting a friend at the bar.

I made my way through the crush of bodies; the Nova Bar was the playground of the suits. Clearly the place to hook up, pick up, and get picked up. People were shouting at each other to be heard over the din of music and loud voices. I saw an empty seat and took it.

I watched the bartender fill orders with balletic grace; pirouetting as he reached for bottles, using both hands to pour their liquids into glasses. He sloshed tequila, triple sec, and lime juice mix into a blender with ice, poured the frothy contents into a glass he'd dipped in salt, and slid it down the bar towards a waitress who put it on a tray. Without missing a beat, he poured the same lime juice mix into a shaker of ice along with vodka, Cointreau, and cranberry juice. Shook it, strained it into a cocktail glass, and garnished it with a lemon slice. He made a martini, another margarita, poured a scotch on the rocks.

I watched him like a cat at a goldfish bowl. On my fingers, I counted how many days it had been since my last drink. Not counting the Vicodin, nine.

He reached for a bottle from the hundreds that lined the wall behind him, poured its amber liquid into a shot glass, and set it on the bar in front of the man seated next to me. Glenfiddich, straight up, my "usual." The man, talking to the woman on his other side, barely noticed the glass in front of him, its translucent liquid glowing as if it had been kissed by the sun. I smelled its warm fumes, could imagine the sensation it would make if, with a quick flick of the wrist, I tossed it down. As if I had done it, I tasted its tart pungency, felt the quick shiver, then the flood of warmth, cares dissolving, tension eased.

"Forty-five minutes to get from Crescent Heights! On Fountain!"

Zeke's conversation began, as all conversations in Los Angeles must, with a lament about traffic, and how long it took to get here, despite the route, outlined in detail, which used to be the speedy alternative. He had sidled up next to me, standing between me and the drink. He wore cowboy boots and a hand-embroidered vintage Nudie western jacket of intricate design, which made him stand out in this crowd of industry executives. His face had even more miles than I'd noticed at the funeral. Its lines were deep, and even in repose, seemed haunted.

"Patrick Caiman had the right idea. He took the money and ran. I heard he left for the Bahamas." Zeke had an involuntary tic, a slight muscle spasm at the side of his eye that made it seem as if he were winking.

"I heard Switzerland."

"Whatever." Zeke scanned the crowd. "Wait for me, would you? I'm meeting someone; I just have to see if she's here yet." He left me alone at the bar and made his way through the crowd. I watched him whisper something to the maître d', leaning in and clasping his hand. The maître d' put his hand in his pocket, without looking to see what had been put into it. Zeke returned to me at the bar.

"I was wondering how long it would take you to call. I never could see you as the holy-roller type." He signaled the bartender. "What are you drinking?"

Glenfiddich, straight up, I thought but said, "Club Soda. Zeke, do you know a kid named Clinton Cole? Small time dealer, sells to some of the high school kids?"

He looked at me in surprise. "You too? You're the third person to ask me about him. Kid left a big hole. He's not as small time as you think."

"Who else is looking for him?"

"Customers who can't find him. They call me. Hey, it's a collegial business. As long as you don't burn anybody, there's enough for everybody, and life is too short, you know what I mean?" He leaned in confidentially. "I have better stuff." He continued to scan the room. "These kids today, they have no taste, you know what I mean? Crank, crack, X, it's all the same to them. They take the drugs they get from their pediatricians and think they're getting high. Not like us. We did real drugs. Weed, coke, mushrooms…" He shook his head with elegiac nostalgia. "We knew how to use drugs, not abuse them. Big difference. We went up, we came down, we made love, got our work done…you didn't see us going on shooting rampages in schoolyards. These kids have no appreciation."

"Which customers?"

He looked at me with a hint of suspicion. "Oh, just, you know, a couple of girls. Nobody that you know."

"Do you know where he is?"

"Who?"

"Clinton Cole."

"I have no idea. Probably couldn't stand the traffic, went off to the Bahamas like Patrick Caiman." He signaled the barman again but still got no response. The place was too busy.

"I have to find him. It's really urgent."

He seemed hurt. "Hey, kid, you got me." He put his hand on his heart. "I mean it. You're family." He looked at me solicitously. "What do you need, blow?"

"It's not that. You remember Julia? Jonathan's daughter? She's disappeared, and the last time I saw her, she was with him. I need to find him."

Uninterested, he said, "Well, if I hear of anything…" I had lost his attention.

"What about Joe Nakamura. You know him?"

"Why? You mad at someone?"

"No. Why?"

He reached into his pocket, found a prescription bottle, shook a pill into his hand, and downed it, needing no water. He leaned his head back, maneuvering the pill down his throat like a snake swallowing a mouse.

"You want to be careful of that guy, Sweets. He's no one to mess around with."

"He came to Clinton Cole's when Julia disappeared. He shot me by accident. I don't know if he was after Clinton or Julia."

Zeke regarded me with his customary ironic detachment, but the cynicism and hopelessness that lay beneath showed through.

"From what I hear, Joe Nakamura doesn't shoot people by accident."

Someone was coming towards us. A statuesque blonde I recognized as Desiree, the woman I'd met earlier at Toby Starr's. Instead of the tight white suit, she wore a tight white dress, very short, with sequins, sleeveless and high-necked. Her heels were high, her hair loose and beautiful, and the make-up that had seemed false in the sun gave her a glow of health in the dimness of the bar.

Zeke introduced us, and we exchanged polite smiles of recognition.

"Thanks for meeting me," she said to Zeke. "I couldn't get through this call without a little help from my friend." She smiled at me conspiratorially, as if I'd understand perfectly.

Zeke clasped her hand and kissed her cheek. Again, I noticed a small unobtrusive exchange had taken place. She put the little packet he had given her into her purse. As she did, she took out some bills.

"Can I buy you a drink?" she asked Zeke. She put the bills down on the table, and I could see that they were five hundreds. "Here, I'll just leave these. Nice to see you again," she added to me, politely. "Oh well. Back to the salt mines," she sighed. With a twitch of her encased perfect fanny, she went to rejoin her dinner partner, who waited for her by the maître d' and greeted her warmly on her return.

The man who took her arm and steered her towards their table was Mike.

CHAPTER 31

Zeke swept the bills into his pocket.

"I've got to run, Sweets, got a few more stops to make tonight."

A moment before, I'd been trying to think of why Joe Nakamura might have been sent to shoot me, rather than, as I'd assumed, either Clinton or Julia. But now, only one thought dominated my attention: What was Mike doing with Desiree?

Well, what did I think he was doing, wasn't it obvious? At least she wasn't underage. The more relevant question was why should it bother me so much?

I felt betrayed.

Mike was my AA sponsor. He was supposed to be modeling sobriety. He was the one who told me to do my fourth step, which as I remembered, was a searching and fearless moral inventory. Did that include meeting high priced call girls at trendy restaurants?

Zeke kissed me on the cheek. I could feel his hand putting something in my pocket. As he pulled away, I felt for it. He had passed me a tiny bag of white powder.

He saw my look of confusion and held up his hand in protest. "A present. For old time's sake."

"Wait a minute…" I held him back. I took out my notebook and scribbled my cell phone number on a page, tore it out and handed it to him. "If you hear anything at all about Clinton Cole, would you call me?"

"Sure thing. And you too. Don't be a stranger." He made a gesture towards me with his head, as he left some bills for the bartender. "Give her anything she wants."

And then he was gone.

The bartender looked at me with a questioning look.

Mike and Desiree. There was no reason for me to stay sober.

I might as well drink.

As soon as I found Julia.

* * *

I got "home" for the first time in days and threw my clothes in the washer, undressed, took off my bandage, and looked at my wound. It was still splotchy and ugly, crisscrossed with stitches, but the purple was fading to a dull yellow.

Pulling one of Gerry Talbot's silk kimonos around me, I went to my laptop. I looked up Stacey Donovan's name in the newspaper archives, and read through the articles that were written at the time of her disappearance. What Jason had told me was true. Stacey Donovan was a fifteen-year-old girl who had auditioned for Poseidon the day before she'd disappeared. It was her second call-back; she'd auditioned before, along with many other young women, but she was the one they wanted to see again. She'd taken the day off from school to audition but was supposed to be back at school the next day. She went to a neighborhood public school within walking distance of her house. Her mother had last seen her heading down her block in the Hollywood hills, walking towards school.

Her disappearance wasn't discovered for hours. Her mother assumed she was in school; the school thought she was absent for her audition. It wasn't until evening, when she didn't come home for dinner, that her mother began to worry. She informed the police that night; it was the next day before her disappearance was investigated.

Everyone connected with the audition was interviewed and, as Jason Ratt had reliably informed me, that included the director Roger Prentiss, as well Elizabeth Esair, the casting director; Patrick Caiman; and Campbell McCauley, who had come to the second audition to read with her; they were going to have scenes together in the movie.

The police interviewed all her friends to find out where she might have gone. The story played out over days, as her disappearance lengthened, and foul play began to be suspected. The similarities to both Caleigh and Julia's disappearance were too eerie to disregard.

Several days into the story, the two detectives investigating the case were quoted about the progress of the investigation. One was Nic Ripetti. The other was Mike Drummond.

I checked the date of the stories—nine years ago. I knew Mike's AA "birthday"; it was eleven months after this. I remembered what he'd told me about why he'd stopped drinking—he'd screwed up badly, and a murderer had gotten away because of it. I wondered if this had been the case.

I was Googling the newspaper archives for mention of either Drummond or Ripetti when the phone rang.

"This is Paulo Navarro," said the voice that made a million little girls swoon. "I heard you wanted to talk to me."

* * *

Thousands of tiny LED lights formed a red star-shaped design on the ceiling above the dance floor, and laser lights of green and purple waved over a frenzied crowd dancing to a propulsive electronic beat. Young women in sexy silky dresses and high stiletto heels writhed and swayed, as young men eddied around them, some in jeans and t-shirts, some in jackets and dress shirts. They moved in a techno-trance, a tilt of a chin, a twitch of a shoulder, expressing attitude. Each danced alone.

"Champagne?" Paulo shouted, offering me a glass. I shook my head. We were in the VIP room, overlooking the dance floor, where he and his pals had a table. The seats were low to the ground, built into the walls, which were lined with real fur. There were six people beside us: four women, two men, all gorgeous. Drinking, laughing, flirting, they all seemed aware of their beauty and magnetic power. None were older than 25.

"I've heard you've been looking for Julia," he shouted.

"What?" I'd only heard the last word. The music was deafening, the beat throbbing and hypnotic. It was hard to hear my own thoughts, let alone anyone's words. It seemed a strange place to have a conversation, but when Paolo Navarro suggested I meet him here, I had gotten dressed and driven back to town.

"Julia! Have you found her?"

"No! Do you know where she is?"

One of the women at the table crawled over the man in between to sit next to Paulo. The man she climbed over pawed her good-humoredly as she passed over him and shouted something to Paulo about an ear nibbling contest. There was a general drunken hilarity as the woman licked the earlobe of the man sitting next to Paulo.

The man closed his eyes and savored the sensations before shouting, "Nine point two!" Everybody laughed.

"But you are looking?" he shouted.

"Yes."

"And you talked to her? She told you…"

Our eyes met. "Yes." We both knew were speaking of the same thing. He flinched.

The woman disengaged from licking the ear of the man on her other side and turned her attention to Paulo. "Your turn!" she shouted. The man on the other side shouted, "It's the Ear Olympics! So far she's averaged 8.9!"

Paulo disregarded the woman, stood, and beckoned me to follow him to the dance floor.

I could see why millions of young girls wanted to take him home with them. His long lashes and soulful eyes gave him the sweet innocence of a lost puppy. He pulled me close to him and held me, swaying to the music, so he could speak directly into my ear, without being overheard.

"I would never hurt her. It was a game. Like this." He gestured to the club. "For show. Nothing. No harm."

"Where is she? What happened to her?"

"I don't know. I swear to you." It was true he made a living looking adorable, but it was hard to imagine this sweet boy doing anybody harm. He pivoted us around in a dance move and pulled me close to whisper into my ear. "Did she say anything to you about a video?"

He extended his arm to hold me at a distance. At my assent, he winced slightly, as if his worst fears had been confirmed. He pulled me towards him and put his arms around me. He spoke softly but urgently into my ear. "Whatever it costs, I will pay."

We were the only couple dancing close, with our arms around each other. A few other couples noticed, and did the same in imitation.

My arms were around his neck. I leaned into his ear. "Do you know who has it?,"

"No. You?"

"No," I said.

"But video is being used…against people." I couldn't tell if the fear in his eyes was for his life or his career.

"By whom?" I asked. "What do you mean?

He glanced around nervously, and whispered into my ear.

"People were told…if they didn't agree to certain business arrangements…on their contracts…the video would get out…"

"Who told you that?"

He wouldn't say, as if speaking of "He Who Must Not Be Named." Instead, he looked at me with such intensity and vulnerability, that it was clear why, when he turned that gaze into the camera, he was worth such big bucks.

"Find the video. I'll pay anything. I mean it. Anything."

* * *

I woke up the next morning to the sound of rain on the roof. I went to the kitchen and made myself a pot of coffee. The ocean view shimmered in the windows wet from the rain.

I opened my laptop and went online. I tried to find out more about Drummond and Ripetti; I found them mentioned in several cases prior to Stacey Donovan but none after. And I could not find out any more from the newspaper about what could have happened to cause Mike to lose his job and need to stop drinking.

Both Mike and Ripetti each had websites, advertising their services as private investigators. Each of them had a page of testimonials from satisfied customers. Neither Marty nor Erika Nussbaum were mentioned among the upper echelon people who gave enthusiastic endorsements of Ripetti and his firm. Services offered ranged from undercover work, to surveillance, to missing persons, skip tracing, evidence of cheating spouses, witness statements, asset searches, and the like.

For a fee, I found out that the blue Impala was registered to a man named Carl Rostenkowski, in Sherman Oaks. I Googled his name and found nothing to indicate who he was or anything he'd done to warrant the attention of Google. Googling Clinton's name gave me less than I already had on the printout I'd made at Mike's.

Mike.

Had something about the Stacey Donovan case caused him to lose his job? What was he doing with that hooker? I went back to my notes. The first time I'd seen him with Susanna Terrell, Marty Nussbaum's assistant, she'd said, "What if he finds out it's you? He'll kill you."

What had she meant?

I looked over the printout of Clinton's associates. Mike had said he'd be talking to them. Who had he spoken to? Why hadn't I heard from him?

On a whim, I Googled the Los Angeles County Department of Child and Family services.

I told the social worker who answered the phone that I was a friend of Rosa Aguilar and had heard her children had been taken into protective custody. I was trying to find them; I had information about their mother that I thought they'd want to know. The social worker told me that information about children in the system was confidential. No matter how much I argued, or what reasons I came up with, the answer remained the same. The law forbade her from disclosing anything about where Rosa's kids had been placed.

Maybe Mike would know a way around this, but I couldn't tell him why I was interested. Mike. I knew what secrets I was hiding from him. What secrets was he hiding from me?

I looked out at the beach, half expecting the pasty faced man to be watching, as he always was whenever I thought about Rosa Aguilar. But it was raining, and the beach was empty. I remembered watching this same view with Julia. How long ago? A lifetime. More than that for Caleigh. But no sign of my pursuer.

Until later, when I was driving back to town, I saw the blue Impala behind me.

CHAPTER 32

Ripetti's office was in the same building as Patrick Caiman's. I parked in the underground garage then went up to the lobby where I had to sign in and give my name to the guard at the desk, who told me which elevator to use to go to the twelfth floor.

A young man wearing a phone headset sat at the receptionist's desk. Although he had a computer in front of him, he was leafing through a celebrity magazine which trumpeted on its cover the story of a famous star's release, then return, to rehab.

I asked for Nic Ripetti. Did I have an appointment? No, but it was urgent. He said Ripetti wasn't in but if I wanted to leave a message...I said perhaps he hadn't heard me: It was urgent.

Ripetti came towards me, his leather jacket slung over his shoulder. "I can't believe you're here. I was just going to call you." He was friendly, but there was something about his manner like a tablecloth taken out and put on for company.

"Are you having me followed?"

"What gives you that idea?"

I didn't say that I'd heard Ripetti kept tabs on everyone for Marty Nussbaum. Instead, I told him about the blue Impala and the man with the pastry face I'd seen wherever I'd been for the last two days. He invited me into his office.

Ripetti's office was sleek, spare, and stylish. No guns, diplomas, awards, or knick-knacks; no indication of the kind of work that went on here. Just a desk and chair, a phone, and a computer, although each was well designed. Across from his desk, a flat panel TV hung on the wall. I commented on the Spartan quality of his office and told him about the feng shui of Patrick Caiman's. He said they put their money into manpower and equipment, not décor. Whereas Mike was a one-man operation, Ripetti ran a company that hired other investigators and operatives, but they were always out in the field. The truth was he was rarely in the office himself.

He asked me more questions about the car and where I'd seen it. I consulted my notes, and told him every time I'd noticed it and every time I hadn't.

"What made you think you were being followed?"

My guilty conscience was none of his business. "What would you think if you saw the same car wherever you went?"

"Wait here. I'll be right back."

Ripetti left me alone. His office was as opaque as his eyes, revealing nothing. Not a paper on his desk, not even a drawer or file cabinet. If there was a hidden camera, it was hidden well.

You'd think someone as guarded as me would be reluctant to pry, but the opposite was the case. Ripetti's opacity was a provocation. The less he revealed, the more challenged I felt to discover what lay at his core. Perhaps this was why I always felt on edge around him, like a leading chord that needs to be resolved.

These were my thoughts when the door opened, and in walked the pasty-faced man who'd been following me, the crumbs still on his shirt.

"Meet Carl," said Ripetti, right behind him. "Carl, she blew your cover."

He introduced us and told me that Carl was one of his operatives whom he'd asked to keep an eye on me.

"Why on earth would you have me followed?"

"I know how worried you are about Julia and that you couldn't sit still and let other people track her down. And I agree Julia's in danger. We both know what happened the last time you found her; I just wanted to make sure there was someone at your back. I'm sorry. I shouldn't have done it without letting you know. I didn't think you'd accept help if it were offered."

I sat down on his chrome steel and black leather sofa, robbed of the self-righteousness I'd felt a moment earlier.

"Have you ever had me followed before?"

When I was at the studio and thought I was being followed, Jonathan said I was paranoid, delusional, because of the drugs. But I couldn't shake the idea that I wasn't the only one who knew what had happened on Coldwater Canyon.

"No, why? When?" asked Ripetti.

I didn't say. "You scared me," I said to Carl. "I thought that's what you were doing. Trying to scare me off."

Carl looked at Ripetti, as if for instruction as to what to say.

"I'm sorry," said Ripetti. "He shouldn't have scared you. He was really supposed to be out of sight." To Carl, he said, "I need to talk to you. Can you wait for me in the conference room?"

Carl apologized to me and then left the room.

"Tell me about the Stacey Donovan case," I said. "You and Mike were the lead investigators. What happened?"

His eyes registered nothing. He looked at his watch. "Look, I really was just going to call you. We finally got a hit on Julia's credit card. At a gas station in Newhall. I was just on my way to go out there to talk to the guy. I don't want to wait."

He picked up his leather jacket and hooked it over his finger. He already knew the answer when he asked, "Want to come with me? We can talk in the car."

The navigation system in Ripetti's SUV said it was 32 miles and would take us 41 minutes to get to Newhall, but it took that and more just to get to the first of the three freeways we'd need to take. That gave us a lot of time to talk.

"Stacey Donovan disappeared eleven years ago," he said. "What makes you think it has anything to do with what happened to Caleigh or Julia?"

"Was Patrick Caiman really a suspect?"

"Yes. We never released the information to the papers, but Stacey Donovan was wearing a heart-shaped locket when she disappeared. We found the locket on Patrick Caiman." He checked for my reaction before going on. "He'd been obsessed with her. Called her at home several times, kept calling her back to audition. Then he wanted her to audition partially clothed…and taped it. He had her audition tape in his office and a duplicate at home. He knew where she lived, knew where she went to school, knew the route she took. His alibi was completely bogus. He said he'd been home sick all day, but he hadn't made any phone calls, and guys like that can't stay off the phone no matter how sick they are. A 'massage therapist' came to see him, but she'd say or do anything anyone paid her to."

"How'd you find the locket?"

"You should ask your friend Mike Drummond. He's the one who found it."

"But he's not here, and you are. So you tell me."

"Seems he and Patrick Caiman had the same tastes in…female companionship. He had mentioned the locket to someone he shouldn't have, someone who was, say, ironing out the kinks after a hard day's work, and this same woman was later performing the same service on Patrick Caiman. She found the locket, knew what it meant, and turned it in. Problem was, by that time, the chain of evidence was so fucked up we couldn't use it anyway. Mike boffing the key witness didn't help either."

"Do you think it was Mike who had the locket, and used her to plant it on Caiman?"

"That certainly came up as a possibility at the time. But there was no way of proving anything either way. He was suspended, but never charged."

The puzzle that was Mike had too many pieces that didn't fit.

"Who else had been at her auditions?"

"Darlin', this was eleven years ago. I don't remember all the details."

"Campbell McCauley?"

"Yeah, maybe. Probably."

"And Marty Nussbaum?"

"I think you're going to have to ask the police these questions. I'm not a cop anymore, and I don't have access to those records."

"When did you go out on your own?"

"When I got shot because your friend was so fucked up he blew a surveillance case. Except I took the bullets, all three of them. And maybe he's the one you should be asking these questions. Except he'll tell you he very conveniently doesn't remember anything that happened.

He maneuvered his SUV as nimbly as a sports car around slower cars.

"You know how it is. You do something you shouldn't, maybe it's not even such a big deal, but it's something you have to keep secret." His tone was conversational, friendly, ingenuous. But his eyes pinned me like a tack. "Because once people know, it'll be all anyone ever thinks about any time your name comes up from then on. It's like sitting on a bench that says 'Wet Paint.' It marks you." My heart raced; my stomach flipped. *He knows about Rosa*, I thought for the first time. He continued, with a sly smile. "Know what I mean?"

Adrenaline surged through my body; my chest constricted, and my legs began to shake. In my panic, I thought of Mike's warning not to trust him, and the queasy feeling I'd had when we were going over Caleigh's crime scene. Was I terrified because he knew about Rosa? Or because I'd gotten into a car with Caleigh's killer? All I knew was that every cell in my body was frightened.

The winds picked up as we drove through the Newhall pass, cutting through the San Gabriel Mountains that bordered the San Fernando Valley on its outer Northern edge. Even the heavy trucks surrounding us were buffeted by strong winds that whistled even through closed windows.

The sun was low by the time we got to the Joshua trees and creosote bush that dotted the landscape of the high desert gateway to the Mojave. Ripetti turned into the gas station/mini-mart where Julia's credit card had been used. The fluorescent lights made a buzzing sound in the still desert air, as maddened insects hurled themselves into their glare. The station was surrounded by sand and gravel from which grew a few clumps of cholla, with its sharp spines and stinging nettles. Beyond that, it fronted a vast unseen wilderness.

"Coming?" asked Ripetti. He opened his door and stepped out into the gas station.

I followed him into the mini-mart.

A clerk in work pants and a checked shirt sat on a stool behind a counter that sold lotto cards and herbal stimulants along with jerky, gum, and candy. His face was lined from exposure to wind and sun, and everything on him drooped, from the sagging pouches under his eyes, to the creases of his disappointed face. He moved slowly. If life had offered him little satisfaction, he'd be damned if he'd give it to anyone else.

Ripetti showed him a photo of Julia and told him that he was a private investigator working for the girl's parents; she'd run away, and they were trying to find her. Someone had used her credit card here. Had he seen her? The clerk barely glanced at the photo before saying he couldn't say; so many people came and went, he couldn't be expected to remember them all. Ripetti looked up at the monitor facing the clerk, which showed a screen divided into four quadrants, each showing what a different surveillance camera was filming: me and Ripetti in front of the counter, views of the aisles, views of the pumps outside. Ripetti took out copies of the credit card slip and asked if we could see the tape from the date and time of the transaction.

The clerk said the equipment was in the back office and nobody was allowed in there; their equipment wasn't sophisticated enough to have a date and time stamp, and besides, they recorded over the tapes if nothing had happened. Ripetti explained that the credit card had posted just a few hours ago; the transaction had taken place this morning. It was just a question of watching today's tape. He remained cordial, explaining that finding the footage would be no problem for him; this was his business; he did this all the time. He showed the clerk Julia's picture again and said that she was only sixteen, her parents were frantic, and it was likely that she had been abducted and was being held by a dangerous drug dealer. He introduced me as her step-mother and said he'd be doing us a great favor to let us look at the tapes.

"Please," I said. "You're our only hope."

He complained that if he rewound the tapes for us, he'd be leaving the place unprotected. What if someone came in to rob him while there was no tape? Ripetti told him he was an ex-cop. He showed him his gun, beneath his jacket, assured him it was licensed, and said he'd offer him more protection than any surveillance camera.

Eventually, the man took us to the back office, showed us the clunky VHS recorder, and stood uneasily, watching the register and us, as we rewound the tape.

We went back to the beginning and fast-forwarded through the herky-jerky motions of people pumping gas, buying beer and lotto tickets. Like a speeded up silent film, we watched as people drove in, got their supplies, and left. We watched their shadows change direction as the sun moved from one side of the sky to the other.

I wished I could smoke; I wished I could have a beer; I wished I could do something to allay my anxiety and fear. I asked Ripetti to stop while I bought a package of cashews and another of raisins and gobbled them nervously as I watched. But then they were gone, and, just as I'd done every day I'd been sober, I had to live through each minute of time on its own terms, without any buffer.

Ripetti put a hand on my back in a gesture of comfort and support. I felt an involuntary physical response. Ever since we'd met, there had been an underlying tension between us; an electric energy that was equal parts attraction and its opposite. The panic I'd felt when he implied he knew about Rosa had subsided, subsumed by his earnest attempt to track down Julia. I was no longer afraid he had brought me here to kill me. But this wasn't the same as trust. I was wary of him, based on what I'd heard, yet drawn at the same time, connected by how much he had helped me from the time he'd saved my life until now.

And by his impenetrability, to which I was drawn because I identified with it so strongly.

The tension created a charge that now detonated at his touch.

It took close to forty-five minutes to scan hours of footage. We went through one complete tape without finding what we were looking for and had just begun another.

"That's her!" I shouted, my voice and eyes registering before my brain.

Ripetti stopped the tape then went forward at normal speed. There they were. Clinton and Julia. Together, just the two of them. They'd arrived in his car, filled the tank, and come in for supplies. She hovered near the magazines, scanning the headlines, while he got chips, soda, cheese, and baloney, bringing each item back to the counter.

We ran the footage backwards and forwards to study it as closely as we could. She was quiet; she said nothing; she hovered in the background. But it was her. And she was okay. She didn't appear hurt, or sick, or held against her will; she scanned the headlines of the newspapers then moved freely in the mini-mart, finding a box of the kind of cookies she liked, adding it to the stash Clinton was gathering, then going back for Tampax.

Clinton gathered all the supplies, including several six-packs of beer; at the counter he bought cigarettes, rolling papers, and condoms. He paid for it with a credit card, and they left. We could see by the simultaneous cameras at the pump that they got back into his car and drove off.

She's alive! She's safe! A surge of joy swelled in my heart, and I asked Ripetti to run the tape over again two or three times. The sight of her brought a momentary relief from the fear that had gripped me since she'd disappeared.

She must be nearby. But where?

We called the clerk in to watch the video, to ask him if there were anything he could remember about them. They were in earlier this morning, a little past 11 according to the credit card slip. "You know, people come in and out, they all look the same."

Not if you pay attention, I thought, noticing the pouches under his eyes and the sweat under his arms; the gut hanging over his belt and the rasp in his voice that sounded like he used to smoke.

Ripetti stayed in the office, running the tape back and forth. I went back out to the magazine stand, as if standing in the space where she'd been could lead me to the place she was now.

Ripetti joined me. "From the things they bought, I'd say they're holed up somewhere, hiding like outlaws. There's a bunch of old mining camps in these mountains. They could be at one of them."

We looked out at the mountains behind the station, a vast expanse of sand and scrabble.

"Wait a minute!"

I'd left my bag in his car, and I ran back there now. Ripetti followed me. I dug in my bag on the front seat to get my notebook, going over the notes I'd made over these last few days. I found the printout of Mike's research about Clinton. The printout about Rosa spilled out too, but that wasn't what was important now.

I grabbed Ripetti's arm. "I know where they are!"

CHAPTER 33

Behind the gas station lay a mountainous region where, in the past, all the old Hollywood studios shot their westerns before it became cheaper to shoot them in Eastern Europe.

Mike's research had uncovered that when Clinton was a boy, he'd been chosen by a newspaper to go to a camp for underprivileged kids in Pico Canyon, up in these mountains behind Newhall. According to his mother, those two weeks were among the happiest he'd spent as a child. Maybe that's where he'd brought Julia.

There were no lights other than our headlights, the stars, and the moon, as we headed up into the mountains. The sky was cloudless, and the spray of stars usually dimmed by city lights, were as visible as diamonds in a jeweler's black velvet box. The moon cast a pale light over the creosote bushes and sycamore trees that sided the road.

We said nothing as we drove from the desert into the mountains, until Ripetti, sharp-eyed, saw the sign for the turnout to Pico Canyon.

My heart pounded as I pictured myself taking Julia in my arms, wrapping her in the safety of my embrace.

When we turned a corner, I saw police cars—lots of them. Harsh eruptions of dispatches squawked from squad car radios, red flares hissed in the road. The swirling red light of a police car swept round in circles, bathing the landscape in an eerie crimson before moving on, like a lighthouse in hell.

We pulled up behind a police car, and both of us jumped out, walking towards what I was beginning to see was another crime scene. Yellow tape was strung up against some trees.

At the sight of the van from the Medical Examiner of the Coroner's Office, I heard myself utter a small cry.

Mike disengaged from a conversation he was having with Detective Norton when he saw me. He came towards me and took me in his arms.

"It's okay. We'll find her. I promise. We'll find her."

It took me a moment to make sense of the words.

"She isn't…dead?"

"She isn't here. It's Clinton who's dead."

Mike had gotten word of the same hit on Julia's credit card that Ripetti had but had figured out sooner that they were at the abandoned summer camp. When he'd arrived, Clinton was dead from a bullet wound. Julia wasn't there. One of the cabins showed signs of having been inhabited. Cooking utensils, a sleeping bag, condoms, and feminine hygiene products indicated both of them had been there. It looked like someone had found them, killed Clinton, and taken Julia.

Beyond the yellow tape, I could see a camp consisting of a few cabins alongside a creek, a campfire, and some cooking grills. The scene was illuminated by floodlights powered by generators. Technicians were taking their specimens and measurements. I couldn't go in; it was marked off as a crime scene.

Detective Norton stood beyond the barricade, and I signaled to him. He came over to talk. He said they were still in the process of collecting evidence. Forensic tests would ascertain the approximate time of Clinton's death. They would get prints and compare them to those found in Clinton's apartment. Perhaps Joe Nakamura had come again, and this time he'd taken Julia with him. Perhaps not.

All I knew was Clinton was dead and Julia was missing.

Seeing the expression on my face, Mike gathered me into his arms and held me close. I felt his kiss against my hair. He said he understood how I must feel and promised he'd find her.

I squirmed out of his arms, uneasy in his embrace now that I'd seen him with Desiree. I couldn't even look at him. I felt I'd lost him as an ally, and I didn't know how I could tell him that.

Did I want to stay with him? Maybe I shouldn't be alone right now.

I said I'd come with Ripetti; my car was at his office. Seeing Ripetti, Mike sagged noticeably, like a spurned lover who sees it's hopeless. I wanted to correct his impression, but I hadn't the strength. Mike no longer felt like someone I could talk to. Ripetti said, when we were done, he would take me back to my car.

CHAPTER 34

I leaned my head against the back rest and tried telling myself that all was not lost; Julia was still alive. But my heart ached. Whoever had her was smarter and faster than me; Julia had never seemed so lost.

The drive that had taken over two hours took less than thirty minutes to do in reverse.

We pulled into the parking structure under Ripetti's office.

"You hungry?"

I nodded.

"I'm a pretty good cook."

I followed the red tail lights of his Bronco west on Sunset, weaving in and out of lanes like the steps of a mating dance.

His apartment was as masculine and unrevealing as he was. All chrome and glass, grey and graphite, on the top floor of a high-rise on Wilshire, with a dazzling view of the city.

"No, thanks; I don't drink," I said at his offer of wine.

He put back the bottle. "Me neither."

"How come?" Half-hoping he was an alcoholic too.

"I don't like to impair my senses."

I couldn't imagine why someone who could drink wouldn't.

How do people get into bed with each other if they don't drink? I'd never had sex when I hadn't been drunk or stoned or both. I knew how to tumble into bed, senses numbed, judgment cloudy, animal desire overriding thought. How to do that sober? How to get from here to there?

Because I'd known, as we'd driven back in the dark, that we would go to bed together. I hurt so much, and I couldn't drink. At least I could have sex. It promised momentary relief, annihilation at last of the endless, nattering self.

Ripetti said he'd like to take a shower and change before dinner; would I like to do the same? He could lend me something to wear. He brought me a kimono and showed me a bathroom of green slate tile and stainless steel fixtures. He pointed out the special features of the shower—(pulse, massage, or fine spray) and left me alone.

I took off my clothes, stepped into the shower, and turned on the spray. There was a tube of shower gel in a caddy. I used it to lather myself in a soothing blanket of foam, cleansing away the residue of murder.

There was a knock on the glass shower door. I opened it to Ripetti.

"Want some company?" he said.

I nodded, and he slipped out of his clothes and came in, closing the door behind him.

CHAPTER 35

I sat in my car parked on a side street facing Wilshire, watching the traffic light turn from green to blinking yellow to red, each color casting a different glow over the darkened street. It was almost two a.m. Only a few cars in each direction.

What I'd thought would kill the pain had augmented it. I'd wanted to lose myself, but I was always there. The release I'd found in a moment of abandon was temporary, lasting only until I'd turned to see Ripetti watching me with eyes as impenetrable as if he'd been wearing shades, that same little "gotcha" smile playing on his lips.

Someone had Julia, and there was nobody to help me find her. I wondered if I'd ever felt so alone. I thought I probably had. Like, always.

My cell phone rang, the caller ID a number I didn't recognize. As I answered, the phone told me I had several messages. Mike had called while I'd been otherwise engaged.

I said hello, but nobody answered. Instead, I heard the beep of a PIN on a touch screen, a nozzle taken out of a gas tank, a receipt ejecting, and the ding, ding, ding of the end of a transaction; a car engine revving up, shifting gears, traffic. Nobody spoke. I almost hung up, when I heard a voice say, "Where are we?"

I froze.

Julia.

My breath caught in my throat. I almost called her name but stopped. If she could speak freely, she would have said hello.

I listened for the answer to her question but heard nothing but the car engine in traffic and the radio playing punk rock.

"Where are we going?"

The radio switched to a talk radio station, then to another in Spanish, then another. Whoever was turning the dial was impatient. A music station was broken up by static. So was the next and the next. Wherever they were, no signal was strong enough.

"I wish it were light out; it looks beautiful here. Almost like a movie," said Julia. "Where are we?"

"Yeah, they used to shoot Westerns out here," said a man's voice.

"Right. Bang bang, shoot em up!" This was a gruff second male voice, with a deep guttural laugh.

"Don't play games." The first voice. "They want her in one piece."

There followed a long silence, with only the sound of the car. It seemed they didn't know the line was open. Then the slow click, click, click of a turn signal. The engine slowed then sped up; the clicking sound stopped. They'd made a turn.

"What mountains are these? Are we back in the city? Because we came down from one set of mountains, and then I think we must have gone all the way through the valley, and now we're headed up into different mountains."

"What are you, studying for a geography quiz?"

"No, I'm just wondering. I don't think I've ever been on this road before. Let's see, the moon is on our right…oh! What is this, Mulholland?"

"Hey, this is…why, you little…"

And suddenly the line went dead.

I was frozen to the spot. Julia was alive. She was being taken somewhere, using her abductor's phone to let me know where she was.

But where?

Somewhere on Mulholland Drive. If the moon was on her right, driving west.

The phone rang again. The same caller ID came up. I answered.

"Try anything, and you're dead," said the gruff voice, before the phone went silent.

I reached for the Thomas Guide, which contained maps of every street in the county. Mulholland Drive spanned the length of the city, from the Cahuenga Pass to the sea traversing page after page in the Thomas Guide. I tried to see where they might be if they'd started at Pico Canyon and the moon was on their right.

Why Mulholland, and where?

Hannah had said the house they'd been taken to was off Mulholland, on Angelo Crest Road. Could that be where Julia was headed?

I was closer. Maybe I could get there first.

CHAPTER 36

Angelo Crest Road was a small street, easy to miss, lined with eucalyptus, giving it a rural look. The houses sat on large land-scaped lots, each one far enough from the other to give it privacy. There were no street lamps. The only illumination came from my headlights. I turned them off, pulled over, and parked.

I made my way on foot, as quickly and quietly as I could. The eucalyptus trees gave off a faintly antiseptic smell, like a doctor's office, strangely comforting. The stars, so visible in the San Gabriels, were completely obscured by the lights of the city which outshone them. The air was moist and cool. Three garbage bins, colored according to recycling laws, stood at each driveway; tomorrow was collection day. The windows in all the houses were dark.

16593 Angelo Crest was the last house on the block, a one story, ranch style stucco that sat alone in a cul-de-sac, looking more like a middle-class family home than a brothel. There were two cars in the driveway. One was the blue Impala, license plate 1NSK569: the car that Carl had used to follow me.

The other was Mike's. I went up to the front door and tried the handle. To my surprise, the door was not locked and opened easily.

I stepped into a large foyer that led to a sunken living room. The sliding glass doors on the opposite side faced a spectacular view of the Valley, resplendent with twinkling lights that sparkled like sequins on the dress of a diva. Traffic lights switched from red to green in coordinated rhythms, while traffic streamed through the streets in intersecting lines of headlights and taillights. To the left, the San Diego Freeway made a river that flowed white in one direction, red in the other.

In the large living room, plush sofas and chairs surrounded a coffee table. There were no glasses, and the decorative bowls were empty. Soft music was playing; the sort of mellow soul designed for late-night adult listening. The lingering smell of perfume hovered in the air. No voices; the house was still. Other than the music, I heard only the sound of my heart thumping.

And then a buzzing sound like flies. And a rhythmic rapping, erratic but recurrent, like an evil spirit knocking for entry.

I didn't know how long I had before the car with Julia would arrive, nor what I would do when it got here. I needed a place to hide but had to know who else might be here and what that strange knocking sound was.

The floors were covered with plush carpet, which muffled my footsteps. I crept down the hall, past two doors that opened onto empty bedrooms. At the end of the hallway lay the master bedroom. Its door was open. Inside, a man and woman were on plush, king-size bed with a satin cover and voluptuous pillows.

The man lay face up, arms and legs splayed outwards. The blood that seeped from the wound in his stomach had formed a large black circle on the red satin bedspread. A gun was beside him on the bed.

His eyes were open, but there was no spirit giving them expression. He was a corpse, not a person. But even from the doorway I recognized the receding hairline and the cream donut features of Carl, the man who worked for Ripetti.

The woman sat on the side of the bed. She was alive, except that her eyes seemed lifeless. They stared straight ahead, fixed and unmoving. Her expression was frozen in the shock of what she had witnessed; she said nothing, saw nothing, did nothing. Desiree.

The knocking sound came from the pull tie of the Venetian blinds. The sliding glass doors were opened, and the wind from the valley rapped them against the metal siding. The doors opened onto a deck that looked out onto a swimming pool and Jacuzzi.

My eyes turned to the body sprawled on the floor.

It was Mike.

Blood poured from his mouth, pooling black. The buzzing sound came from the flies around his wound. Beside him lay a stepladder, knocked over on its side. It looked as if he'd been shot as he stood on it and had crumpled to the ground. The clock that had hung on the wall now dangled from where it had been secured. Its back was opened, revealing a space where, I guessed, something had been removed.

I hurried over to him and bent down. He was deathly pale and did not move, but I felt a weak pulse.

"Mike." I heard the edge of insistency in my voice, a lifeline thrown to him; he must grab it and come back to me.

Mike stirred slightly at my touch; his eyes flickered recognition. He moved his mouth and a dreadful gurgle came out, blood continuing to flow from him.

"Can you hear me?" I clasped his hand in mine and put my face close to his. His unfocused eyes met mine, mute with pain, pleading.

I put my cheek to his, mine warm his cold, as if I could transfer my vital force to him as he had to me when he took me to that first meeting. I was aware of all he had done for me; nothing else mattered.

I called 911 from my cell phone. I told them there'd been a shooting. One man was dead but one still alive. Send an ambulance, quickly. Hurry, please, God, hurry!

Mike continued to make guttural, rasping sounds, like a death rattle. Beads of sweat formed on his brow. I took his hand in mine and realized he was clutching something in it.

I felt his eyes were trying to speak as he could not use his voice.

When he felt my hands around his, he relaxed his grip and released what he had been holding onto: a tiny video camera that had probably been hidden in the clock, recording whatever had taken place in this room.

"Woooo…eu…" Mike tried to speak, but the sounds were unintelligible. He could not utter words; the blood continued to seep from him, and he grew even paler at its loss. But with his last gasps, he was trying to tell me something; I could see it in his eyes. I put my ear directly to his mouth.

"Wooo…wooo…"

I repeated what I heard back to him, hoping he could elaborate, but he made the same sounds, like grunts but without any consonants.

"Wooo…eu…eu…"

He fell silent.

I sat cradling him, telling him, and God, that he was just going to have to live because I didn't understand. I held him in my arms until the ambulance arrived.

CHAPTER 37

A crime scene is a little like a movie set—a lot of people milling around, each with a specific job to do. Uniformed policemen barricaded the scene and kept guard while others went door to door to interview neighbors about what they might have seen or heard. One technician dusted prints while another collected and analyzed the splatter of blood. Paramedics had come for Mike and taken him away but only after a route had been established, protected, and secured so that he could be moved with as little contamination of the scene as possible. A uniformed policeman had interviewed me briefly then asked me to wait outside until I could be interrogated further by the investigator. He did the same with Desiree. She was shivering in shock, and someone had thrown a blanket over her bare arms and taken her to wait in the back of a police car. Black and whites barricaded the street, red lights flashing a warning to everyone not to go farther.

If, as I had suspected, Julia's abductors were bringing her here, they would not come now.

The ambulance left, but the medical examiner's van remained. Investigators and technicians dusted and measured, collected and documented, drew and photographed. Police put up yellow tape to isolate the house.

Detectives Norton and Martinez arrived, and Norton asked me to remain where I was until he had finished examining the scene.

I sat on the curb and waited. The night was chilly, and I got my suede jacket out of my car but still I shivered. I'd been in a state of heightened alert since arriving at the house, but now the adrenaline was beginning to drain. I struggled against the encroaching exhaustion, knowing the despair that would accompany it. I wanted to stay in the illusion that there was something I could do, decisions I could make, which would affect the outcome. If I just handled things well, Mike would live; Julia would be safe. As dire as the stakes were, I still preferred to think I had a role in the outcome. It was too depressing to feel the full extent of my impotence.

I fingered the camera in my pocket. It was small enough to fit in the palm of my hand. I had not turned it over to the police. I knew it was evidence, and I knew withholding it was a crime. I also knew that if there were sex videos of men as prominent as the ones who'd done "enjo kosai" with these girls, it would not be long before someone, somewhere, would get it and post it and it would be visible to everyone in the world with access to a computer.

I felt a hand on my shoulder and looked up into the face of Detective Luke Norton. He looked grim.

"He was your friend, wasn't he?"

"Yes."

"I'm sorry."

He offered a hand to help me get up. I took it and stood. He asked if I were okay. I said yes, although I knew it wasn't true.

I told him about coming to the house and finding the bodies. I told him that Carl was an operative who worked for Nic Ripetti, and I thought that Desiree was a prostitute who worked for Toby Starr. I told him about seeing them together the night before. Mike was her client, I'd thought.

He asked what I was doing there. I told him about the call from Julia and the conversation I'd overheard. She'd used her abductor's phone to alert me she was being taken to Mulholland Drive. Since this was the house where the "enjo kosai" took place, I thought it might be here. I'd found out the address at Patrick's office and confirmed it at Toby Star's.

Did Mike know about the call from Julia? No. I'd been so disappointed to see him with Desiree; I no longer felt I could trust him. He'd phoned me earlier, but I hadn't gotten the call. Together, on the speaker of my cell phone, Norton, Martinez, and I listened to the message that Mike had left on my voice mail.

"Brett, it's Mike. Listen, call me. I got a big break in the case. I don't want to leave it on your voice mail, but I think I know how we can find Julia. So call me. It's urgent. Hey. Kiddo. It's going to be okay."

We listened to the message again. Martinez asked me if I had any idea what he was referring to; I wished I did, but no.

I asked what Desiree had said. Norton said that right now they were gathering information, not giving it, and they'd be bringing Desiree to the station for questioning. They were going to want me to come as well.

At the end of the street, a dog was barking, protesting the presence of so many intruders. The bark was high-pitched and urgent; because it was not heeded, it persisted.

I showed them the number that had been used to call my cell phone; whoever owned that cell phone had Julia. Martinez made a note of the number and asked me to give them the phone; the lab might be able to determine more about where the call had originated. I gave it to her gladly.

She asked again why I'd thought this was where Julia was being taken.

"A hunch. They were on Mulholland, and they were bringing her to meet someone, someone who 'wanted her safe.'" I showed her the notes I made. "I knew this was the house where Julia and her friends 'did sushi.' But now—if they were coming here, they'd have been scared away." I tried to keep the frustration out of my voice, but one more time, I'd seemed so close, only to have her beyond my reach. "Anyway, everything that went on in that room is on this." I took the camera out of my pocket.

"Carl worked for Ripetti, and Ripetti was collecting dirt for Marty Nussbaum. I think Ripetti recorded everything that went on in this room to be used as leverage should the participants ever prove troublesome." My voice broke, "I found it in Mike's hand. I think he was shot retrieving it."

"You should have left it there. It's evidence." Norton frowned.

"When I'd first found Julia, she'd said, 'there's video…' I thought this might be what she meant. It probably shows Julia having sex for money. She's only sixteen…"

The exhaust of the police cars overpowered the smell of eucalyptus.

"I shouldn't have withheld it. But if it ever gets out, posted on the Internet…"

"It won't." Detective Luke Norton seemed solid and true, steadfast as a German shepherd. But I handed him the camera because I had no other choice.

"Check the rest of the house too. There are probably other cameras in other rooms. Who knows? Maybe Calcigh was murdered here. If she was, it could have been recorded too."

CHAPTER 38

I **sat in the** interrogation room, drinking the dregs of a stale cup of coffee. A large glass panel against the wall that looked like a mirror fooled nobody; I knew I could be observed. But I wasn't doing anything interesting, just waiting for Luke Norton and Theresa Martinez to come to talk to me.

Norton came in alone, carrying his own cup of coffee in one hand and the video camera in the other. He took a seat across from me.

"It wasn't what you thought," he said. "He wasn't cheating on you with a hooker."

I started to protest that my relationship with Mike did not include the concept of "cheating," but I was more interested in what he had to say.

"He's a good detective. He found out that, ten years ago, Desiree was a child actress who'd been raped by Marty Nussbaum. Her mother agreed to a settlement to keep it quiet. Kind of gave her an idea of what she could do for a living when she grew up."

"Did she audition for that child-in-the-brothel movie that Stacey Donovan auditioned for?"

"Got a small part in it, too. And several other movies over the years. She was a real favorite of Nussbaum's. Her mother told her it was a small price to pay for a job, and actresses did it all the time. As she grew up, he lost interest in her, and her career never went anywhere after that. Couldn't make the transition out of child actress, so she grew up to be a very expensive call girl who knew her way around the movie business. Mike thought she might know something about what had happened to Caleigh and Julia."

"Did she?"

"Campbell McCauley was one of her clients. Mike had something he needed to talk to McCauley about, but McCauley was always surrounded by bodyguards. So he used Desiree to set up this tryst. McCauley came with a bodyguard anyway."

"Carl."

"Carl found Mike tampering with the camera and shot him. Mike shot back and...well, you saw the result. We're bringing in McCauley for questioning now."

He'd brought in the video camera I'd found in Mike's hand, and he hooked it up to the television monitor in the room. "I think you're going to find this interesting."

We watched the tape together, fast forwarding to get to the part he wanted me to see.

It was about as erotic as surveillance footage at an ATM, with the same grainy, herky-jerky quality. There was nothing even slightly titillating or stimulating about watching a series of men performing sex acts with a series of women.

We fast forwarded through the "enjo kosai." I didn't really want to watch Hannah having sex with Paolo Navarro, Caleigh or Julia with Campbell McCauley. Luke fast-forwarded till he got to the spot he wanted me to see.

Norton slowed it back to normal speed. Caleigh and Patrick Caiman. Not having sex but dressed and speaking.

Patrick said, "You know your father tapes everything that goes on in this room. Eventually, he's going to see this. So tell him what you told me. What would you like to say to your father?"

Caleigh was too young to look so old. Her eyes were heavily made up, but the eyeliner and mascara were smudged; her eyes were puffy and unfocused. She looked bloated from too many drugs, too much to drink. She was tipsy; she was giggling as she surveyed the room.

"Where's the camera?"

Patrick pointed to the clock on the nightstand. "It could be there…" and then pointed to the television on the wall "or there…" and then to the vase on the credenza "or there…But it's here. I'm sure of it. So what do you want to say to him?"

Caleigh giggled. "We're going to tell on you, Daddy! We're going to bring you down!"

She looked wildly around the room, unsure where to aim her invective. "All my life, all I ever heard from you was how stupid, or ugly, or clumsy I was. 'A moron would know that, Caleigh, don't you even have the brains of an idiot?' 'You're too fat, Caleigh, nobody's going to love you if you look like that.'" Her lip quivered, and her voice shook as she imitated the cruel things her father had said to her. "Well, if I'm so ugly, how come so many men like me? You told me I was nothing better than a whore. So guess what, Daddy, now I really AM a whore! And lots of men love me. Patrick loves me, don't you?"

"Tell him what you told me. Tell him what we know."

She looked away from the camera towards the vase. "I don't know where you are…I don't know how to talk to you…" She kept looking at different places in the room before just looking up at the ceiling and addressing the overhead light. Her voice was strong. "I'm going to tell about that girl, Daddy, the one you killed. You told me you needed me to keep you from doing all those bad things to other girls, that if you did them with me, you wouldn't have to find anyone else. I know that you killed her, Daddy, and that Ripetti covered it up for you. You said if I ever told you'd kill me too. But I don't need your money anymore, Daddy. I can take care of myself now. You thought I was stupid, like one of Mamma's dolls. But Mamma's dolls can't talk, and I can. And I will! Because maybe I'm stupid, but I'm smart enough to HURT YOU! Just like you hurt me!" Her expression was suddenly as plaintive as the little girl she'd so recently been. "Why couldn't you ever say anything nice to me? I don't think you ever gave me a compliment, not once in my whole life!" She turned to Patrick. "Are you sure he's going to see this?"

"Oh, he'll see it. And he'll find out that he's not the only one who can use dirty little secrets to his advantage."

"We're telling, Daddy! And I don't care what happens!"

Her expression was pure hatred before her face crumbled, and she began to cry. Patrick took her in his arms and comforted her.

"He's going to kill me…" she said.

He stroked her hair. "I won't let him."

She pulled away from him, doubled over, and held herself in a little ball. "He's going to kill me," she repeated and then added, "He'll kill you too…"

"I think I'd better go have a talk with Marty Nussbaum," said Norton, as he turned off the machine.

CHAPTER 39

It was dawn by the time I got back to Gerry's, and I fell asleep instantly. The phone rang and woke me. I fumbled for the receiver. The caller ID was a 404 area code, from Toronto.

"Hey, Brett. How's the house working out for you?"

It was Gerry Talbot.

"Great. No problems. How are things up there?"

"Brett—I'm going to need it back a little sooner than I'd thought."

My heart sank.

"Are you coming back? I thought you were in production until June."

"No, I'm not, but…" He put his hand over the phone, and I could hear him talking to someone there on the other end.

"Are you at the house now? I'm going to send someone over for the keys."

"Today? Gerry, please, I need a little time to find another place. What about the car? Do you need the car too?"

"Sorry, Brett."

I had barely hung up when the doorbell rang. Two men were at the door. They were each dressed in black pants, dress shirts open at the neck, and dark glasses, and although one was shorter than the other, one had a pock-marked face and the other didn't, they seemed like clones. I couldn't say I recognized them from the reception at Marty's, but they wore the same battery pack and headset and had the same demeanor as the men who'd worked security at that event.

"Do you work for Ripetti?" I asked.

They didn't acknowledge the question in any way.

I asked if I could have some time to pack. One of them said that would be okay, and they'd wait while I did it. The other one asked if I needed help. I said no, but he followed me upstairs anyway.

I called Ripetti from my cell phone. I got no answer.

Upstairs, I put my clothes in a duffel. I really didn't have much. I wore mostly jeans and sneakers these days. Everything I had fit into the one bag I'd brought with me. That and my laptop made up the sum of my possessions.

Good thing too because, when I gave up the keys to the house and the car, I had to take it all with me. I wasn't about to leave it there. I didn't know that I'd ever be back.

* * *

I walked up to the coffee shop in the Trancas shopping center, ordered coffee and a muffin, and sat at a small table outside. Detective Norton had told me which hospital Mike had been taken to, and I called there now to get an update on his condition.

I felt a familiar dread as I waited, while a singer on the Muzak lamented that he was all by himself, but didn't want to be. I thought about what it took to compose that song, its wail of fear and loneliness, and whether its writer imagined it would one day be sonic wallpaper for people on hold. I used these thoughts to distract myself from the awareness that one more time I was waiting to hear about someone who might die because of me.

Mike had saved my life. No other way of saying it. He'd taken me in, fed me, housed me, helped me…loved me. Because I suddenly realized, of course, he loved me. Not in any way I'd ever been loved before; not because I was tall and thin, or smart, or funny, or pretty, or successful, not even because I was broke and miserable. He loved me because…I had no idea why he loved me, but he had. And I had repaid him with suspicion, withholding—and lies.

I was dishonest, so I couldn't imagine anyone else being different. I was so contaminated by my own garbage that everything I looked at seemed dirty. Now he hovered between life and death because of me. How casually we say "Go to hell." This was hell.

"…condition still gravely critical."

I thanked her and hung up.

I had no car, no place to live, barely any money. I had failed as a woman, a writer, a mother, a detective, and a friend. As a child, Julia had been entrusted to my care, and all I'd given her was a model of addiction, a lesson in how to waste your life and throw love away. When she'd come as a teenager needing help, I'd failed her again. I'd been led to her a third time, at a dealer's house, poised on the brink of disaster, and I'd stood helplessly by as she embarked upon a journey that seemed destined to end in death. At best.

And then there was Rosa. Always Rosa.

I looked at my notes. They all swirled before me. What difference did any of them make now? The damage had already been done. It was too late.

Was it? Wasn't Julia still alive? Come on. What if this were a script. What would Jinx Magruder do?

How the hell should I know? I never could write without drugs.

I felt in my pocket and found the little plastic baggie Zeke had given me. Maybe that's what I needed. One good snort of coke would put everything into focus.

What was the point of staying sober? Rosa Aguilar was already dead, whether I stayed clean or not. I could see no value of my sobriety to anyone, least of all me.

Fuck it.

I'll snort this. I'll go in the bathroom. I'll use a bill, rolled up. Then I'll call Zeke. Maybe I can stay with him a few days. The one bridge I haven't burned.

The coke will keep me from drinking.

And if it doesn't, so what?

I decided to do it.

But first…The coffee shop was a hot spot. I opened my laptop and Googled Yolanda Aguilar, Rosa's daughter's name. To my surprise, I got a hit.

It appeared in a news story from a local paper in Duarte. She was a member of a 4-H Club which was holding a sale to raise money to send a delegation to the National Leadership Conference. There was a picture of the Club, and Yolanda Aguilar was third in a line of girls. She had dark hair and a shy, sweet smile.

I put the baggie back in my pocket, heaved up my duffel, and took a cab to Mike's house.

* * *

Yellow tape surrounded it, and there was a police lock on the door. That was okay. I didn't need to get in. I still had the key to the

Woodie he'd let me use when I stayed with him. And that was in his driveway, without yellow tape preventing access.

It was the car he'd been working on when I came to see him about Julia, the one he called his "Drunkmobile," for picking up drunks and taking them to meetings. He had yet to paint it or replace its mildewed wooden slats. But I knew he'd been working on the engine and judged it safe to drive.

I opened the trunk to put in my laptop and duffle. A folded blanket smelled of old vomit. Mike used it in his 12-step work, and I found the odor strangely comforting; it reminded me of what he'd done for me. If worse came to worst, I could wrap it around me and sleep in the car. I'd be okay.

When I got in and opened the glove compartment, to my surprise, I saw a gun.

Feeling the weight of it in my hand, I remembered what Mike had said about not wanting a gun in the house any more than he'd want alcohol and for the same reason. There were moods when he didn't trust himself not to use it.

I put it back in the glove compartment. I could always shoot myself. In the meanwhile, I had work to do.

CHAPTER 40

Duarte was an hour's drive east from Mike's. On the way there, I heard on the radio that the final approval of the merger between Poseidon and Alliance was being withheld, pending new developments in the investigation into the murder of Caleigh Nussbaum. Her father, Marty Nussbaum, had been brought in for questioning by police; his lawyer issued a statement that he was not considered a suspect, simply a material witness. He was cooperating fully with the police, and he expected the merger to go forward as planned.

Whereas Eastman, in Brentwood, occupied the mansion of a former movie star, the high school in Duarte was a sprawling complex of cinderblock buildings on an arid strip of land near the freeway. I parked in the circular driveway in front of the school. The air was smoggy and smelled of car exhaust. I got out of my car and waited.

When the bell rang, kids teemed out of the school, all talking at once. Spanish and English were only two of the many languages spoken. I couldn't identify each language, but it was a broad mix; Tugalag, Farsi, Thai. Still, their unspoken language was universal; teenagers with boundless energy, razzing and shouting, high-spirited, happy to be out of school.

The kids paid little attention to me as they walked in clusters. I searched each face as they streamed past me. I recognized Yolanda Aguilar as soon as I saw her. I'd only seen her picture in the paper that morning, yet as she came towards me, one of a group of girls speaking in Spanish, I felt as if I'd always known her; as if we were bonded by something deeper than birth.

"Yolanda."

She looked at me without recognition. If she had spent her days and nights thinking about me, as I had her, it was without realizing that it was me who haunted her dreams, as her mother did mine.

Her friends turned to see who she was looking at. Their lack of recognition registered as hostility. They knew I didn't belong here, and they didn't like me.

"Yolanda…" I said again.

She had thick black hair and large brown eyes; the slight jut of her chin showed the determination that marked her as nobody's victim; this girl was a survivor. Her initial response was wary. Her eyes blazed with innate defiance.

"I knew your mother…" I stammered.

Her expression softened. I had her attention.

"You knew my mother? How?

"I knew the Engelmann's…" I started to lie. "My daughter was a friend of their children…" She looked at me with no comprehension.

"I always wondered… if you were okay…"

She made a slight grimace and walked away, rejoining her friends, saying something dismissive about me in Spanish.

"Yolanda…!"

She stopped again.

"It was me. I was driving the car."

I saw her eyes widen as she realized the implications of what I was saying.

"I'm going to turn myself in. I'm going to tell the police. But before I did…I just had to find you and tell you…" The words were so inadequate, but they were the only ones I had. "…I'm so sorry for what I did."

I saw that she too had dreamed of this moment since that night, created and rehearsed tirades to heap upon the person who had shattered her life. Now that it was here, she was robbed of speech; there was too much to say. We held each other's eyes, like lovers who have searched the world over and finally met.

Her claque of friends was oblivious to our drama. The cell phone of one of them had gone off, and she'd answered it, and now she squealed, laughed, and showed something on her phone to her friends. They too shrieked in that way universal to adolescent girls.

As Yolanda and I stood staring at each other, one of her friends came over to show her what was on the cell phone.

"Mira, está Coco y su bebé."

Yolanda looked at the cell phone video but waved it away, continuing to stare at me, the anger within her welling.

"You drove the car that killed my mother?"

"Yes."

The veins in her neck pulsed with blood rising to her head.

"And you come to tell me this, why? You want me to forgive you? You want me to say it's okay?"

I shook my head. I wanted nothing from her but this, to face her and tell her the truth.

Words seemed to form in her head but stopped at her throat, choking her; too many of them coming at once, too many feelings, too strong to put into words. Her hands shook with what I could only imagine was the urge to strangle me.

Her friends saw her and surrounded her, looking at me with hostility and suspicion.

What she had to say to me could not be put into words. But it could be expressed. From deep within her, she brought up a wad of saliva which she spit at me with all her might.

As they walked away, they showed her the video that had arrived on the cell phone.

* * *

I don't know how long I stood there. I know I was still standing there long after Yolanda and her friends had left and the other kids who had streamed out of school had dispersed. It took me that long to absorb what I had done and what I knew I had to do now. It was only as I walked back to my car that the full implication hit me. Not only of what I had done but what I had seen that I had been blind to until now.

CHAPTER 41

This time, I needed no Thomas Guide to find Clinton's apartment. The same Camaro was on cinderblocks, untouched in the intervening days, the same dirty palm fronds were in the gutters. I parked the Woodie. As I looked up at the sign with its missing letters, I remembered the smell of drugs in the room, the sight of Julia taking the pipe from Clinton, the crackle of the drug as she inhaled. The knock on the door, twisted sheets in the bedroom. And Julia staring at her cell phone saying, "Brett, there's video…"

And the last thing I saw before blacking out: Julia had flipped her cell phone off the balcony as she and Clinton ran down the stairs.

I opened the glove compartment to look for a flashlight and saw Mike's gun. I took it out and cradled it. I stuck it into the back of my jeans, under my suede jacket. I got the flashlight and went back to the "El Encantador" apartments.

Clinton lived on the second floor, and he and Julia had gone out the back, through the kitchen. Just as there was a balcony along the front of the apartments, there was also an iron balcony and fire escape leading down from the rear. It went down into an alley fronting a carport and shed where the garbage bins were kept. It was here that I had seen Julia drop her cell phone.

Julia had said "there's video," and I thought she'd meant video of the "enjo kosai." But what if the video was on her cell phone? What if Caleigh had videoed the murderer and sent it to Julia before she was killed? And what if the murderer had been looking for Julia and her cell phone ever since?

It was a hunch but a good one, at least the only one I had to go on.

I knew that the police had already searched this area as part of the crime scene; nonetheless, I felt compelled to do it for myself. I had written a scene for Jinx Magruder where she went over a crime scene the police had released and found a clue they had missed. Come to think of it, I had written that scene more than once. So I knew what to do.

The police divide the scene into grids, carefully patrolling each vertical and horizontal line. I began the slow and methodical work of searching the area of the stairs, the alley, the garbage, the carport, for the cell phone that Julia had shed. It was painstaking work. I was on alert. Chances were someone had stolen it. And yet, if they had, it would have been used, and it hadn't.

I opened the dumpster. The smell of rotting garbage was overwhelming. Did I have to go through it? I was willing but thought I'd try everything else first. I searched along the side of the dumpster in the grunge of the shed. I took off my suede jacket and got down on my belly and searched the underside. My eye fastened on a lump beneath the bin. I stretched my hand under. I shone the flashlight on it, and reached for it, but the lump turned out to be a

McDonald's bag with the rotting remains of a hamburger and fries. I left it there.

I was beginning to sense the futility of this search. If I had seen her drop the cell phone, surely the gunman had too and had already retrieved it.

But then why was someone still searching for her, searching hard enough to find her with Clinton in their hideout?

I put my jacket back on. I scoured the garage, the carport. I knew the police had already done this, but I did it again. I found nothing they hadn't found; I found nothing.

I didn't know which direction Clinton had gone, so I had to search the alley all the way in one direction and then all the way in the other. I walked up and down, my eyes peeled for any sign of cell phone, wanting to find it so badly I imagined seeing it where it wasn't. Other apartment houses backed onto the alley; other car ports, other garbage bins. I was looking for a cell phone, but all I saw was pot holes, garbage, tossed fast food wrappers, gravel, and grit.

A moment before, I'd felt euphoric at the idea that there was still something I could do. But as I searched in vain, that sense of purpose faltered. One more time, I'd deluded myself. How stupid, how futile, to think that I could still be of use to anyone, that it wasn't too late for me to rescue Julia.

That was what I was thinking when I saw the phone.

There it was: tiny, flat, razor thin, lying in a clump of grass between two apartment buildings across the alley from Clinton's. Thrown from the balcony with sufficient force to land here.

I grabbed it. I tried to turn it on. The battery was dead. But if there was a media file on it, I'd bet some techie would be able to retrieve it.

I was standing in the alley holding the phone, punching its buttons, when I saw that I was directly in the path of an oncoming red Hummer, speeding towards me. Joe Nakamura was driving. The car was about to run me over.

And Julia was in the passenger seat.

I dove out of the way, crashing against the garbage bins in the alley, knocking them over so that their contents spilled on me. In the moments it took me to get out from under, the Hummer had gone, and I was not able to get its license plate. I had knocked over all three bins. The bottles for recycling had spilled out and broken; the alley was covered with glass along with newspaper and cardboard containers. I had gravel burns on my arm from where I'd skidded and fallen. I staggered to my feet, picked the broken glass out of my arm, brushed myself, and ran down the alley in the direction of the car.

I had almost reached the end of the alley when I saw Joe Nakamura coming towards me, pointing his gun. He had shot me once; I did not want him to shoot me again. I stopped, my autonomic nervous system sending signals to my brain beyond my control, freezing me in my place, my hands reaching up, including the one holding the cell phone. I could feel Mike's gun beneath my jacket in the waistband of my jeans, but nothing in the lesson I'd received from Ripetti told me how to reach for it with Nakamura's gun pointing right at me. Wraparound glasses covered his eyes, but his lips were tight and cruel. The smell of sweat and fear came from me, not him. He came close, pointed the gun into my gut, and reached for the cell phone. I held onto it.

"Give it to me, or I'll kill you." A simple enough equation. I stood there pondering the choice.

"Where is she?" I said knowing she was in the Hummer close by. "I'll give it to you if you let me see her."

He stood so close I could feel his breath on my face. He too seemed to be weighing his options. Perhaps he saw someone coming to the alley with his garbage because he didn't shoot me; rather, he used the gun to clobber me on the side of my head. I staggered away from him, blinded by flashing lights. The next punch had me reeling. It was easy for him to kick me in the leg and send me tumbling. Then he was on top of me, straddling me, punching me again. He stood and stepped hard on my arm, so that my hand involuntarily opened, and the cell phone fell out. He pocketed it and ran from sight.

The man who'd been taking out his garbage came over, as had several neighbors, surrounding me, clucking, and I heard murmurs of questions and the answer "her boyfriend beat her up" and clucks of tongues and murmurs of concern, as an old man bent down and asked if I were okay.

I sat up, still woozy from the blows to my head.

"Somebody call an ambulance," I heard someone say, but if an ambulance came I'd never find that Hummer.

"It's okay; I'm okay…" My shirt and suede jacket were dirty and bloody. I wiped the snot and blood with the back of my hand, swallowed hard, and staggered out of the alley, around the corner, and back to my car.

CHAPTER 42

I got back to the Woodie, blotted up the blood as best I could, and sat for a moment, trying to catch my breath, assessing the damage. No bones appeared broken; I opened my shirt to check my incision. The stitches had held; he'd only punched me in the face. Maybe it was adrenaline, but I felt alive and alert.

Martinez had returned my cell phone the night before. I took it out and called Luke Norton. I told him that I thought Caleigh had taken video of the murderer and sent it to Julia and that the media file was still on Julia's cell phone. I put my car in gear, and pulled away from the curb, driving as I spoke, looking for the Hummer. "She knows who the killer is. That's why they've been looking for her—to get her cell phone." I told him about my encounter with Joe Nakamura, who had Julia with him. I told him about getting beaten up.

"Is Joe Nakamura the killer?"

"I don't know. We won't know until we get her phone."

"Are you okay? Do you need to get to a hospital?"

I said I'd go later. Right now, it was more important to find that Hummer with Julia in it. I told him I could drive up one street and down another, but it would be a futile search on my own. I needed the police to help me. Even so, I did just that—drive up one street and down another, checking every intersection.

"They're in a red Hummer. They just left Solano Avenue. I'm not sure which direction they're headed."

I looked down each residential street I passed. No sign of the Hummer.

"Can you put out an APB? They're somewhere in Panorama City, but they won't be for long."

"What's the license plate?"

"I don't know. It's a Hummer, and it's red."

I could hear the frustration in his voice. "Brett, I can't stop every red Hummer…"

"I can't find them myself! She's in the car with him! And now that he's used her to find the cell phone, he doesn't need her alive anymore! How many red Hummers can there be in the Valley?"

He said he'd see what he could do.

I had reached Van Nuys Boulevard, with three lanes of traffic in each direction, a divider in between. It was lined with gas stations, supermarkets, and stores selling the basics every Los Angelino needs: mufflers, transmissions, auto parts.

"There's something else I have to tell you."

I couldn't have this conversation while I was driving. My heart was pounding too hard, and my vision could not be relied upon. I crossed over into the farthest right lane, pulled into a parking space, and stopped the car, although I left the motor running.

"The reason I've been so suspicious of everybody is…three years ago… I killed someone."

I sat in my car, aware only of my racing pulse and the contraction in my chest that was never less intense no matter how many times it occurred.

"In my car, on Coldwater Canyon. I was drunk and high on cocaine. Her name was Rosa Aguilar. I kept going. Nobody ever found out."

There was stunned silence on the other end. Tears welled up in my throat, but I pushed them down. I did not deserve them, and this was not the time. I watched the light ahead turn green, but I stayed put.

"Brett, that's a felony."

"I know." I said out loud the detail that had caused me the most anguish. "She was a single mother. She had kids." I knew there could be no forgiveness for that from God, the law, or myself. "I found her daughter today. She's in foster care, in Duarte. I told her who I was. I promised her I'd turn myself in."

"Brett." His voice was kind. "Brett, I have to Mirandize you."

"I'll waive my rights." I vaguely knew I shouldn't do that, yet I couldn't see why I should be entitled to rights. Had Rosa had them? "Whatever. The point is I was driving the car that hit her before she died."

I exhaled, and it felt as if it were the breath I had been holding since that night on Coldwater.

"Where are you?"

"Van Nuys. I'm looking for that Hummer."

A red SUV sped past me, and although it wasn't the Hummer, it was similar enough to make me jump. And in that moment, as I watched it make its way towards the freeway onramp, I realized where Julia must be.

"Meet me at the lodge on the Poseidon Ranch, in Malibu. Bring a warrant. For me, yes, but also a search warrant for the ranch."

How could I have not figured it out sooner? I pulled out of the parking spot and eased my way into traffic.

"I thought they were taking Mulholland to the house on Angelo Crest. They were taking it in the other direction, towards Malibu. Poseidon didn't shoot their westerns out there in the San Gabriels; they shot in the Malibu Hills on the Poseidon Ranch. The Nussbaums use the lodge. That's where they took her."

"Brett, I had Marty Nussbaum in here all morning. I have no evidence, no reason to hold him. There's absolutely nothing linking him to Caleigh's death other than that he's her father. And that other thing that Caleigh mentioned on the tape? We don't have a shred of evidence of any kind."

"Bring a search warrant!" I shouted. "But I warn you, it might be hard to get. He's got something on everybody."

I made my way onto the freeway onramp.

"I'll come in. I promise. As soon as I find Julia."

CHAPTER *43*

If everyone in a car had been riding a chariot on the back of a tortoise, we might have made faster progress than driving the 101 freeway in rush hour. The Drunkmobile's needle hovered below 15 MPH and never rose above. I turned on the radio, tuned to talk radio, and listened to a conversation about the merger between Poseidon and Alliance that created the largest media conglomerate in the world. Pundits were weighing in on the implications of the merger while callers fulminated on one side of the issue or the other. One factoid that came out of the conversation was that the stock that Marty Nussbaum owned in Poseidon put the value of his personal stake in the merger at five billion dollars. Some research was needed to discover whether this was the largest personal payout ever or whether some of the young computer whizzes who had created the new media had equaled or bettered it. But pundits agreed that, as far as old media went, this was the jackpot.

* * *

Poseidon Ranch was a large undeveloped space in the Santa Monica Mountains which had been bought by the original Poseidon studios as a place to shoot its B Westerns. It was considered "Private Protected Open Space," which meant it could be privately owned yet protected from development.

The land had originally been inhabited by the Chumash Indians and, after that, ranchers who had used it for grazing cattle in the last century. I drove past rolling grasslands and savannas before heading up into a mountain road bordered on either side by coastal sage scrub and chaparral.

I tried to picture what I would say or how even to approach the Nussbaum ranch. I ran a few scenarios in my mind, alternating between stealth and forthright knocking at the door. I was lost in thought when I noticed the Hummer coming towards me in the opposite direction.

It sped past. Joe Nakamura was in it, but Julia was not. I hoped this meant that he had brought her to the ranch, and left her there. I had no time to think about it. He made a U-turn, and came towards me, bearing down.

I sped up, but on these deserted mountain roads, the old 40's Woodie, souped up though it might have been, was no match for the Hummer. I couldn't outrun it, and I couldn't evade it. It came towards me, its grill a menacing sneer.

In the four years I'd been on *Murder*, I'd argued forcefully against car chases. I thought they were stupid. They were expensive to shoot; they didn't advance the plot; they were just a way of taking up airtime and providing false adrenaline. They bore as little relation to reality as production numbers in a musical.

I thought of that now, as I saw the Hummer speeding towards my rear bumper with no apparent intention to slow. My tires screeched as I swerved around a corner, going faster than the Woodie was ever meant to go.

The road spiraled upward through the canyon, with no streets branching away on either side. To the left, it sloped down towards the Valley; to the right, a rugged stretch of scrub and brush was flat and dry, before rising up into the mountains. I turned my wheel sharply and drove off the road onto the rocky soil.

The Hummer turned in pursuit. I kept going as fast as I could, off-road now, bouncing along the rutted terrain, over rocks, sage scrub, and chaparral. The Woodie was built before seat belts were invented. I bounced in the seat like bric-a-brac in an earthquake. I spun the wheel, avoiding rocks, trying to avoid shrubs. For the Woodie, the terrain was treacherous. To the 4-wheel drive Hummer, it was sport. The rocks and shrubs crunched meekly beneath its wheels as it bore down on me with implacable will.

I made a U-turn and headed back towards the road. I heard a popping sound, and the sudden lurch made me realize I had blown a tire. I continued driving as quickly as I could, the car veering on three wheels, sputtering and smoking. As I lumbered towards the road, the Hummer pulled up easily alongside of me. I looked to my left and saw Joe Nakamura smiling as he pulled the trigger.

The sound of the gunshot ricocheted through the canyon, popping in my ear, its echo enveloping all other sound.

I saw a burst of light in an all-black sky, showering shards of dancing lights, crystalline facets that glinted and darted through prisms of color. *I'm dying*, I thought and felt myself floating towards a radiant white light.

I heard a loud crack and felt my head smash against something hard. Warm liquid oozed down my face. When it reached my lip, I tasted it with my tongue: blood. I tried to touch it with my finger, but my arm was pinned beneath me. I opened my eyes, and saw a twisted steering wheel and shattered glass, a ripped seat, and the sky through a smashed windshield. I was lying on my back, pressed against the passenger door, looking up at the floor of the car.

I smelled gasoline and heard a hiss. I tried to open the door I was jammed against, but it wouldn't yield. The air in the car felt hot. I lifted myself gently and was relieved to see I could move. I felt my way to the driver's side, which was up in the air.

I was pushing my shoulder against the door when the car exploded. As if shoved by a mob, I was propelled into the air. The sun was bright in the neon blue sky. Puffs of clouds formed shifting shapes that drifted towards one another, merging before floating apart in new configurations. The rolling hills rose and fell like the tide, sparkling and glistening in the warmth of the sun. I felt myself spinning in circles, tumbling in an arc as graceful as a wave. I let go, releasing all tension. Set free, abandoning hope and with it striving; all that was left was a calm sense of peace, and, yes, I would have to say, joy.

I landed with a thud on a jagged surface, nestled between a rock and a tree, at least thirty feet from the car, which was now engulfed in flame.

The heat was intense, bending the air into rubbery waves. I crouched behind the rock and watched Joe Nakamura and the driver get out of the Hummer and run towards the flame and smoke that had been the Woodie. I couldn't hear their muffled conversation, but it appeared congratulatory, a job well done, because they left the smoldering remains of the car, got back into the Hummer, and drove away.

I took a moment to catch my breath and test the arm that had been pinned, on the same side as my surgery. It moved. I slowly tried each movable part of me, and one by one, they all worked fine. My clothes were torn and dirty; my head was bleeding, as were my arms and face. I was twisted and sore but not broken.

My breath returned and with it, fear.

I fear; therefore, I am.

Miraculously, Mike's gun was still stuck in the back of my jeans.

I watched with apprehension as the car burned, a plume of black smoke spiraling into the sky. In the hot summer months, when these hills are dry and the Santa Ana winds blow in from the desert, the brush ignites easily, and flames rage through the mountains with unstoppable force.

Returning to the ruined remains of the car, I used my toe to loosen the soil. There was nothing salvageable from the car, but I wanted to keep it from doing any further damage. My jacket was torn and soiled. I used it now as a sling, scooping up as much dirt, gravel, and rock as I could, to fling over the fire to keep it from spreading. The heat was intense. I wished a car would come along I could flag down for help, but none did.

When I had extinguished the last of the embers, I looked around to get my bearings. The road cut north south through the folded mountains, following the path of an ancient canyon, through rocks of buff colored sandstone. If I was to get to the lodge, I'd do well to follow it. I tied the remains of my suede jacket around my waist, and set out on rubbery legs.

CHAPTER 44

Now, my obsession was not for whiskey but for water. This need was beyond compulsion; it was survival. I licked the sweat off my arm; it only made me thirstier.

I don't know how long I'd been trudging when I saw a road turn off to the right. A wooden sign by its side said "Private Road."

Was this the turn-off to the Poseidon Lodge? I couldn't be sure. In any case, it would lead to a house, which meant water.

The landscape changed. I had been trudging uphill. Now the private road went down into a dell that became greener and lusher, signaling the presence of water nearby. I began to pass scrub oaks and cottonwood, and even willow trees, as the road descended into a glen of green.

I tried to smell for dampness and listen for sounds of water. I heard the breeze, the birds, and the sound of my own footsteps, and eventually, what sounded like a running stream.

I said a prayer of thanks and made my way to it, maneuvering over the rocks that lay on its banks. Squatting by the stream, I scooped water into my hands, splashing it on my neck and face then slurping it into my mouth in greedy gulps.

But I didn't want to be stuck here once night fell, and I couldn't count on daylight to last much longer. I made my way back to the private road.

I must have walked half a mile before I finally saw a thick iron gate that blocked the road from further entry. A red LED light indicated video surveillance, so I didn't approach the gate but left the road and went deep into the woods to the side, windmilling my way through a bramble of shrubs and bushes that scratched my arms and face as I cut through them. I approached the gate from way off to the side and saw that it attached to an electronic wire fence that extended past the road on either side. On the western side, the fence continued as far as I could see, through a vast savannah dotted with sycamore and clusters of small oak trees, which sloped gently down towards the ocean. So I followed the perimeter on the other, more heavily wooded side, looking for a possible opening. The dell eventually sloped upwards, rising into a mountain, and the gate rose with it into chaparral that was taller than me and too dense to penetrate. I pushed my way through anyway. The bracken tore at my exposed skin but hid me from view, and eventually, I saw the gate end at a place where the mountain rose into the steep face of an almost vertical cliff.

There was no path to follow, but there was nowhere to go but up. The woods were dense, rising from rocky soil. My sneakers were not made for this terrain. I took each step gingerly, testing each rock I landed on for stability before shifting my weight to it. With each footfall, I heard rocks fall below. I made my way slowly, using hands and feet.

I was thirsty again,; parched. The sun was lowering in the sky, and the air turned chilly. I tried putting my jacket on, but it was little more than ribbons. And as I looked up at the cliff with its sharp outcropping of stone, I thought I'd be better off without it, and retied it around my waist. As I grabbed hold of a rock, I felt my toe slip; the ridge I was standing on gave way, and I heard the rock tumbling below me. I gently felt for another rock to stand on and flattened myself against the granite, taking a few breaths. My hands and face were raw and scraped; my sweat mingled with blood. I licked it, hoping it would hydrate me. I shimmied up the precipice towards the next hold of hand and foot, and as I did, my jacket got torn away, and I watched it fall: the last remaining vestige of my former success, lost, not worth chasing. Mike's gun was still in the back of my jeans.

I found comfort in the sight of the bushes and shrubs that rose from the mountain with no visible soil. If a tree could grow out of a rock, perhaps there was hope for me.

When I thought back to all that had happened, I shuddered with regret and despair. When I looked forward to what lay ahead, I knew I wouldn't survive. But when I asked myself, "Are you dead yet?" No. "Are you okay right now?" Yes.

Then I'd think back or ahead, and I'd have to go through the ritual over again.

I zigzagged along an indentation that might have been a trail a hundred years ago, pausing often to catch my breath. The sweat on my skin evaporated, and I grew cold. Night would fall soon; I had to hurry.

The moon rose, pale at first, then brighter by contrast as the sky grew dark. I climbed as long as there was light, but when night fell I knew that, hungry and thirsty though I was, it was too dangerous to go on.

I leaned against a boulder, ignoring the creeping things I knew must share my shelter.

The night was dark but not silent. The wind rushed through the trees sounding like waves. I heard twigs break as unseen creatures did whatever it is they do to survive in the wild. I thought of water every moment. Where did my fellow creatures drink? A bird called, and in the distance, a coyote howled.

I was exhausted. I had barely slept in two days. I fell instantly into a deep sleep.

* * *

My eyes opened with the first light of the sun, coming over the mountain behind me. My body ached from sleeping on rocks. I stretched, blinked, and tried again to get my bearings.

My throat was cotton, my tongue swollen. I thought I heard traffic. I listened closely, disbelieving my ears. But there it was—a rising and falling whoosh and rush that sounded like cars on the freeway.

Scrambling over the rocks I'd lain against, I reached a ridge that looked down on a lush landscape of trees and plants that bordered the banks of a rushing stream. I had fallen asleep not thirty feet from water. What had sounded like traffic was the wind rippling through the leaves.

Sweet water tumbled down from the same mountaintop I had just crossed. The sun had risen over the mountain, and the stream glinted in the sunlight.

I clambered down and fell to my knees beside the stream, scooping up water into my mouth. As if the water became the blood in my veins, my body came back to life, revived, like a stalled engine receiving fuel. I splashed water on my neck, my face, then went back to sit on a rock by the stream.

The sun was warm. Its pale early light was reflected in a shimmying corridor of pink in the rippling stream. The column expanded with the rising sun, undulating in gentle rhythm. The trees made a rustling sound in the breeze, but otherwise, the air was still. There was an occasional coo of mourning doves. Each breath filled my arms and legs with the tingling feeling of being alive.

As I inhaled, the breeze became a part of me, moving the blood through my veins, expanding my chest and lungs. As I exhaled, my breath became the breeze that rippled the stream and swayed the trees.

In that moment, there was no difference between me and the world around me. The rhythmic dance contained us all, no boundaries or separation. I knew why I hadn't been killed either time I'd been shot. There was something I had to do, and I hadn't done it yet. And if I died trying, it didn't matter because I am a part of this beauty, and I will go on regardless.

CHAPTER 45

I decided to follow the path of the stream, thinking I would be less likely to get lost that way. I hopped from rock to rock, lighter of step and heart, now that I'd had a good night's sleep.

I felt excited, as I often did as I was coming to the last act. I still couldn't see it all clearly, but a shape was forming.

Suddenly I felt an unaccountable tugging in my stomach, like sadness or remorse. It was like being caught in a net; the harder I tried to ignore it, the more tightly I was bound. It was such a contrast to the excitement and confidence I'd felt a moment before that I sat on a rock to try to deconstruct it.

It was like a memory but without content. Just a feeling. Haunted, desolate. So familiar. Why now?

The stream tumbled over rocks whose colors glinted beneath the rushing water. The banks were lined with trees with a rich understory of fern; the sky clear and blue beyond a lattice of green. A salamander trundled from the pebbles. A school of fish darted in the current, their silver sides sparkling. Bigger than fish you'd expect to find in here, fish as big as trout or bass. Like the ones Marty put in his artificially stocked trout stream.

Oh, Jesus, this is where I fucked that guy on the company retreat!

It had been night, and this was day, but I recognized this part of the stream that tumbled over a small waterfall, the rock outcropping at a certain bend, the willow trees, the rye grass.

The details were dim; they did not include his name, nor anything about him, save that we'd met at the bar and recognized each other as fellow renegades. But I remember lying with him here. That is, I remember coming out of a blackout, finding myself on the bank of this stream, pants down, shirt up, arms and legs wrapped around a stranger, too far gone to stop. The sour taste of drunken kiss and tongue, the spinning vision, lurching stomach; passion fueled by desire, but also by hatred for Jonathan, Lynda, and myself. Then sinking back into blackout, the kind that lets you function but obliterates what you do from memory.

For the first time, I was glad I didn't drink. Up until then, I'd never been able to think about alcohol without grieving its loss. Now I was grateful for sobriety because it meant I never had to do that again. For twelve days, I hadn't thrown up or fucked a stranger, and each morning I remembered what I'd done the night before. Sleeping with Ripetti might not have been the smartest choice, but at least it was a choice, entered into with awareness.

It took a moment for the true meaning of the memory to sink in: I had been here before. I was on the grounds of the Poseidon Lodge. I had managed to evade the surveillance and make my way over the mountain through the back way.

I knew how to get to the lodge from here.

* * *

I walked carefully, watching the ground to avoid stepping on twigs that might snap, or stones that might tumble and make noise.

Something silver glinted in the sunlight, just off the trail; something I might not have noticed had I not been trying to step so carefully. It had fallen behind a stone, and was half-buried in an accumulation of dead leaves and mud.

A silver card case.

The caked and soiled business cards belonged to Patrick Caiman. He had been here.

Well, of course, Patrick could have been to the ranch many times; he used to work for Poseidon.

But these had his Red Hat information, not Poseidon's. And although the case was slightly tarnished and showed the wear of being out in the elements for a while, it was still recognizable as good silver. It hadn't been here long.

It was evidence. What should I do with it? I had already handled and disturbed it.

I pocketed the case. Feeling for the gun, I practiced releasing the safety, to make sure I remembered how, then locked it back. I stuck it in the front of my jeans. Without my jacket to conceal it, I might as well keep it where I could reach it more easily.

My eye was caught again, by a glint of color, not far from the spot where I'd found the card case. It was a tiny shred of wool, lime green. Just like the cashmere sweater Caleigh was wearing before she was killed.

* * *

The trail led to a clearing, high on a hilltop, with a panoramic view of the Pacific Ocean, where the Poseidon Ranch sprawled. The property consisted of a main house and several outlying buildings. The grounds were lavishly landscaped, with a wide and colorful variety of plants, pruned and shaped and meticulously cared for. Bougainvillea ran up trellises on the main house, a huge Spanish hacienda built in U-shaped mission style around a courtyard. Except this was a mission on steroids: it was as large as a hotel. The mid-section of the U was three stories tall; this was where the guest rooms were. I knew because I had stayed in one with Jonathan. The two ends of the U were two-stories each; these were the private quarters where the Nussbaums lived.

The outlying buildings were home to the groundskeepers, housekeepers, and maintenance people who kept the house running and ready for the Nussbaums whenever they decided to come.

There was an Olympic-size pool and a pool house that for most families would be considered a nice sized home. Of course there were tennis courts.

It was still early morning; no sign of activity. Quiet and still, the occasional plaintive coo of mourning doves was the only sound. A rich aroma of lilac and jasmine perfumed the air.

If Julia was alive, she was here; I was sure of it. I just didn't know where or how I would find her. Or, more importantly, how I would get her away.

One of the legs of the U was the private wing, the bedrooms on the second floor. How to get up there?

I cased the house, keeping hidden in the foliage.

A staircase in the back led to a small landing and door. This had to be a fire exit. I closed my eyes and tried to recreate what the lodge looked like on the inside. Were there fire exits? Of course there would have to be in a structure this size in an area so vulnerable to fire.

The back of the house appeared deserted. I took a deep breath, checked to see if anybody was watching, and made a quiet—I hoped—dash for the back staircase. I climbed the stairs, which led to a landing. I tried the door. It was locked.

Some of the rooms had private balconies. But each was discrete and separate, none of them connected, either to each other or to the landing I was on.

The overhang of the roof jutted out about three feet above my head; I couldn't reach it. At first. Then I crouched down and sprung up as high as I could and managed to catch the edge of the roof in one, then the other, hand. I dangled, wishing that I had spent less time gazing at the ocean contemplating suicide and more time at the gym doing lat pulls and chin-ups. It took all my strength, but I scrambled onto the roof.

It was flat. I crawled along on my belly to the edge of the roof on the side of the building I believed housed the private wing.

I looked down on what I thought must be the master suite. It had a large balcony and commanded a view of the ocean from the Channel Islands to Palos Verdes and out to a seemingly infinite expanse of glittering blue and white that ended only at the orange-brown stripe at the line of the horizon.

I counted the balconies and made a rough calculation as to which would be the right one. I took a chance, said a prayer, and lowered myself towards it, staying to the side of the sliding glass door. I dropped to my feet as gently as I could but heard with dismay the small thud my feet made at impact. I pressed myself against the wall and waited, holding my breath. Nobody came outside to check. I tiptoed silently towards the door and looked in. I had hoped to land outside Caleigh's room. I had guessed wrong. I had landed outside Erika's.

She was dressed in a nightgown but was not in bed; rather, she was pacing up and down and drinking from a crystal glass. A silk peignoir revealed the outlines of her bony shoulders and stick-thin arms. Her hair was askew and wild, but she wore make-up. The veins in her neck stood out like ropes from her tight, tense jaw. She downed one drink and went to the dresser and poured herself another from an open bottle on top of the dresser.

Her husband came in, wearing pajamas. The windows faced the ocean and were open to the breeze, which billowed the curtains making it possible to hear their conversation

"She's asleep."

"Shouldn't you be with her? Tucking her in, telling her bedtime stories? You're so good at it, and you get so much out of it." Her voice dripped with contempt; she all but spit the words.

He sat down heavily on the bed. "I told you. It wasn't like that. You always saw what wasn't there."

"I saw the way she looked at you. Always trying to please you, competing with me, trying to show you who loved you the most. Well, she loved you so much she was going to cost you five billion dollars."

"I don't believe that."

"No. You saw it with your own eyes, heard it with your own ears, and you still don't believe it. Well, she can't do that now. One more time I've protected you. And one more time, I get no thanks." The sound she made was intended as a laugh, but it was mirthless. "Don't worry, I'm used to it."

She went to pour another drink from the bottle, but it was almost empty, and the drink she poured was the last of it. She shook out the last drops, frowning as if it were just one more thing in her life that had let her down.

I crept along the balcony and looked inside the windows of the next room I came to, but these curtains billowed into an empty bedroom with a bed that had not been slept in. I didn't find the room I was looking for until I had rounded the corner and reached another wing of the house.

Caleigh's room had been done in a western motif but decorated for a young girl. It had a wrought iron bedstead, with large pillows with ruffled shams, and a hand-made quilt folded over the foot rails; the bed was covered with a duvet of white muslin. On the floor was a hand hooked throw rug with a rose design, the bed stands were wood, with a vase of pewter holding freshly picked flowers.

A young woman lay in the bed on her side facing the window, her dark wavy hair spread over the pillow and partly spilling over her eyes. Long lashes lined the lids that covered her eyes; her complexion was pallid and sallow. Even in sleep, her features had settled into an expression of despair, devoid even of the hope of hope.

Julia. At last. The most beautiful sight I'd ever seen.

The window was open. Before I could climb in, Erika came into the room and sat on the side of the bed, silently watching her sleep.

Erika brushed the hair gently from Julia's face. Julia stirred; her eyes opened, and she recoiled at Erika's touch.

"Has anybody told you how much you look like your mother?"

Julia froze, not answering.

"Please don't be scared. I'm sorry for the way we brought you here. I'm sure it frightened you. I wish we could have done it differently. But we needed to find you to talk to you, and we didn't know how else to do it. You did a good job of hiding. You were hard to find."

Julia said nothing, but her fear was palpable.

"Nobody here is going to hurt you. I just wanted to talk to you. You didn't come to the funeral, and I had to see you. You see, before

Caleigh died, she told me that she had something to tell me. And then she…died. I never found out what it was. You and she were so close. I was hoping maybe you knew what it was that Caleigh wanted to tell me."

Julia remained silent, trembling with fright.

"After your child dies, you're haunted by all the things you might have said and didn't, all the things you wish you'd told her and hadn't…I've been going over and over in my mind all the times I know she was trying to talk to me, and I was too busy or too distracted…too focused on Caleigh's father to take the time to talk to my own daughter. And now she's gone. You're the closest thing I have to her. I thought if I could talk to you, I might be able to get some closure. Such a stupid word. As if losing a child weren't something that will haunt your days and nights for the rest of your life. Still…I was wondering…do you know what it was she was going to tell me?"

Erika looked to Julia, hungry for the words she might say, but Julia had no words for her.

"Darling, you must trust me. I won't hurt you."

"Please. I just want to go home."

"Of course. I just need to make sure that when you get home you don't spread the same lies that Caleigh was spreading. You knew she was sleeping with Patrick Caiman, didn't you?"

"Yes." It was barely a whisper.

"And that her father found out about it? And threatened to kill Patrick if he came near her again?"

Julia looked frantically towards the door, seeking escape.

"Did she tell you how afraid she was of her father and his temper?" Julia cringed, as if afraid of being hit. "Caleigh's father has a violent temper. All through my marriage, I've been one step behind him, cleaning up after him, protecting him from himself. But now…I'm sorry, I just can't." She buried her head in her hands. "He's gone too far. I can't cover for my husband when he killed his own daughter."

Julia got up out of bed. Erika grabbed her by the wrist and held her. "You know that's what happened, don't you. That Marty killed Patrick for taking Caleigh away from him. And he didn't realize that Caleigh was in the room and saw him, and so then he had to kill her too."

Julia pulled herself away and ran to the door. Marty blocked her exit.

"That's what happened! Tell him! Tell him you know he killed his own daughter."

Marty pushed Julia aside as he came towards Erika.

"Goddamn it, you are not going to pin this on me."

Erika lunged for Julia. "Tell him! Tell him you know what he did. That everybody knows what he did. That he'll go to jail for the rest of his life, that he'll get the death penalty for what he did." Erika held Julia in front of her, shaking her as if she were one of her dolls. "Tell him!"

Julia wrested herself free.

"He didn't do it! You did!"

Marty and Erika both stopped. "I saw you. Caleigh took a video while it was happening and sent it to me. It was you! Not him, you!"

Erika slapped Julia hard across her face then grabbed her by the wrist, yelling, "Joe!"

I came in the window holding my gun.

"Let her go."

They all turned to me. Erika, in her surprise, let go of her grip on Julia. In Julia's look, I saw gratitude, relief, and love.

I pointed the gun at Erika. "Come on, Julia, let's go. We're leaving."

"*Joe!*" yelled Erika, and I heard footsteps clattering up the stairs. In an instant, Joe Nakamura was in the room, training his gun on Julia and me.

"Give me that." He reached his hand for my gun. I did not surrender it, rather kept it pointed at him, using both hands.

"I'm taking her home."

I shepherded Julia towards the door, keeping Marty, Erika, and Joe Nakamura in range.

"Kill me if you want, but there'll be a lot of explaining to do. If you shoot me, my blood will be all over the room. And if you strangle me, like you did Patrick and Caleigh, Julia will be a witness—and if you kill her there'll be more explaining than even you can put a spin on."

I turned so that I was walking backwards, keeping them in range.

"Come on, sweetie, I'm taking you home."

I corralled Julia out of the bedroom and hurried us down the hall towards the large stairway that led to the main foyer.

We were halfway down the stairs when Marty came after us.

"Get back here, both of you."

Julia went rigid at the sound of his voice. I kept us both moving.

"I said, bring her back."

I placed myself between him and Julia, training the gun at his belly.

"I'm taking her home. And I'll shoot you if you try to stop me."

I unlocked the safety; we could all hear the click. How I'd love to shoot him for what he did to Jinx Magruder. But that wasn't why I was here.

"Don't be stupid," Marty said. "Of course Julia will go back to her real parents. That's in everybody's interests. There are just a few things we need to get straight first."

Erika came out of the bedroom, followed by Joe Nakamura, who pointed his gun at me. I pivoted slightly, so my gun was now pointing at him, instead of Marty. He came close. My finger trembled on the trigger, itching to shoot the man who shot me. My eagerness must have shown in my face because he stopped short. Marty continued.

"Put that gun away. I'm sure there are things we can all agree on."

"You mean get our stories straight," muttered Julia.

Marty looked past me. A small smile flitted across his lips. I turned my head; Ripetti was at the foot of the stairs.

He wore his gun, but it was holstered. Still, guns were pointed at me, held by the two men flanking him, the same security men in black suits who had escorted me out of Gerry's.

"That's right, Brett," said Ripetti, the little half-smile at the edge of his mouth. "Surely you, of all people, know the value of keeping quiet about an accidental death. You know that not every murder needs to be reported. Perhaps 'murder' is too strong a word. 'Vehicular manslaughter' is more accurate in your case. But the prison time feels the same."

He reached for my gun, confident that I would surrender it. I did not.

"I've already told the police. I'm turning myself in. Just as soon as I get Julia back to her dad."

I continued to walk her downstairs. I had no plan. I didn't know how I was going to get her out of there. And once out, I didn't know how I'd get her back home. But I had gotten this far one breath at a time, and that's how I had to take it now: one step, one breath at a time.

It wasn't until I had reached the bottom of the stairs that, in a coordinated movement, Ripetti, his henchmen, and Joe acted in concert. Before I could react, the two henchmen grabbed me, wrenching my arm backwards, forcing the gun out of my hand. Joe took Julia, and Ripetti grabbed me away from the henchman, holding my own gun to my head.

"Mike's gun," he said. "Just what you'd use to kill yourself." I could feel its barrel cold against my temple. "You're so brave. And so stupid. Don't you know we can kill you, and nobody will even notice? You're a loser and a fuck-up. You mean nothing to anybody. You won't even get an obit in the trades."

It's one thing to say those things to yourself. It's another to hear someone else say them. I shoved him in the stomach with my elbow. He gasped, and I struggled out of his grip. He took aim, but I ducked, whirled around and kicked the gun out of his hand before he could shoot. He grabbed me by the shirt and hit me. I went reeling. .I scurried on the floor towards the gun, but one of the security men stomped on my hand as I reached for it. The pain was blinding. In spite of myself, I doubled over in a fetal position on the floor, holding the hand which must have broken bones.

Joe had handed Julia over to the other henchman, who held her while Joe trained his gun on me. I heard the blast of his gun, but one more time, he missed me. I had scurried over to the henchman holding Julia. I bit his leg as hard as I could. He cried out and released her in surprise. I grabbed her arm with my other hand, and bolted for the door.

We ran outside. I didn't need to look back to know that the men were coming after us. Marty rushed outside shouting to me to come back, and I heard the clatter of Erika's mules, following behind the men. I kept Julia in front of me, blocking her from the guns I knew were pointed at us, but she stumbled, terrified, crying. I pushed us both forward. The Hummer sat in the circular driveway in front of the house; I thought if we reached it, we could gain cover if not a means of escape. But Julia hung back out of fear. I dragged her by the hand.

"Stop it. Right there."

The command was given by a voice used to being obeyed. Erika tottered out on her mules, holding Joe Nakamura's gun in both hands. I recognized the look in her eyes, the insane determination of the addict on a mission. I had seen it in my mother's all my life—and in my own. My mother had never killed anyone. Erika—and I—had.

Suddenly, improbably, I felt a rush of love for my mother! Every time I'd seen Erica, I'd seen my mother, and my projection had blinded me to the truth. My mother was a drunk, just like me. An inadequate mother, due to her addiction. Just like me. But she had never pointed a gun at me, as Erika was now. And she had not certainly not killed me, as Erika had Caleigh.

I decided to call her, if I ever got out of this alive.

Erika took aim and, steely-eyed, fired.

I dove in front of Julia, knocking her to the ground and covering her with my body. I don't know how long I lay there, listening to us both breathe. The gurgling sound of blood filling the airway passages came not from me, but from the man lying in front of us, dying in a pool of his own blood. Marty twisted his head to look in shock and betrayal at the woman who'd shot him in the back. I followed his gaze to see Erika slowly lower her gun and walk back into the house.

I did not move. Ripetti, Joe, and the henchmen were still walking towards Julia and me, guns drawn. I heard another fusillade of gunfire. Then silence.

The next voice was kind and caring. "Brett. Are you all right?"

I looked up into the deep brown eyes of Detective Luke Norton, kneeling beside me.

I climbed off Julia and sat up. Police were swarming over the grounds.

Ripetti was sprawled, crumpled and contorted, lying in a pool of blood. He looked up at me. His mouth twitched slightly, as if trying to smile.

"You…beat me…" he said. "…don't let that get around…"

It was the last thing he said before he died.

Luke Norton helped me to stand, and I did the same for Julia.

"You were right about how hard it was to get a warrant. Otherwise we would have been here yesterday," Luke said. "When nobody would let us in, we came over the fence. Looks like we made it just in time."

He began the process of organizing yet another crime scene, calling the coroner's office and the forensic technicians. My right hand was useless, but now I didn't need it. The police began taking the statements of everyone there. Suddenly, Erika emerged from the house, still in peignoir and negligee, holding, not a gun, but one of her dolls.

"What seems to be the matter?" She gave Luke Norton her eerie hostess smile.

Norton seemed flustered. "We came with a warrant," he said. "Brett and Julia were being shot at by these men."

Erika didn't seem to hear him. She wafted past him, the baby doll in her arms.

"Caleigh?" she said to Julia. "Come back in the house, sweetheart. It's all right now. He'll never hurt you again. I promise."

Erika surveyed the bloody landscape with eyes that were cloudy and glazed, as if lost in another world. She looked insane. I think that was the point. All these witnesses had seen her pull the trigger; she was already planning her defense.

She looked at me strangely, evidently trying to remember who I was. But then there was a slight lifting of the fog, and the smile returned. "Ah, yes. Did you ever find Julia?"

"Yes. She was with you."

"I'm so glad," she said. She turned to the doll in her arms.

"You see?" she cooed softly. "Nothing to be afraid of. It's all going to be all right. Mommy's here to protect you. You're perfectly safe."

She drifted back towards the house and paused at the doorway.

I was sure that what she did next was purposeful, in case any of us were required to testify at a competency hearing. She undid her wrapper and lowered the shoulder of her nightgown. She put the doll to her breast and the nipple into its little bud mouth. Then, with a look of serenity on her face, she glided into the house.

CHAPTER 46

Later, when Luke Norton read me my rights, I realized I should get a lawyer, even though I was not backing out of my confession. I pled guilty to vehicular homicide while under the influence of a controlled substance and leaving the scene of the accident. I hid nothing, presented no extenuating circumstances. At my attorney's urging, I presented evidence of my sobriety and the service I had performed to the community by helping to solve Caleigh's murder. As this was my first offense, the judge had a lot of leeway. I could get anything from a suspended sentence to fifteen years.

I was out on bail until the sentencing hearing.

As it turned out, Julia's cell phone wasn't needed. Not only was Caleigh's video stored on an external server somewhere; Marty, in addition to doing surveillance on his enemies, had also been recording himself. He had wired his offices to capture his business dealings, of which Erika was unaware. She invited Patrick out to the ranch to talk to her, and it was on this surveillance video that she could be seen, admitting that not only had Marty killed Stacey Donovan in the course of a prolonged period of rape and sex games, he had also come to Erika afterwards, a quivering mass of terror, and she was the one who had orchestrated disposing of the body. It was she who suggested taking Stacey's locket, so the evidence could be planted where it would do the most good. She admitted this to Patrick so he could see how effective she could be at getting done what needed to be done. She apologized for the inconvenience it had caused him, but there was really no permanent harm. Once he transferred ownership of *Space Wizards* to Poseidon, he would share equally in this payoff, which would be far larger. Patrick refused. He'd been waiting too long to get this revenge. Now that he knew Marty killed Stacey Donovan, he would get the truth out even if it meant he would never make a dime. Erika showed Patrick a contract she'd had drawn for his rights to *Space Wizards*, and urged him to sign it. Patrick was adamant. She called in Joe Nakamura to help convince him. Joe slipped a cord around Patrick's throat, increasing the pressure until Patrick finally signed each and every copy. Joe killed him anyway. Erika hadn't realized it, but Caleigh had come in and recorded it all on her cell phone. When we saw the video she sent to Julia, we saw Erika looking up in surprise, realizing that her daughter was there, seeing the phone, and ordering Joe to strangle Caleigh too. Joe hesitated, not believing that Erika could possibly want him to kill her own daughter. Erika insisted. Caleigh filmed it all. The last thing we saw was Erika grabbing the garrote out of Joe's hand and coming towards her daughter. At that point, the screen went blank.

Erika claimed temporary insanity. Her attorneys claimed that the shock of finding out about her husband's crime had sent her into a fugue state during which she remembered nothing of what she'd done. Even when confronted with the proof on video, she maintained that she had neither ordered Joe to kill Patrick nor killed her own daughter. An alternate self, born of trauma, had taken possession and done these acts for which she could not be held responsible. At first, she claimed she had shot Marty by accident. When her security people had alerted her there was an intruder on the premises, she shot wildly in an attempt to defend her home and hit her husband by mistake. But when she became aware that this was no bar against inheriting, she changed her story, including his death too in her insanity defense.

There were legal precedents on both sides of whether or not Erika could inherit money from a spouse she had killed. On one side was a legal maxim that no one should be allowed to profit from his own wrongdoing. On the other was a finding that a person who was mentally ill at the time of the killing may still inherit. It was this side that would prevail. Erika had five billion dollars at her disposal to make it prevail. Eventually, she would make a plea bargain to negligent homicide in the case of her husband, insanity in the case of her daughter, and would be sentenced to serve time in a psychiatric facility until such time as she was deemed cured.

* * *

"There was something I never could figure out before." Detective Luke Norton forked some Pad Thai into his mouth. He had called me and said he had some "unofficial" information that he thought I'd like to know, and we'd arranged to meet at a restaurant near the station. "When your friend Mike Drummond set up that meeting with Campbell McCauley and Desiree, he hadn't gotten the video yet; it was still in the camera in the clock. And yet, he already knew enough about Campbell McCauley to use against him. How'd he get it?"

I waited for the answer, but Norton offered me some spring rolls, enjoying my curiosity.

"We found it all on an external hard drive in the glove compartment of that crazy car of his. Not the one you took, the other one, the one he drove. What is it, an old Mercury?"

"In his Woodie?"

"Yeah. How does he get around in that thing?"

"That's what he was trying to tell me," I said. "After he was shot. I couldn't make out what he was saying. He was trying to tell me to look in the Woodie." One more time, Mike had been trying to help me, and I was too caught up in my own wreckage to understand.

"You were right about Marty Nussbaum having something on everybody. Nic Ripetti got it for him—surveillance, wiretaps, even stealing notes and memos from offices and trash. Somehow, Mike got copies of it all and hid it on an external drive in his car. How did he get it, do you know?"

I thought back to the night I'd overheard Susanna Terrell saying to Mike, "What if he finds out it's you? He'll kill you." One more thing I'd misread.

"Maybe from Marty Nussbaum's assistant," I suggested.

"Anyway, however he got it, he'd read the notes that Ripetti had stolen from Campbell McCauley's therapist's office. Wait 'til you hear this: Campbell McCauley knew about Marty Nussbaum and Stacey Donovan. Seems he went to that house on Mulholland with a call girl on the day that Stacey Donovan disappeared, and they both saw Nussbaum there with Donovan—this was eight hours after the poor girl had disappeared. She'd been with Nussbaum at that house all day. McCauley and the prostitute, whose name was Joanie Jones, gave statements to the cops at the time, blowing Nussbaum's alibi. But then, mysteriously, Joanie Jones OD'd, their statements disappeared, and one of the cops lost his job over it."

"Mike."

"Seems Drummond was dumb enough to use cocaine with a material witness. It was laced with something, and she died. She and McCauley were the only witnesses, and McCauley knew better than to say anything about it, and it gave him his career. But he was terrified of Nussbaum and talked about it to his shrink."

"How did the locket get found on Patrick Caiman?"

"Don't know for sure, but my guess is Ripetti planted it. He and Drummond were both offered jobs with Nussbaum, but Ripetti was the only one who went for it. Moonlighting while he was still on the force, and then full time when he left. Mike thought it was Ripetti who made the statements disappear, but he made it look like Mike had done it, and Mike lost his job. It was in his notes on his thumb drive. Of course, nobody had to twist his arm to use blow with a witness."

I understood finally the root of the animosity between Mike and Ripetti; one more thing I'd read wrong.

"Marty had something on you, too," said Luke helping himself to seconds. "He used Ripetti to keep everyone under surveillance, gathering dirt to use as a bargaining edge. Ripetti hadn't seen the accident, but I guess you were acting so erratic afterwards he began following you and managed to put two and two together. He had a copy of the receipt for the bodywork you'd had done on your car. Kept quiet about it, just waiting for the best time to use it."

So I wasn't paranoid after all. Just completely twisted when it came to picking men. I was eager to finish the lunch with Norton so I could get to the hospital to see Mike. He was dozing when I got there. He had a tube running from his midline and IV fluids flowing into his arm.

"It's amazing the lengths some people go to get drugs," I said.

He opened his eyes and smiled. I sat on the chair near his bed and pulled it close to him.

"How're you doing?"

His eyes, usually so clear, were cloudy; his smile was hazy. "Nurses round the clock, Demerol in the vein. How bad can it be?"

"Don't get used to it."

He drifted back to sleep for a moment before jerking awake and taking me in.

"You? How are you?"

"Twenty-three days."

His face took on that look of pleasure that AA's took in each other's sobriety.

"Good girl."

I showed him my cast, and told him I'd had to take two pain pills before it was set, but none since, and no longer needed them. He nodded approvingly.

"I've asked Boots to be my sponsor. You were right about needing to work with a woman. I'm reading her my inventory this weekend." I paused. "You're in it."

"Me?"

"I was wrong about you so often. I just didn't understand. I had too many secrets."

"We all do. That's why we need each other. We understand each other the way other people don't."

"Yes, but…I owe you so much."

"Pass it on. That's how it works…"

"No, but…" There was so much I wanted to tell him, but I

barely knew what it was and knew it would take a long time to find out. So much of what I thought I knew was wrong. I'd asked Boots to be my sponsor because I wanted my relationship with Mike to be free to go in any direction. How, when, or what, I couldn't say; I was on my way to prison, after all. I could promise nothing yet could not deny what I felt for him. If I had to give it a word, I'd pick love. But for the moment, it was better to leave our relationship undefined.

I was in no hurry to leave. I pulled my chair closer and sat by his side, keeping him company while he slept.

When the doctor came in to check on him, Mike woke up. The doctor said he'd need another surgery; a bullet fragment had nicked his thoracic duct, and there'd been some leakage. But, barring unforeseen complications, they were predicting a good outcome, though a long period of rehabilitation lay ahead.

"What about pain medication?" I asked. "After the surgery. Will he need to take it?"

The doctor seemed surprised by the question.

"She's worried about me," said Mike. "I'm a drug addict. Clean, now. She's worried I'll get re-addicted."

The doctor frowned. "You'll need something for pain management."

"It'll be okay," I said. "If he sends you home with anything, just call me every four hours before you take it."

I squeezed his hand.

* * *

When news of the wiretaps and surveillance came out, all of Hollywood was on edge about what private information might be thrust into public view. Marty Nussbaum did, in fact, have something on everyone. As the details began to seep out, the town absorbed and adjusted to what became known. The targets of the wiretaps had basically wanted sex, money, and advantage, and all they had done were in those pursuits. Everyone could understand. Before long, people who had not been wiretapped began to plant stories inferring that they had so as not to appear unimportant.

Marty's death left a hole at the helm of the newly merged Alliance/Poseidon, and Jonathan was appointed CEO. Erika's temporary incarceration left a vacancy on the boards she'd sat on, and Lynda graciously took her place.

* * *

While I was awaiting sentencing, I arranged through the court to meet with the family of the woman I had killed. I made it clear that in no way was this a substitute for punishment. I simply needed to talk to them, to tell them personally how sorry I was for what I had done.

They refused. If I wanted forgiveness, I would have to look elsewhere. I asked my lawyer to communicate to them my need to make amends. They would be doing me a favor if they would let me help them in any way.

My lawyer returned with a message from Yolanda. She wanted to enroll in a chef's academy when she graduated from high school. She didn't want to clean other people's houses like her mother had, and she knew she had a talent for cooking. With proper training, she could make a good living as a chef and caterer. Her mother had been working two jobs to save for the tuition: forty thousand for a two-year program. Would I help pay for it?

I gulped. I had no money and was already in debt. My high earning days in the TV business were over. I was headed for prison, where my earnings would be next to nothing. I did not know how I could possibly come up with forty thousand dollars.

But I hadn't known how I would find Julia. I hadn't known who had killed Caleigh. I hadn't known how I could possibly live without drugs and alcohol.

I instructed my lawyer to tell her she could count on me.

For a start I wrote and sold a three-part article about all that had happened. Just as I turned it in, the magazine was sold to a subsidiary of the Alliance/Poseidon Corporation, or APC, and the new editor killed the story. Nonetheless, they were contractually obligated to pay me, and it gave me enough start paying Yolanda's tuition.

Then Jonathan offered to option the article. He thought my experience finding Julia and solving Caleigh's murder might make a good series, particularly if I transposed it to a different milieu, say Silicon Valley. He said you couldn't sell stories about the entertainment industry. Also, he was wary of implicating Poseidon or its new corporate parent, Alliance, whose interests he now had to protect. The Caleigh story could be the pilot.

At first, I wanted to say no. I'd had enough of "the industry." It paid well, but for me, it seemed to take more than it gave. But then I realized the money could go to my amends to Yolanda, and I agreed. I'd sell the source material, and someone else could write the pilot and run the show. I knew I never wanted to work in television again. And besides, I was facing time.

I was sentenced to two-to-five years in prison, with eligibility for parole after one. I was taken directly from the sentencing hearing in handcuffs. I surrendered my belongings, was strip-searched, given an orange jump suit, and taken to a crowded cinderblock holding cell where I waited with the other women who would also be taken to prison.

At two in the morning, they woke us up and told us we were being transported. They took us to another cinderblock room and lined us up facing the wall. They attached us together in a long chain, a belt around each of our waists, with handcuffs coming out of the belt. Then they attached us to each other in chains around our ankles. Then they disappeared to do paperwork. I had completely lost control over my life.

CHAPTER 47

There is nothing like being cuffed and shackled to a chain of other prisoners to really make you take a hard look at your life. After four hours, we were taken to a white van with windows covered in mesh, blacked out so that we could see out, but no one could see in. As they took us along the road running parallel to the railroad tracks towards Fontana, I looked out at people driving, alone or with others, listening to the radio, stopping at fast food restaurants, going about the business of their ordinary lives and knew that it would be years before I tasted such freedoms again. I wondered how I would ever live through this. But even as I listened to the other prisoners cry or mutter under their breath about the bad boyfriends and worse breaks that had caused them to end up here, I knew that I had no one to blame but myself and the choices I'd made.

I tried to tell myself that drugs and alcohol had brought me here and that if I stayed clean and sober, I never had to do this again. But that provided little sop to the fact that I was doing it now. Some of the prisoners I was chained to were tough and ugly with scars and tattoos and enough attitude to scare the bejesus out of someone like me, which I guess was the point. Every time I told myself that this could be a benchmark, a low point, that nothing life held could ever be as bad as this, I would look at my fellow prisoners, imagine being raped or knifed, and thought *No, it could get worse.* Then I would remember that it wasn't happening now. All that was happening now was that I was being taken to prison. I spoke alternately to God and to myself, not really believing in or trusting either. To God, I prayed to get through this. To myself, I said, *This happens to people. People go to prison. They get out. This will be over one day. You will survive.*

We arrived at what looked like a huge college campus, except it was surrounded by two rows of twenty foot tall electrified razor wire. As we drove in the first gate, I saw a rabbit, or the rotting remains of one, who had unwittingly touched the gate and gotten roasted and fried. The message was clear.

We waited in front of the gate while the prison guards checked the driver's paperwork and checked the van for bombs with a wand. We were waved in. The front gate didn't open until after the back gate was shut. My life in prison began.

We were taken to a holding cell, thirty of us in one big room with one toilet in full view. I was shoulder to shoulder with some serious, hard time criminals, and I prayed again, *Please don't let me get killed in here.* Then the COs came in and told us all to take off all our clothes, all of us in that room together. We had to bend, squat, cough, and duck-walk across the room. *This will be over soon*, I told myself.

And eventually, it was. We were given orange pants and top, a state-issued box containing toothbrush, toothpaste, deodorant, five pieces of paper, five envelopes and stamps, and a handbook of rules we were to memorize. Finally, exhausted, hungry, humiliated, and degraded, I walked across the yard to a big cinderblock building and my first cell. A small room with a bunk bed for two, a metal desk and a toilet, a big metal door with a tiny window. My first roommate was already on the bottom bunk. I climbed up to the top, we said our names, and I fell asleep.

After four weeks in receiving, eventually I was processed and issued "prison blues," two pairs of jeans, two t-shirts, and slip-on tennis shoes. I was assigned to the lowest security cellblock and yard and given a job. Because of my crime, I was assigned to a drug and alcohol program, which I attended after my kitchen duty, preparing breakfast, a job that started at four a.m. to allow me to spend the regular morning work period in treatment.

Once a week, some people from the outside brought in a panel for an AA meeting. Because I was in treatment, I was allowed to attend although there was a long waiting list and not everyone who wanted to go was allowed. I began sponsoring a girl in my yard, and it was the beginning of feeling that my life might have some value after all.

In prison, I learned that there's a place in my mind that no one can touch. Even in chains or in lockdown, my thoughts are my own. And it was those thoughts that determined the quality of my experience. I couldn't control which thoughts arose, but by choosing which ones to heed, I could control my attitude. I learned that while my mind contained my thoughts, it was bigger than my thoughts. Bigger even than the walls that confined me. In prison, I learned how to be free.

My job paid 21 cents an hour. As soon as I could, I saved enough to buy a notebook and began writing this down. Because AA requires anonymity at the level of public communication, I changed my name for this memoir, and I'm calling it fiction.

I know what bad shape the publishing industry is these days, but my hope is that somehow this book will get out. If you've bought it, you're helping to pay Yolanda's tuition, and you're part of the amends I need to make.

I'm very grateful.

THE END

ACKNOWLEDGMENTS

You don't publish your first book at my age, or take as long as I have to complete it, without accumulating a large number of people to thank. The complete list would rival the page count of the novel. Here are a few: To Cubby Selby, in memoriam, for the phone call that began this book. To my teachers and fellow students at the Bennington MFA Writers Program which incubated it. The Virginia Center for the Creative Arts, in whose nurturing womb it took hold and flourished. Jerold Mundis, writing coach extraordinaire who guided, cheered, and midwifed it into existence. To Mary Murphy, for 35 years of sharing the truth about writing. My writer friends who meet regularly in New York and Los Angeles to do the same. To all those who read parts, but in particular Honor Moore, James Ellroy, Lawrence Block, Paula Lumbard, Joanne Parent, Amy Schiffman, Ellen Geiger, who read various drafts, and Alan Howard who read more than one. To Kirsten Grimstad, who read every single one. To the Writer's Guild of America, and all the members who went out on strike to get pension and health benefits, without which this book could not have been written—and to all those on the other side, which granted them. To too many friends to mention, who keep me sane and sober, and make my life worthwhile; my family and dogs, for their contributions to my wonderful life, and once again, to Kirsten, who taught me that artists don't have to be lonely to be good.

Diana Gould has written pilots, movies, epi-
sodes and mini-series for network and cable. She
was writer-producer of *Dynasty*, executive story
consultant on *Knots Landing*, created and produced *Berrengers*. Her script for the TV-Movie, I
Love You—Good-bye won the Population Institute
Award, and she served on the Board of Directors of the Writers Guild
of America. Her short story "The Monkey's Daughter" was nomi-
nated for the James Kirkwood Award at UCLA's Writing Program.
She received an MFA in fiction from Bennington, has taught fiction, screen and playwriting in the MFA program at Goddard, and
coaches writers privately. Additionally, she teaches at InsightLA, a
mindfulness meditation center in Los Angeles, and works as a spiri-
tual care volunteer with Vitas Hospice. *Coldwater* is her first novel..

Author photo by Aloma Ichinose